# Paradise Café

### Dale Rominger

Published by The Backroad Café, 2023.

This is a work of fiction. Similarities to real people, places, or events are entirely coincidental.

PARADISE CAFÉ

**First edition. March 15, 2023.**

ISBN: 979-8215132371

Written by Dale Rominger.

For Jim

A longtime friend

# 1

# The Palimpsest and the Café

I'M SITTING AT AN OUTSIDE table for two at Paradise Café, Hearst Food Court, Hearst Avenue, Berkeley, California, United States of America, Earth, Solar System, Solar Interstellar Neighborhood, Milky Way, Local Galactic Group, Local Virgo Supercluster, Observable Universe. I think it's important to keep things in perspective.

I've claimed this table for the writing of my palimpsest. The word refers to an old manuscript, usually of papyrus or parchment, upon which two or more texts have been written, the earliest having been scraped off or erased. The earlier text can be completely or only partially obscured. When the second text only partially hides the first, both texts can be read. Allegorically, a palimpsest is something that has many levels of meaning or development or history. The point is that I am not writing my autobiography. At this point in my life, it just doesn't make sense to hide the first text, pretending it isn't there. It won't do to skim over the surface, pretending nothing is written underneath. It does make sense for me to be completely truthful with myself, and subsequently with you. I'm as old as parchment, or at least I feel that way most of the time now. And yes, in an attempt to honor the pedigree of palimpsest, I will mostly leave my laptop in my bag, except when research is demanded. I am writing on a yellow legal pad with a medium-blue ballpoint pen. This is going to take some time. And to add a little spice, I am slightly dyslexic, so this writing by hand without a spell checker is going to be a train wreck. It will also be very time consuming when I finally type all this into a computer, for into a computer it must eventually go.

My name is David Robert Bainbridge. I'm seventy-four years old, slim, but certainly not skinny. I have a full head of gray-white hair. Actually, more white than gray, but not sun-blinding white. For the past several months, I have been letting it grow. Not sure how long I will do that. I have some vague notion of a ponytail. Some years ago, when I was in Tokyo, I saw a middle-aged Japanese man with a ponytail down to his butt. I was impressed. But the real reason I am letting my hair grow at this point in my life will, no doubt, become obvious to even the most dim-witted Freudian. I have a gray-white, neatly trimmed beard and moustache. I've had both since my mid-twenties. I'm five foot ten inches tall. I have prostate cancer.

Lately, I've had the good sense to forget my dreams.

I have, in an informal way, requested sanctuary at Paradise Café from Melissa Jennifer Davis, the owner. We go some way back. Her husband, Jorge Francisco Amado, died in a small plane crash. Their son was also in that light airplane, and while eventually losing both his feet, he did, mercifully, survive. Sadly, he doesn't have much time for Melissa Jennifer Davis these days. Melissa Jennifer Davis has a keen mind, a kind heart, a wonderful body, and a rather unfortunate face. All the individual parts are fine, better than fine as a matter of fact. Angelina Jolie cheekbones. Scarlett Johansson lips. Charlize Theron eyes. Ashley Judd nose. Sandra Bullock chin. And a Halle Berry smile. Thing is, when they all get together, it just doesn't work. Still, it's not important. Melissa Jennifer Davis is important. Paradise Café is important. I've come here because this is the first place I met with Michael Andrew Walker Johnson. (I never refer to Michael as Michael, but only as Walker, for reasons that will become clear later.)

When I first started visiting Paradise Café, the place was owned and run by Melissa Jennifer Davis's mother, Mary Jane Davis. I remember Melissa Jennifer Davis coming around quite often after school. She was at home in the café and would often approach my table, sometimes take a seat, and open a conversation on any number of topics. I mostly found these encounters delightful. I was in Berkeley for close to seven years, so I got to know Mary Jane Davis and Melissa Jennifer Davis quite well. After leaving Berkeley, I would return to the city and the café once every couple of years. On one such visit, I discovered a now-grown Melissa Jennifer Davis to be the new owner of Paradise. Mary Jane Davis had decided to retire and sold the café to her daughter for one dollar.

That was a long time ago. Now I *am* the old parchment. And I will no doubt misuse the word "palimpsest." I will use it to refer to myself. I will use it to refer to that which I'm writing. I will use it to refer to the process of exposing myself. If you can't handle this abuse of language, I would suggest you stop reading now. However, I will not stop writing, and what I write may prove interesting, amusing, or revealing. I've also decided that each day, I will write what my mind, or spirit, or heart—take your pick—requires, so hold on to your metaphorical hat. For your convenience, I will title and number each entry.

Dyslexia was something Walker and I shared, though for me it was an annoyance while for him it was a problem. I guess it's hardly worth mentioning now, but I do because we lived with it in the days before a million dissertations had been written on the subject.

Damn. I must pause. Unfortunately, whenever I think of dyslexia, I think of Samantha Esther Cunningham, and now I can't get her out of my mind. She was a friend.

Well, there you go! The palimpsest thing. The over-writing of the still-visible first text I just pretended had been scraped away.

And we've only just begun. I must not overwrite that truth. Point is, Samantha Esther Cunningham was a bit more than a friend.

# 2

# Samantha Esther Cunningham and the Kiss

WE WENT OUT TO DINNER one evening under the pretext of discussing church business. I was the minister and she the church moderator. It made sense. Christians like sharing meals together, for obvious reasons. We sat at a table by the window overlooking the sea. We drank wine and watched the sun set. People do that. It was an enjoyable evening, though I must admit there was a bit of sexual tension in the air, in that space over the table between us. That surprised me. She wore a tightly fitting black dress, low cut, though not inappropriately so. However, in the interest of accuracy, when she leaned forward to emphasize an important issue concerning the church, I couldn't help but notice her rather attractive cleavage. This pleased me. On the other hand, she wore black stilettos, which did not please me. I think it is important to emphasize that I found, and still find, stilettos problematic. I view stilettos in the same way I view foot binding in ancient China. So you won't be surprised to hear that after dinner as we were walking to her car, I asked her why she, an intelligent and reasonable woman, wore stilettos. She looked me straight in the eyes and said, "They make me feel sexy."

I did wonder why she wanted to feel sexy having dinner with her minister. I mean, she could have said something like, "I just like these shoes," or "These shoes go well with this dress;" but she said, "They make me feel sexy." Well, fair enough. There is nothing wrong with a church moderator feeling sexy. And she was sexy. Maybe she still is. Can't old people be sexy? Maybe I should look her up.

After dinner, we got into her car and drove to the church parking lot where mine was waiting. She pulled up alongside my car. We started with the goodbyes when she leaned forward and kissed me on the lips, with a little tongue. It felt great. Again, in the interest of truth, I must emphasize that that kiss was the full extent of my marital infidelity. I didn't feel guilty. In fact, for years, I was disappointed I hadn't responded with more enthusiasm. For months afterwards, when I masturbated, I thought of Samantha Esther Cunningham, her tight black dress, nice breasts, soft lips, wet tongue, and black sexy stilettos. Not every time I masturbated, mind you. Maybe every tenth time. And no, I didn't feel guilty about masturbating with Samantha Esther Cunningham in mind. However, I did feel overwhelming guilty that her stilettos turned me on.

I should say in the interest of full disclosure that my principled stance on the morality of stilettos has had absolutely no impact on the fashion industry. In this regard, my principled stance on stilettos is like all my other principled stances throughout my life. As I sit here now at Paradise Café, I must admit, must write down, that I've been something of a fake all my life. What I mean is this: I could always have gone further. Most of the time I didn't. I always told myself I had gone far enough, but deep inside, I knew. I could have gone further.

Anyway, the reason Samantha Esther Cunningham entered my mind while speaking about dyslexia is that one morning, sitting in her kitchen (post-kiss) as she was grinding coffee beans, which she made a point of telling me she did every morning, she said to me that dyslexia was falling out of favor. Not her words, but that's what she meant. Apparently, on the scale from no dyslexia to horrendous dyslexia, most of us experience some dyslexia. I had to take her word for it. She had a PhD in something having to do with psychology and learning theory. But it was a blow. Being a straight, white, middle-class, educated male, I had no claim to victimhood, which was all the rage at the time. Claims of victimhood I mean, not being a straight, white, middle-class, educated male. I was eager to be liberated and so acknowledged that "my people" had in the past oppressed fucking everyone. They continue in the present, and truth be told, seem to enjoy it. In this regard, Walker always had an advantage over me. He was dyslexic and gay. All I had was a limp form of dyslexia, which I nonetheless embraced with all the enthusiasm of a desperate man. My thinking was that a well-intended, straight, white male confessing to anyone and everyone who would listen could garner some sympathy for being dyslexic. And maybe dampen some of the guilt of privilege. Mind you, I didn't overplay it, but it did help from time to time. However, to be honest, for all the effort, I got very little out of it. Privilege is not forgotten or forgiven just because you reverse numbers, confuse "class" with "glass" (it's all about linguistic voicing), and can't pronounce the word "familiarity." Nonetheless, you can see that Samantha Esther Cunningham's morning comment over the noise of the coffee grinder was disturbing.

I told Samantha Esther Cunningham just that and she said, while handing me a hot cup of coffee, "You're liberated, not castrated."

I took the coffee cup, noting that our fingers touched and that her words in no way addressed my distress over losing my only passport for entry into Victimville. They did, however, speak to the after-dinner kiss. I thought it best to let it pass, which I did. But dear me. Samantha Esther Cunningham. Haven't thought of her in years. And I have to say, the thought of a woman sticking her tongue in my mouth because she likes me isn't all that bad. Since Jessica died six years ago, not one woman has offered to stick her tongue in my mouth, not without substantial financial reward that is. Jessica and I were in one of those desert patches in our marriage when I was looking at Samantha Esther Cunningham's cleavage, so if I do say so, I did damn well in controlling myself.

Did I mention that the tight black dress stopped just above Samantha Esther Cunningham's knees and that she had great legs?

For the sake of moral accuracy, I do want to repeat that the Samantha Esther Cunningham kiss was my only act of infidelity. Samantha Esther Cunningham's lips were the only lips other than Jessica's that touched my own, and Samantha Esther Cunningham's tongue was the only tongue other than Jessica's that I tasted in forty-three years of marriage.

Oh well, there I go again. There were Walker's lips. Palimpsest: seventy-four-year-old parchment scraped clean and used again, only sometimes not scraped completely clean. Let's be honest. We are forever trying to retell our lives as though our past has been scraped clean. We are willing to bleed to have it scraped clean. I must not become discouraged.

However, in fact, I don't think the Samantha Esther Cunningham kiss should be called infidelity now that I'm writing about it. She kissed me and I didn't pursue it. And honestly, can one be unfaithful while masturbating? I'm thinking, not so much. If the charge of marital infidelity is spirited my way, it would have a better chance of hitting home if the target were Walker. I was in love with him, and for a moment in time, a moment that lasted six or seven months, I wanted to embrace a physical component to that love, as did he. Indeed, we tried, but it just wasn't there. We talked and talked about it, but it just didn't happen. As it turned out, I really am straight and not somewhere midway along the continuum. If I were bisexual, that would have found full-blooded actualization with Walker. So I guess you can say, while I was not physically unfaithful in my marriage, I did engage in emotional infidelity, which I'm not proud of. Still, I will not take refuge in the insipid phrase, "the heart wants what the heart wants." That's just a way to justify avoiding responsibility. The marriage of Cartesian dualism and Hollywood rom coms has not served us well.

The physical, the emotional, the moral. Sometimes not an easy mix. And it takes both the head and the heart to find our way. Now that Jessica is dead, the emotions and the morality of fidelity are not my problem. However, the physicality of longing can be.

About a year after Jessica died, I thought about finding an escort. What a word, "escort." It has the power to dislocate, to dismiss, to diminish. It's Orwellian. It's sexual Newspeak. Truth is, an escort is a prostitute, but linguistically scraped clean of sin and, hopefully, disease. The internet helps in this verbal subterfuge.

I'm talking about sites in the uptown locations of the web, where the light still shines. Here the internet normalizes, legitimizes. It's all just good, wholesome consumerism. Rent a car, order a pizza, find a lawyer, secure an Airbnb, buy a plane ticket, download a book, read a newspaper, hire an escort. It's what you do from home at the kitchen table.

Finding an escort on the internet is not cruising down dark streets looking for women standing under dirty, dim streetlamps. Women who never look like a young, innocent Julia Roberts. Pretty woman, indeed. You're not looking for a quick fifty-buck suck and fuck. No, you're looking for that uptown girl on her uptown website. The one who costs—the more expensive, the more morally justifiable. The high-class wardrobe and makeup. And the stilettos, of course. Articulate, intelligent, friendly. Beautiful with, perhaps, a higher degree. Well-traveled. A companion. The kind of woman you can take to a suite in the Four Seasons Hotel. A pro, not a prostitute.

I never went through with it. I like to think that my decision was primarily grounded in my commitment to ethics, morality, and justice. But I must confess, I also thought I would not be able to sustain disbelief long enough to enjoy the experience. Because hiring a woman to have sex with you is an act of fiction, a making-believe, a willing suspension of disbelief. Paying for love where there is no love takes Oscar-winning performances from both of you, and it is love you are looking for, not just sex. If I paid enough, she might be a pro performer, but I certainly would not be. Unless you are just a body with a penis, what you want is what you have lost, and I lost Jessica.

Someone said to me once, "If you can't bring yourself to hire an escort, find a fuck buddy." Ah, we move from the language of deception to the language of juvenile crudeness. I said, "I prefer the term 'friends with benefits,' but either way, finding a buddy or friend at my age seems unlikely in the extreme." For a fraction of a second, I considered asking Melissa Jennifer Davis if she might want a friend with benefits, but the thought evaporated as quickly as it had appeared.

There is, of course, pornography, now that it has been democratized and civilized. I mean, you can do porn anywhere—in your bedroom, study, office, bathroom, kitchen, living room, attic, basement, even the back yard if your Wi-Fi goes that far. But somehow, porn is for males fifteen to fifty-five. It just seems embarrassing for a man my age to indulge.

So here I sit at Paradise Café without Jessica, without Samantha Esther Cunningham, without an escort, without a buddy or friend, and without Walker. Alone, writing on a yellow legal pad with a medium-blue ballpoint pen making one dyslexic mistake after another.

# 3

# Michael Andrew Walker Johnson and the Womb of the Mother God

FOR YEARS I HAD A PHOTOGRAPH of Michael Andrew Walker Johnson on my study wall, on every study wall I've ever had. He is young and in San Francisco. It's a black and white photo of him leaning against a street post. Above his head fastened to the post is the street name—Castro. The post had been used for years to display fliers, advertisements, logos, and goodness knows what else. At the time of this photo, most had been torn off, exposing layers of urban history.

His hair, black in the black-and-white photo, is short, not covering his ears, but falling across his forehead. He has a moustache, which was unusual for him. His eyes are slightly squinting in the sun. He is almost smiling. White shirt and, I think, a corduroy jacket. His hands are in the front pockets of his jeans. Walker, the post, and the road sign are in sharp focus, but everything behind him—people, cars, buildings—is tastefully blurred. It's Walker we are meant to look at, and why not? He looks damn good. San Francisco Castro District cool.

Walker is not actually one of his middle names. The name Walker was added after he spent an extended time among Native Americans in the Pacific Northwest. His spiritual journey took him first into a very liberal expression of Christianity (which I will make clear in a moment), then to Buddhism, and eventually to Native

American spirituality. It was in the Pacific Northwest, under the influence of not a few hallucinogenic mushrooms, that he came upon the name Walker. I don't really know if he discovered the name or if it was given to him by the tribe. He was rather secretive about it but did make it clear when he returned home that from that day forward, he would be known as Walker.

Walker was a student training for the ministry, and I was assigned as his pastoral advisor. A committee told me he was openly gay and handed me his file. I was flattered. You see, it polished my liberal, inclusive credentials. It rewarded my advocacy. It sanctified my struggle for justice. It redeemed my risking professional advancement and personal attack. I accepted his file with humility.

In the file, along with a lot of mundane information—address, telephone number, age, that sort of thing—was his faith statement. Everyone wanting to train for the ministry has to write a faith statement and Walker's was, well...unusual. To be honest, I don't remember much of what he wrote. Hell, I don't remember any of what I wrote when it was my turn. But I do remember him writing about the womb of the mother god. I'm willing to bet the little money I have that he was, and probably still is, the only person who, when interviewing for the right to train for the Christian ministry, wrote in their faith statement about the womb of the mother god. I have images of him describing a birth canal and emerging spirits, but at this point in my life, after all these years, I don't know if he wrote about such things or if my own imagination created them. What I do remember is that I thought he was a bit crazy.

Also in the file was a paper describing my responsibilities as his advisor. I was to be a "spiritual guide" when needed and a "practical advisor" to help him get through the mundane, but necessary, bureaucratic steps in training toward, hopefully, ordination—at which point he would have to write another faith statement. You can't have too many faith statements.

My instructions also told me that under no circumstances was I to make the first contact. That apparently awesome duty was his. Something didn't smell right about that. It made me uncomfortable, as if the student's initiative, or lack thereof, was a determining factor of their character. It also seemed to imply a particular power dynamic in the relationship that was unacceptable to me. I waited a week and didn't hear from him, so I called. We met a couple of days later at Paradise Café. Little did I know at the time that, when I reached my mid-seventies, our story would still be in full flow.

Walker was wonderfully outrageous and creative. I felt ponderously conventional and established by comparison. He was a dancer. He was a singer. He was a poet. And he was smart. I was, well, just me.

In time, mutual caution became mutual respect. Respect became friendship. Friendship became love. In time, he was ordained and called to the only ministry the church could, at that time, tolerate a gay man being called to. He became the AIDS Minister. I have to tell you, and this is no big reveal, that being a gay minister back then was no picnic, and it probably still isn't. It could be exhausting.

For example, Walker and I attended a regional conference of our denomination and Walker, the AIDS Minister, was to present a proposal, for what exactly I don't remember, but it was, of course, controversial—it was about gay men dying of AIDS. Some guy, an ordained guy, got up and spewed out his gay bigotry—prejudice, emotional and spiritual violence—attacking not the proposal but Walker himself. Walker did what he had to do. He kept his cool, addressed the issues, and got his proposal passed. It's what happened next that could bring you to your metaphorical knees.

The ordained guy, the gay bigot, came up to Walker and pleaded with him to come to his room in the evening to help him work through his homophobia. It's the double whammy that is so damn exhausting. The attack and then the request for the victim of the attack to "heal" the attacker.

Before Walker was called to the AIDS ministry, he applied for the position of associate minister in a local church. The church rejected his candidacy and then asked him to come back to help them address their gay prejudice. After that, they asked him to candidate again and, you guessed it, they turned him down again. Not good. It's something deep and disturbing. Something deep in the individuals. Something deep in the community. Something deep in the institution. Something deep in the ideology. Something deep in the theology. It's something dangerous, like something sensed but not seen in a deep, damp, dark basement.

Walker asked me to come to the bigot's room with him, because he was just too tired to deal with the double crap alone. As I sat there in the room with Walker and the gay bigot, for the first time I felt in my gut, in my heart, deep in my brain, the kind of shit Walker went through. Years later, I understood why he found more peace in a native community in the Pacific Northwest and changed his name.

I'm sure you know that ministers are ordained. It's a ritual that can be quite meaningful. It's important, or at least it should be, though it does have its ambiguities. One part of the service of ordination is called the "charge." Essentially, it is a brief speech or sermon to the ordinand about their upcoming ministry. A charge can be somewhat ecclesiastically formulaic, a listing of responsibilities cloaked in theological language and scriptural references; or a charge can be *not* those things. Michael Andrew Walker Johnson asked me to give the charge at his ordination.

I need you to understand something. Walker was ordained to the AIDS Ministry in 1986, and back then it was a big deal. AIDS was ripping through the San Francisco Bay Area like a 9.5 plus earthquake. No cocktail or pill back then. There was an almost complete disregard for the disease at the beginning because it was the "gay disease." This was discriminatory and political. For some it was theological. Hatred can always find a theology.

Walker was the first AIDS minister in the area, and the ordination was held in a big Berkeley Congregational church. This was not an ordination to a local church. This was an ordination to a community of the ignored, shunned, unclean, soon forgotten. That big Berkeley church was packed. And as I stood up to deliver my charge to my friend, I looked out at the front row filled with men with AIDS. They were not well. They were dis-eased. They were hard to look at. And yet, they were also excited, focused. They were there for Walker. I'm sure they all died during Walker's ministry. They were his parish.

Sometime before Walker's ordination, I had taken a photograph of an old weather-worn wooden cross. It was in an English graveyard, overshadowed by numerous grand stone grave markers, standing apart, and surrounded by weeds. It was an embarrassingly humble marker. On it was nailed a man. I had the photo framed, took it to the ordination, and presented it to Walker as a gift. Then I spoke. I think it is important you know what I said. It is important to me that you love and respect Walker, and the charge may help you in that endeavor.

*Charge for Michael Andrew Johnson*
*Ordination*
*Sunday, September 21, 1986*

*I would like to give your charge in part in a picture.*

*The photo has many images that will be released if you only look at it. I give you images because you too speak in images. Your ordination paper was filled with narrative images. Your poetry and your dance create images of a different kind, but images, nonetheless.*

*I would ask you to hang this particular photo in a place that suits you best, but I have some stipulations. Hang it in a place where you can see it often, every day, if only at a glance. Hang it in a place where you can sit quietly with it, alone and undisturbed.*

*The picture was taken in a small churchyard in southern England. You need to know that it is not a very substantial grave marker. All around it, dwarfing it, are massive stone crosses and gravestones. They are infinitely better equipped to stand the pressures of wind, rain, sleet, snow, and time. This grave marker stands only two feet tall. It is made of wood. It is poor. It stands with the weeds, and I think it may have been forgotten. I am not at all certain that it still stands today, though I like to believe that it does.*

*At first glance it is a photo of death—this is, after all, a grave marker in a graveyard. At first glance, your ministry too is about death, of harrowing days, with people who have been largely ignored or forgotten by our society and our churches.*

*At first glance, it is a fragile and vulnerable marker, easily pushed to the ground, trampled upon, and forgotten. I am sure that when it was first placed at the grave, it was clean and new and filled with expectation. At first glance, your ministry is fragile, easily trampled upon, vulnerable to the pressures of hatred, fear, and ignorance. And at first glance, after the excitement of this day has passed and weather and time have taken their toll on you and your parish, it could be forgotten or ignored.*

*At second glance, however, we see a figure in the shadows and realize that the photograph presents a very human view of God. It is a view that reminds us that death is not what we thought it was, and, therefore, that life is not what we think it is. At second glance then, it is one of the most important images we have, as your ministry may be one of the most important images the church has. Neither the image on the photograph nor you and your parish should be forgotten, and I charge you to continue to remember and to remind. You cannot afford to forget. If necessary, let the photo remember for you.*

*The more you look at the photo, and the more you look at your ministry, the more you see life and not death. I charge you to explore the images offered in this photograph, to keep them alive and foremost in your heart and mind, to carry them with you as you go throughout your day and your life.*

*As you contemplate what ordination will mean for you in the short and long run, do not lose sight of the person on the cross. He is not on the cross because he was important in the hierarchy of his religion. Ordination is an institution that was created and is perpetuated in part to separate some people from other people. I charge you to walk the line of gaining spiritual and practical strength from ordination without forgetting that you declared your ministry to be one of encounter and dialogue. Hierarchy and separation change the quality of encounter and restrict dialogue. Do not let your priesthood get in the way of your ministry.*

*I charge you to let God choose where, when, and for what reason you may suffer in the name of Christ. Look at the photograph and remember that Christ has already suffered and died to save the world. Though, of course, we still have a significant role to play in the drama of life, do not die the numerous false deaths of the professional ministry. Do not die in health, in spirit, in friendship, in playfulness, in love. Do not become a dead man preaching life to others. When you look at the picture, see that you are in Christ and Christ is in you, but that you are not called to replace Christ or to protect Christ. If you must die for your ministry, then let it be for God's will and not for your profession.*

*Remember, the Holy Spirit is not sent to be your career guidance counselor but is the heart and mind of God speaking to you about your life and the lives of others. Let God choose for you when, where, and for what reason you celebrate and rejoice. Remember that there is no time to wait to love and laugh. Let the Holy Spirit fill your every moment or, at least, as many moments as possible.*

*Please do not forget that after the crucifixion is the resurrection. You are a spirit created to be alive. Your dance and poetry are two of the greatest expressions of that life. They both give life to the world and to you. They are avenues for the Spirit to rejoice and for you to be re-created. Something in me shouts that if you stop dancing and writing, you may wither spiritually. Do not take away time or energy from either, thinking that you are making more time for your ministry. Your dancing and poetry are celebrations of life, and the spirit of your ministry will wither without them both.*

*Finally, remember that there are many people who truly love you. You are so busy, your days are so filled, that it is easy to forget that people do indeed love you. You must leave time to nurture love.*

*I have seen you tired and saddened and feeling alone. You are never alone, though sometimes you may need to make the effort to touch as we will also need to do. The image in the photograph tells you that ultimately you will never, can never, be alone. Christ did not travel the road to the cross for his own aggrandizement, but to tell you that you are not alone. You are saved. God bless.*

Years later—and I mean years—Walker wrote the following in an email exchange we had: "*I don't actually remember what you said at my Coronation, but I do remember you saying it as I sat in the pew and listened.*" If I hadn't found the charge printed on aging, fading paper in an old, dirtied folder tucked away in a closet, I would not have remembered either. I was amazed I still had it. Thing is, preaching, like newspaper journalism, is ephemeral. But if you write it down, it may have a chance. I never wrote my sermons down, but I did the charge.

I copied the charge into my laptop and finally wrote it once again on my yellow legal pad paper while sitting at Paradise Café. As I physically wrote it onto my pad just now, I was struck by a line I could not write today, now these many years gone: "*...that death is not what we thought it was, and, therefore, that life is not what we think it is.*"

Actually, even sitting here with the sun streaming through the wooden latticework above my table reflecting off my yellow paper, death *is* what I thought it was. It is *death*. It is fucking *death*. What more could it be? As for life...well, what do we think it is at the end of the day? I really don't know, and I'm running out of time to figure it out. And for some reason, a reason I do not understand, a mystery that is unfathomable to me, I think it is important before my time is up that I figure it out. I'm in my third act, and there is no encore. Trust me on this. No encore. Death *is* death.

And so, this absurd palimpsest on long yellow paper. If scraping and bleeding are necessary, let it be so. However, there is one sentence in the charge that I can write today: *"Remember that there is no time to wait to love and laugh."*

# 4

# Jessica Margaret Phillips and Acute Panmyelosis with Myelofibrosis

MY TABLE FOR TWO IS just left of the door. Paradise Café is located near the rear of Hearst Food Court, which is good, because this area of the court gets the most sun. In the old days, most of the food establishments in Hearst Food Court were traditional US American—hamburgers, sandwiches, pizzas, that sort of thing. Now as I look down the court to Hearst Avenue, I see the TC Garden—Chinese; Aki's—Japanese; Comuaru—Korean; Chianglai—Thai. There is also Top Dog—traditional American; O'Doul's—which doesn't sound Traditional American, but must be, and Le Petit Market—well, you can figure that one out yourself. None of this is a problem for me. I've been to all those countries and love the food. It's just interesting how things change.

Above me is the wooden lattice creating its pleasant pattern of shadows and light across my table. The sun feels warm. Melissa Jennifer Davis has just placed a caffe latte and croissant in front of me with her Halle Barry smile. This is no Starbucks caffe latte. No, it is not! Melissa Jennifer Davis makes caffe lattes the old fashioned and correct way, served in a clear pint-sized glass with all three layers that constitute a proper latte visible for one's inspection. The top layer is white foam, the middle layer is coffee-brown milk, and the bottom layer is deep, dark coffee. I'm just saying. If you're going to make the damn thing, make it right.

When Jessica was alive, I didn't just call her Jessica. I also called her Jess and Jessie. But here, in this palimpsest adventure, I will only refer to her as Jessica. I'm not entirely sure why, but if feels right.

I can't tell you how many times we sat at Paradise Café when I was in seminary and she was studying journalism down the hill at Cal Berkeley. I say "down the hill" because the seven seminaries were up the hill, actually on the hill. Thus the name Holy Hill known far and near.

We often sat at this very table. I can actually see her now. She is young—in retrospect, we were very young back then. Her light brown hair reaches her shoulders and sweeps across her forehead. She is wearing a white blouse with short sleeves. Her left arm is resting on the table. She is wearing an old watch, brown leather strap, and if my memory is correct, it was given to her by her father years ago for a birthday. In front of her is a pint glass filled with a strawberry smoothie, whipped cream on the top. Her right elbow is on the table, her right hand holding a long iced tea spoon which has just captured a heathy dollop of whipped cream. She is smiling at me, wide, happy, beautiful. She never wore makeup. What you saw was what you got, which was fine by me.

She's been gone six years, and I can still see her sitting there. I can see her young. I can see her old. I can see her middle-aged. I can see her blissfully happy. I can see her angry. I can see her bored. I can see her lost. I can see her frightened. I can see her heartbroken. I can see her dying. I can see her dead. I miss her.

She died of acute panmyelosis with myelofibrosis, a rare blood or bone marrow cancer with a survival rate of less than three years. Trust me, the details are not important. The only detail that matters is that it killed her in less than three years. The rarity of the disease haunted me for those first years, and if I'm honest and scrape even lightly on my parchment-like skin, it still does.

My prostate cancer is somewhat common among older men. My father had prostate cancer, so my odds increased automatically by fifty percent the day I was born. It still sucks, and it can still kill me, but I can hardly be surprised. But acute panmyelosis with myelofibrosis just isn't fair. It's against the odds. No hand is ever that bad. It begs the unanswerable question, why me? I must emphasize that these unreasonable, almost infantile musings, are mine and were never Jessica's. As she said to me one night as I railed against the universe about the utter unfairness of acute panmyelosis with myelofibrosis, "It doesn't matter, I got the fucking thing, who cares if it is rare or fair?!"

Hans Theodor Woldsen Storm, in *The Rider on the White Horse*, wrote that, at a commemoration of death, the "banquet table seemed to sag under the silence and loneliness." People who gathered at Jessica's commemoration of course called it a celebration of life. But for me, at the time, the silence and loneliness engulfing my being crushed the banquet table. Crushed it! It took some time before I was able to celebrate anything.

We met in college. I was a junior and she came in with the new freshman class on a beautiful fall day. I saw her, not across a crowded room, but across the campus, from afar. My first impression of her was, well, somewhat impressionistic given the distance between us—both the sense of "in the style of impressionism" and as a very personal and subjective impression. A few days later, I saw her again in my philosophy class. To me she was stunning. Interestingly, Walker never saw it. He said she was certainly pleasant looking, but stunning? He thought not. I watched her coming and going on campus and in class for almost three weeks. I was afraid to approach her. But one day she acknowledged my existence.

Volleyball was a big deal in our small liberal arts college, and I was a setter on the best of the best teams. We never lost. That's how good we were. One evening, the gym was filled with teams playing, people watching, and people just milling around—nothing like being part of a volleyball evening buzz. My team had won its game, and I was sitting on the floor, my back against the bleachers, when I saw Jessica walking toward me.

I had never been very courageous when it came to women. My first girlfriend in junior high school almost ditched me because I wouldn't engage in the first-kiss experience. And I don't mean my first kiss with her, but both our first kisses ever with anyone.

So, when I saw Jessica coming my way, I did look up and make eye contact but didn't say a word. However, as she passed me, she said hi and ruffled my hair with her hand. Two days later—must be a pattern here—I asked her "out" for a walk. After the walk, we were together until the day she died of acute panmyelosis with myelofibrosis.

# 5

# The Palimpsest, Megan Margaret Williams, and the Smile

THE SUN IS SHINING as I sit at Paradise Café, latte in hand. It's always shining this time of year in Northern California. If there were a god and that god took any interest in individual human beings, let alone creating them, that god created me to live in warm climes wearing loose fitting clothes. For reasons beyond my comprehension, I have denied that possible god all my life by living in cold, gray, wet places. Could it be that that god is actually real and is punishing me for my misbehavior? If so, it seems a bit meanspirited and disproportionate.

Besides the issue of divine punishment and the ethics of faith, I only mention this because I love the sun and the warmth. And so, on my morning walk from my apartment to Paradise, with the sun warming my journey, I was susceptible to grace.

I was ambling down Le Conte Avenue, bag over my shoulder with my laptop (for research purposes only you remember), my pen, my yellow legal pad, and my good intentions. I turned left on Euclid, and I saw two women walking toward me. One had a baby wrap carrying an infant whose head was resting in peaceful sleep on her chest, the kind of sleep only babies can experience. The other woman was pushing a stroller occupied by a small child. She looked to be no more than three or four years old. As they grew near, I stepped off the sidewalk to allow them to pass. When the stroller reached me, the little girl gave me a small wave with her right hand and said, "Hi."

The woman pushing the stroller stopped, and we made eye contact. She smiled an okay, so I returned my gaze to the child, gave a small wave, and said, "Hi there."

She was a cutie, no doubt about it. Her hair still bright blond, sharp blue eyes, and a smile that embraced her whole face.

"My name is Megan," she said with her full-face smile. It was so genuine and beautiful it almost broke my heart, the way beauty can sometimes do. I looked into her eyes and was astounded.

I said, "My name is David, though a lot of people call me Dave. It's nice meeting you."

"It's very nice meeting you," she said and looked up at–I presumed–her mother.

The stroller started to move forward once again, and as they passed, each woman smiled at me. The woman with the stroller gave a slight nod of the head and said, "Hi." I nodded back.

I stood there and watched. Unbelievably, there were tears in my eyes.

# 6

# Michael Andrew Walker Johnson and the Poetry

FOR THE LIFE OF ME, I can't remember what Jessica and Walker had been talking about, but after he returned home to New York, he emailed the following, "*After Jessica talked about my dealing with things in poetry, the very first words that came were: 'What is loneliness at night? A caravan of jugglers tossing bits of life....' The rest evolved after that. By the way, when I thought 'caravan,' I was thinking of the British use of that word, and more like roadies or internal migrations, passing by in the night through neon lights.*"

You can't know Walker without reading at least some of his poems, and I want you to know Walker. It's important. So, keeping faith with the palimpsest, I will open my laptop, copy them onto my yellow legal pad, and scatter them throughout my musings. I will start with this one:

> It's all made up.
> And therefore one must keep on making it up
> In a way that keeps creativity alive,
> Because once created
> They will shut it up in conventions
> And for co-opting the Creator.

# 7

# Jessica Margaret Phillips and the Kids Thing

JESSICA AND I NEVER had children, by choice, not because of medical determinism. After we left college, we ended up in Columbus, Ohio, with another couple from the same school, working jobs that we knew would be temporary. After about a year, we bought a Toyota Land Cruiser and prepared to drive to Alaska. This was to be our first adventure together, and while the Alaskan Highway is now paved, back then in the good old days when Land Cruisers weren't luxury vehicles used by mothers to take their kids to and from school but were real four-wheel drives driven by real men—or at least men pretending to be real men—the highway was all dirt all the way. It was, to say the least, a challenge. We spent a month in the state and then took the ferry system back down to Prince Rupert, BC, disembarked, and drove southeast from the coast to meet up with a friend in Missoula, Montana.

After college, I found it hard to settle down, or more accurately, to find a way into my future. I applied to a PhD program in philosophy. I applied to become a psychiatrist, which first demanded that I go to medical school. Thus, I applied to medical school. I had to begin with a rather basic biology course. I found it so boring, I quit. However, for some time, I had been reading books about archaeology, and that seemed to hold my interest, so I walked into the University of Montana anthropology department and announced I wanted to be an archaeologist. Three years later, I had an MA degree in anthropology and a teaching gig at Rocky Mountain College in Billings. It was while we lived in Billings that I decided to head to seminary.

I applied to Yale and Berkeley and was accepted in both schools. Since Jessica and I knew the East Coast, we decided to get to know the San Francisco Bay Area and the Pacific Rim.

However, before starting school again, we thought we needed a break, a treat, so we traveled to Greece to visit a couple of friends who owned a cottage in the small town of Areopolis on the Mani peninsula. During three romantic hot weeks in Areopolis and the Mani coast, it became clear we could no longer avoid the question of marriage, though we didn't exactly approach the topic directly. At the end of our Greek escapade, standing in the Athens airport at four in the morning, Jessica asked, "Do you want to have children?"

Kids. The answer to that question was probably no, but I guessed Jessica might answer in the affirmative. Amazingly, we had never discussed the issue. Hell, we were young. We hadn't even talked about marriage. In a matter of seconds, I contemplated saying yes for fear of losing her but decided it was best not to start a marriage with a major deception. I said, "No, I'm afraid not."

"Right answer," she said and then went on to explain that in a former life, she had had ten children and ten was enough for all her lifetimes. I thought she was kidding about the lifetimes and the ten kids, but I never asked her. To this day, I don't know if she was joking or serious. Bottom line, we got married and never had children.

I tell you all this for a reason. While never having children, three times in my life, during our marriage, I dreamed I had a little girl. The first time she was, perhaps, around four years old. She had blond curly hair, blue eyes, a nice smile, and was pretty in her way. The second time she was older, maybe nine or ten. It was the same girl. In each dream I loved her completely, overwhelmingly, with a love I had never experienced before or since. About nine years ago, before Jessica died, I dreamed of her again. This third time she was around twenty and had become quite confident and beautiful. Again, the same girl, now a young woman. It was her. It was clear I was her father and she loved me. I was, once again, overwhelmed.

I miss her and wonder if she will appear again. Perhaps at her wedding. One thing is certain. She needs a name.

I have decided to call her Megan.

# 8

# The Palimpsest, the Character Flaw, and the Pig

I THINK NOW'S THE TIME to mention a minor character flaw of mine, at least minor compared to my other character flaws.

I swear.

Here's the thing. I started swearing when I was a kid on a New Jersey boardwalk. My mother had two sisters, and given that the extended families were matriarchal and none of us had much money, we often spent vacations in one or the other's homes. I had three male cousins, all older than I, and one summer, we sold newspapers on the boardwalk. My oldest cousin would drive us to the railroad station. We took the bundled papers right off the railroad cars and threw them in the back of the station wagon. Quite a thrill, I must say. As we drove to the boardwalk at speed, we cut the wires and put the sports pages and the magazine section, if there was one that day, into the main news section. We were selling *The News & The Mirror* on the boardwalk to people in their late teens and early twenties. We started selling about eleven and went until three in the morning. My cousins planted me in one spot, telling me not to move on punishment of death, while they walked the boardwalk and ventured into the cafes and bars. I can't remember how old I was, but I'm surprised my mother let me do it. I stood there shouting "Morning paper, *News and the Mirror*." The girls would come up to me and say it wasn't morning, and so I would shout, "Almost morning paper,

*News and the Mirror.*" Got a laugh every time and sometimes a kiss on the cheek. Anyway, the thing was, my cousins swore like truckers. Hell, they all carried knives! Not domesticated pen knives, but big, ugly knives. Point is, if being a man meant swearing, then swearing it would be.

I'm not proud of this character flaw, but, as I have said, it seems one of the least of all my failings. Swearing does not merit lost sleep and ethical angst, at least not the way I swear. What bugs the hell out of me is that many of my male colleagues often use swearing to demonstrate their machismo.

In my first church in a small town south of San Francisco, a seventeen-year-old boy and a sixteen-year-old girl were killed in a motorcycle accident. The girl was from my church and the boy from the Catholic church the next town over. The priest and I decided to share in the two funerals. On the day of the boy's funeral, the priest and I stood outside his church watching people arrive for the service. The priest offered a running commentary on the appearance of the women approaching. At one point, he leaned toward me, indicating with a nod a woman coming our way, and said, "Boy, does she have fucking big tits." I proclaim without hesitation or prejudice that he was a pig, as I hasten to apologize to all pigs everywhere.

At that time, there was a lot of talk about the feminization of the ministry, emphasizing that the qualities of a good pastor were the same qualities most generally associated with women: sensitivity, caring, empathy, collaboration, altruism, and of course, love. If I had been able to summon any sympathy toward this unholy man, spewing disrespect if not violence toward women, I might have found it in the swamp of his fear—the fear of being trapped in an effeminate profession; a fear ill-founded, since the ministry has been dominated by men since the day Jesus got up and walked away. His swearing and disrespect of women were complicated by the fact that if he adhered faithfully to his church's doctrine, he could only find macho hard-dick pleasure in masturbation, and no doubt not without a little guilt. Violent language was his substitute.

Am I a pig like he was a pig? I do swear, but I like to think of my swearing as adding color to my speech or, at times, necessary force. I did let Samantha Esther Cunningham kiss me, and Walker too. But in all honesty, I don't think I'm a pig like he was a pig. God, I hope I'm right about this, because it's a bit late to mend my ways.

But fuck me, I just remembered that Samantha Esther Cunningham (pre-kiss) once told me that my swearing was "kind of sexy." I believe I was pleased at the time.

# 9

# The Palimpsest, New Sneakers, and Summer Sun Tea

MELISSA JENNIFER DAVIS just brought me my latte and croissant and a black coffee for herself. From time to time, when it is not too busy, she will sit herself down across the table from me and start talking. This was one of those times. Without hesitation or remorse, I immediately put down my pen, slid the yellow pad to the café wall on my left, and listened. On this morning, she missed her son.

"He was never the same after the plane crash and the amputation of his feet," she said. My immediate thought was, who could blame him. He had been trapped in the crashed plane on a snow-covered mountain next to his dead father for two days.

What Melissa Jennifer Davis was remembering was the little boy before the crash, not the surviving adult male who has drifted away. I sat, I sipped, I chewed, and I nodded. I said very little, in part because there was nothing to say and in part because something she said about being a little boy took me back to a small house in New Jersey across the street from a small church. The pastor of this small church was my father, Patrick Daniel Bainbridge.

I need to make some things clear. That small church was Patrick Daniel Bainbridge's first and last. He made it a short three years before packing it in. He left to pursue his real love and passion—James Joyce—but that's another story for another time.

Truth is, Patrick Daniel Bainbridge couldn't handle the juxtaposition of healing, forgiveness, love, and new life with the banalities of who got the keys and the sometimes-libelous relationships in the congregation. Joyce was anything but banal and libelous to Patrick Daniel Bainbridge, at least not at the time. Sadly, he would learn differently.

I don't remember much about the church except that, every year, our dog won the best behaved and most beautiful church dog of the year contest. Even as a small boy, no more than six or seven years old, I knew there was something suspect about this.

I have vague memories of the small white house. I remember one Sunday morning, dressed in my little gray suit and no doubt black tie, I found a can of black paint, mysteriously open, and a paint brush. As I waited for my mother and brother and our walk across the street to the church, I painted my red wagon black. I found this so successful, I put the can of paint and the paint brush in the wagon, went around to the front of the house, and started painting the house black. Ah, to be creative again. But I digress, because that's not the memory Melissa Jennifer Davis sparked in me.

As you entered the kitchen of the white-black house, the sink and fridge were to your right. Straight in front of you was a table that could accommodate four people. Cozy, yes. And beyond that was the door leading to the back yard.

It was summer, so the inner door was open. The screen door had one of those long springs to pull it closed. Out the door, it was two concrete steps down to the yard. On the top step, to the side so the screen door would not hit it, would sit a huge, clear-glass jar of sun tea. For those of you unaware, my mom filled the jar with water, dumped in a load of tea, and put it on the back step to sit in the sun. I think it sat there for hours.

Here's what I remember: the one day of my life I felt free.

It was Saturday, the first day of summer vacation. That meant three months of no school, and to me, at that age, three months was forever. I sat at the end of the kitchen table looking through the screen door to the back yard. Our back yard went on for miles—again, so it seemed to me—and ended in woods that continued until you reached the railroad tracks. I was eating a tomato sandwich—white bread, sliced tomatoes, mayonnaise. We didn't know much back then but somehow survived. I was drinking sun tea in a tall glass with more sugar than you want to know about. As the sugar settled at the bottom of the glass, I stirred it with a long Howdy Doody iced tea spoon. Google it if you must.

I wore a white t-shirt and Levi's—there were only white t-shirts then,; no colors, no words, no logos, no images of any kind. My feet didn't reach the floor and swung back and forth impatiently. Why impatiently? Because on those feet was a new pair of Converse sneakers. Those sneakers and my feet were made for running.

After I had finished my tea and sandwich, I ran around the table and through the screen door, flew over the steps, and hit the ground running. My mother yelled from the kitchen, "Don't slam the screen door!" I heard the door slam shut.

My new sneakers enabled me to run faster than I had ever run before. A cesspool in the yard had overflowed, and a wasp nest had settled in the muck. As I approached, I was astounded by how fast I was running. Surely, I could almost fly. It was almost as if I were outside myself, observing this magical moment. The dreamlike speed gave me the courage I needed, so I ran through the pool of filthy, shitty water and the nest, scattering wasps into the air, and continued straight to the woods, onwards to the tracks. There I would place a penny on the track and wait for a train.

The forever summer had just begun. I was free from the almost debilitating dyslexic burden of teachers who didn't understand or even care. I was free from the routine of black spelling test stars and failures. It was sun tea and brand-new sneakers.

Sitting at Paradise Café, memory almost took me back. Faster than light and free as a bird. It was exhilarating, intoxicating, but not complete, not a full incarnation of a little boy's experience so long ago.

My God, what would I give for just one moment of that feeling now? I yearned and ached for it. Unfortunately, I fear I have nothing left worth giving so that the mundane and sacred negotiation can begin. Summer does not last forever. Sun tea without a boatload of sugar probably isn't all that good. And Converse sneakers cost a fortune these days. Ah, such is life and the certitude of aging, which we all must do until we don't.

# 10

# Michael Andrew Walker Johnson and the Poetry

BITTER TIMES
      Embrace in trenches
where we huddle
Heads into our knees
leaning against each other
Whistling of cruelties
overhead, missiles and slanders.
I die here
edge of wilderness,
love and barbed wire
Tomorrow another form
shucking. Old skin itches and splits
Leaves the carcass behind.
emerge, speaking the dark languages.
Soft, behold: litter of bodies
splayed across the swallowing mud.
There, yesterday's tears
already being made into wine.

# 11

# Barry Patrick Olds and the Brotherhood of Christian Businessmen

I WAS SITTING AT MY usual table looking toward Hearst Avenue. I had just removed my legal pad and pen from my bag when Melissa Jennifer Davis came through the café's open door, placed my latte on the table, and took the chair across from me. She looked serious.

"Barry Olds wants to talk to you," she said.

"Who's Barry Olds?" I asked.

"Have you seen the five guys who come to the café and take a table indoors?"

"The ones who look like they just arrived from the 1950s? Yeah, I've seen them. They're here quite a bit," I said.

"That's them. Olds wants to talk to you. He asked me to ask you if it was okay for him to come out and sit with you for a minute. I'm sorry. I'm just passing on the message," she said.

"Why the hell does he want to talk to me?" I asked. "I don't know him. He doesn't know me."

"Actually, I think he does. But like I said, I'm just the messenger."

In order to let Melissa Jennifer Davis off the hook, I agreed. The legal pad would have to wait.

Barry Patrick Olds came through the door and turned toward my table. He, like his companions inside, wore a gray suite, a nondescript tie—a tie that could only offend people who detested boredom—and shining black shoes. His light brown hair was cut very short, almost in a crew cut. He was, of course, shaven, and his skin looked scrubbed clean. His fingernails were perfect. His smile exposed the kind of straight, healthy, gleaming white teeth I've always been jealous of. My guess, he was in his mid-thirties.

"Mr. Bainbridge, do you mind if I sit down?" he asked, standing erect with a cup and saucer in his left hand.

"Go ahead," I said, and so he did. "What's this about? Do we know each other?"

"We've never met, but I know you," he said with his beatific smile.

Melissa Jennifer Davis came out carrying my croissant and what looked like a blueberry muffin and placed them on the table.

He took the muffin and I the croissant. I was already breaking off a piece of pastry when Barry Patrick Olds said, "We should give thanks." He began to raise his left hand across the table, obviously assuming I would hold it as we prayed. In an instant, he realized that was not going to happen, so he placed his hand on the table and began to pray aloud.

I found all this somewhat presumptuous. I interrupted him.

"Mr. Olds, perhaps it would be better to continue your prayer in the nearest closet. What do you think? Shall we do a Matthew? I'm sure Melissa will be accommodating. I'm quite sure your salvation is all but guaranteed, so I don't think there's any reason to make a public display. And why don't you call me David if you're comfortable with that?"

It took Barry Patrick Olds a moment, but to his credit ,he smiled, reached for his muffin, and took a big bite.

"So, Barry, what can I do for you?"

He placed the muffin on the plate, wiped his hands on a paper napkin, took a sip of what I now knew to be tea, and said, "My brothers and I..." He paused, glanced at the café wall beside us, indicating that his "brothers" were sitting very close on the other side of the wall. "My brothers and I," he repeated, "are the board for the Brotherhood of Christian Businessmen."

"No sisters in the Brotherhood?" I asked, knowing the answer.

"No, David. We adhere strictly to the sacred scriptures. I don't believe I need to say more about that," Barry said.

"No, Barry, you don't."

"And I certainly didn't sit down to begin a discussion about biblical literalism versus interpretation," he said and laughed lightly.

I too chuckled and said, "Well, Barry, I'm glad to hear it."

We both took a sip from our drinks.

"David, I want to be straight with you," he said.

"That would probably be best," I said.

"I'm not here to attempt to justify the Brotherhood's biblical and theological understanding of Jesus Christ's ongoing ministry. I'm here to ask for your help," he said.

Now that did intrigue me. We both knew I was a million miles from the Brotherhood's understanding of Christianity. That became clear over grace. So it was surprising that he would be asking me for help. Once he said, "the Brotherhood of Christian Businessmen," I assumed he was hoping to evangelize me into said Brotherhood.

"I'm listening," I said and reached for my croissant.

"Thanks, David. I was hoping you would say something like that. May I continue?"

"Go right ahead," I said. "But don't forget your muffin." He smiled.

"As chair of the board, I'm always looking for ways to further the Brotherhood's mission. It is our belief that America, once a great Christian nation, has strayed from its faithful path. The Brotherhood wants to aid the country in getting back on track. I admit we are small. We only have one hundred thirty-two Christian businessmen in membership, but I'm not ashamed to say we do have a lot of money." He paused to take a bite of muffin. The declaration about having a lot of money didn't surprise me in the least.

"It is our belief that the country can only prosper if it becomes, essentially, a Christian theocracy, but with a forgiving and open heart, of course."

"Of course," I said.

"Well, we are businessmen, not politicians, but we firmly believe that we might reach this national goal in part by establishing one business after another, very large and very small, Christian businesses, kind of business theocracies, if you will. And so, we are in the process of buying up businesses up and down the country. Well, to be honest, not yet up and down the country. We are starting here."

"Here?" I interrupted. "What do you mean, 'here'? You don't mean Paradise Café, do you?"

"By 'here' I mean Northern California, and specifically the San Francisco Bay Area. Might as well start in the devil's playground," he said and laughed again. "David, did you know there is a devil under every bush in Berkeley?"

"No Barry, I didn't know that," I said.

"But to answer your question, yes, by 'here' I also mean this café."

My latte was getting cold. I sighed and sat back in my chair. I looked up through the latticework above me, longing for the sun. All I wanted to do was sit at this outside table by the door of Paradise Café and write my palimpsest on a long yellow legal pad. I didn't come here to listen to this kind of bullshit. I was sick to death of this kind of bullshit. I had left this kind of bullshit behind. My heart sank thinking that my sanctuary had been breached by the Brotherhood of fucking Christian Businessmen.

And yet, even as my despair threatened to overwhelm me, I realized it could have been worse, much worse. In another time, a time more rational and reasonable, Barry Patrick Olds would have sounded completely and ultimately bat-shit crazy, but this is not one of those times. As I sit here in Berkeley writing in my yellow pad, this is a time when millions of US Americans have cut their tether to reality and are willingly floating into a golden-showered never-never-land of alternative facts, mendacity, and insanity. This is a time when upwards of sixty-six million US Americans believe in QAnon, when hundreds of them would gather in public waiting for the return from the dead of John F. Kennedy and John F. Kennedy Jr. coming to announce that Trump was King of America. This is a time when hundreds of thousands believed lizard people from another planet, disguised as humans, controlled the government. In this time, Barry Patrick Olds was just an old-fashioned US American Christian fundamentalist who wanted to turn the United States of America into a Christian camp. In other words, no big fucking deal!

I leaned forward, placing my elbows on the table. I looked Barry in the eyes and said, "Barry, I don't see how I could possibly help you in what I consider a poorly conceived mission. And I'm quite confident Melissa will not sell Paradise Café to the Brotherhood."

"David, she's seriously thinking about it. Why do you think we come here so often? Paradise Café is to be our first step," he said, with a slight, not mischievous, but sinister smile.

How did this day go so wrong so quickly? My sanctuary, such as it was, was under threat. I didn't even pause to ponder why Melissa Jennifer Davis would sell Paradise Café at all, let alone to five Christian fundamentalists whose vision was to take over the United States and who had no respect for her as a person and a businesswoman. All I could think was, *What about my damn safe place?* I looked longingly at my yellow pad. My dried out and cracked old parchment of a life was waiting to be written upon. It frightened me to think what might happen if I failed in the telling—the scraped, bruised, bloody telling. This really was my last-chance-saloon moment.

I didn't care that the latte was now cold. The croissant sickened me. The sun had not yet crept over the table. I looked at Barry Patrick Olds, and I could see that he could see I was shocked. He gave me no time to regroup. "Can I continue, David?" he asked politely. I nodded. "The board would like to hire you as a consultant."

Well, you could have knocked me out of my chair with a whisper. The day actually could get worse.

"Barry, you've got to be kidding," I said.

"No. I'm not kidding. We prayed about this long and hard, and the Lord has insisted," he said.

"What could you and the Lord possibly want with an old progressive like me?"

"We want you to help us get access to the gay community. A lot of the businesses in this area are owned by gay people. Our mission is to buy them out and cleanse the businesses for Jesus. We want you to help us," Barry Patrick Olds said.

I just stared at him for the longest time, then I said, "Absolutely not!"

"No, David, there is a way. We are going to pay you more than handsomely," he said, reaching into his jacket pocket, bringing out a pen, writing a number on a napkin, and sliding it across the table to me. I didn't look at it.

"David, I know you could use the money. Your wife's death was expensive, and I believe I'm right in saying you haven't fully recovered, financially speaking. As I told you, money is not our problem. Gay people are our problem, and you love gay people, and apparently, they love you. Our Lord and Savior assures me, you are our way in."

"Barry, go fuck yourself."

# 12

# Michael Andrew Walker Johnson and the Kiss

*He was the gay friend, and I was the straight friend. Then he kissed me, on the lips.*

*The kiss was not an advance. It was not an invitation. It was simply a spontaneous gesture of loving friendship. The kiss was not sexually threatening, exploitative, or manipulative. And yet, all my self-defined noble deeds, all my self-exaggerated risks, all my self-conceived bold public statements, all my self-important theological and biblical arguments were exposed as painfully bounded in one moment of lips touching lips. The unease I felt became articulated in a question: Did I truly love this man, or was my love actually restrained by the fact that he was gay?*

*As it turned out, others saw the kiss, the result of which was one, the quasi-public questioning of my sexual identity and two, a thought for my soul to ponder. The thought was really another question: Was my commitment to justice constrained by my unwillingness to be identified, not with, but as one of those treated unjustly? The issue of sexual identity has been made profoundly complex and important due to an equally profound and complex history of homophobia in our church and society. However, if I truly believed that a gay person had as much ethical, theological, or anthropological integrity as any straight person, then why would I care if others thought I was gay or bisexual? Any hesitation was not a matter of guaranteeing a correct identity. In many ways, before the kiss and the questions, I no doubt made it clear to everybody and anybody that, while I supported gay rights and had gay friends, I was straight. Justice was one thing; my identity was another. It went deeper. It went to the integrity of my being.*

*Until that kiss, my love for gay men and lesbians was conditional, and my support of gay people was qualified. In a church and society that metaphorically stitches pink patches on our clothing in the attempt to identify those who must be rejected, conditional love and qualified justice are not good enough. For the sake of love and justice, it doesn't matter if I am gay or straight. It does matter where I stand when others inflict spiritual, emotional, and sometimes physical violence on people.*

I WROTE THAT MANY YEARS ago, after Walker and I kissed. It was published in a collection of essays gathered and edited by a colleague. I doubt many people read it. Still, I stand by what I wrote, though today I would obviously update the language, making it more inclusive. I should note, it was not Walker's intention to catch me up short when he initiated the kiss. He wasn't trying to expose my insecurity or hypocrisy. He just loved me.

Here's what happened.

I mentioned earlier that we went to a regional conference together. On the ride to a place called Asilomar, we got laughing about what a gossip-fest these conferences were, and Walker thought it would be a fun idea to spend as much time together as possible, let it be known we were sharing a room, and stay physically close, often touching each other in casual friendly ways. Nothing sexual or romantic, just close friendliness. I'm certain when we parked the car and Walker leaned over and kissed me, that was *not* the beginning of our little game. It was just him and me. I doubt he thought much about it. I never asked.

Since truthfulness in the interest of self-actualization is the reason I'm sitting here hunched over a legal pad, I'd be remiss not to mention that I kissed him back. Do I feel better at this moment for writing that down? Not really, though it needed to be said. Did I ever tell Jessica? No, I did not. Why not? Well, perhaps that question is still hidden below the surface of the parchment.

Through our relationship, Walker and I have actually spent very little time together when you add up the years. There have been long stretches when we didn't see each other or even communicate. Then there would be a visit or a flurry of emails. In one of these flurries, we talked openly about our relationship and the love we had for each other. I kept those emails—they were important. But one day, I went to Outlook and all my email had been emptied out of my numerous folders except for the most recent. I searched and swore but couldn't find the damn things. I actually felt significant loss. That was years ago, and I can still remember the feelings. At the time, I hadn't thought about going straight to Google mail, given I have a Gmail account. But when I was preparing to leave Maine, it occurred to me that those emails might still be held in some Google computer farm by some river tucked away in some far-off landscape. I went to my Google mail account, and, while I found 167 emails to and from Walker, there was no sign of that flurried moment of tender sharing. That poignant, important, loving moment was not there. Now the emails are impressions, residual moments alluded to.

In those 167 emails there were occasional passing comments about our relationship. In one, Walker wrote: "*I haven't forgotten you are a real man. One aspect of the real manliness about you I have always enjoyed, aside from wishing I had married you!!!, is your fierceness. Your dick is not your only spear (or shaft, depending on pun).*" I could not find what I had said to him that caused him to write that. Spear. Shaft. Pun. I have no idea. However, it was pure Walker.

An email from me to him: "*Not sure I have all that much to say but wanted to say hi anyway. I was sitting here in my study the other night reading and suddenly remembered that I love you. Not that I forget that, but it was one of those sudden awareness moments that makes you pause and look up from your book as though someone suddenly entered the room. I do marvel at this simple fact. Not that you are not worthy of love! That would be an absurd notion. It's just that given all the years we have known each other, we haven't spent all that much time together. It is a marvel, and an enjoyable one.*"

Walker's response: "*So much to respond to in your email. First, I do love you. Why has this never gone away? I don't know. And you're right, we don't see each other much, but that first openness to you in Berkeley has remained constant. I am always glad to know it is reciprocated. The thought of you is always accompanied by love and warmth.*"

In the lost emails, me the straight man and Walker the gay man, we wrote about the surprise of our love, the, perhaps, improbability of it. We accepted and mourned the fact that I was not gay. We remembered our fleeting but nonetheless genuine exploration to discover if I were perhaps repressing a part of me that could flourish with Walker. We tried and tried again, but no hidden suppression to be liberated. Bottom line, though I had wished otherwise at the time, I'm straight.

All the trying, all the exploration, all the hoping happened long after the kiss in the car at Asilomar. I don't know who saw us, but by the end of the three-day conference, the word was that we were having an affair. Sometimes you really can count on all the people all the time.

And so, it's palimpsest time. The lunch crowd has come and gone here at Paradise Café. Melissa Jennifer Davis is cleaning tables, looking a little frazzled. She has just brought me a very welcome but not requested large glass of red wine with the words, "For your writing." The traffic is heavy on Hearst Avenue at the end of Hearst Food Court. As always, the sky is blue at this time of day and this season of the year. And I've reached the point at which I always turn away. But not now, not this time. It's blood time, scraping time, reading the original text time.

What would I have done if Walker and I had discovered that I was bisexual?

Let's be honest. I was emotionally unfaithful to Jessica. Couples talk about fidelity, more than not thinking about physical fidelity, when they declare their love and intentions. But surely emotional fidelity is important as well. No, I did not tell Jessica about the kiss or about the emails, and certainly not about the exploration.

However, Jessica wasn't stupid. She knew my relationship with Walker was essential to me and that my feelings ran deep, but she never talked or asked about it. Walker and Jessica? They were, I think, good friends. I never noticed awkwardness or tension between them. But I'm betting she knew or at least suspected. How much, I will never know.

What would I have ultimately done if I were bisexual? I honestly don't know, but it would have been messy, and it would have been hurtful, and it would have been painful. I knew a man married to a woman who was having an affair with a man. He told me that he was not being unfaithful to either partner with a certitude that was, perhaps, nothing more and nothing less than a kind of ethical camouflage. I told him that his assertion was bullshit, though obviously convenient for him. That kind of ethical gymnastics is not for me; is not me. If you're in love with two people, declaring those loves and acting on those loves, there will be consequences.

Some time before leaving Maine for Berkeley, I received this from Walker: "*If you had been gay, we would still be lovers, long-term mutual evolvers.*" If that's true, I'd also be divorced and, as a result, heartbroken.

# 13

# The Palimpsest and the Family

THERE WERE ALWAYS FOUR issues to discuss with people planning to marry, and I mean all people. I don't care if they are straight, gay, trans, or something I've never heard of yet. Having said that, I guess my assertion doesn't apply to sologamy. I mean, if you're going to marry yourself, then I'm thinking you've already discussed these things with yourself. And yes, sologamy is a real thing.

In any event, the topics for discussion. Communication: Do you actually talk to each other? Sex: Are you doing it and how's it going? Finance: Are your relationships to and uses of money compatible? Children: Are you planning to have them, and have you talked about how to raise them? Now, if I were still in the biz, which thankfully I'm not, I'd add another topic for their consideration. Extended family: Are you aware of your intended's relationship with their family and their expectations of you in that family?

I'm not boring you with this stuff because it's all that important to you, but to say that Jessica and I were pretty damn good on the first four when we started out. No, Jessica wasn't perfect, nor was our marriage. If I'm making it sound like that, you'll have to forgive me. I was with her since our college days, and now she's dead, so give me a break.

Jessica's relationship with her family was loving, open, and valuable. It was one of eternal return. She was always, with open arms, returning to her family. This dumbfounded me. To me, family was, is, something to be avoided, to be run from, at pace. If I were somehow magically to recall all the fights Jessica and I had over the decades, the vast majority of them would have been about family. As I said, other stuff we pretty much nailed. Communication? No problem. We talked through the good and bad times, and it probably saved our marriage on a few occasions. Sex? I'd say we did pretty damn well, though you will understand that, even in a palimpsest confession, the details are inappropriate. Finance? We worked that out right at the beginning. Children? We agreed not to have any—problem solved. But family? Well, we inhabited different galaxies on that one.

Don't get me wrong. I lucked out with Jessica's family, big time. They were respectable in the ways necessary and disrespectable in ways that warranted applause. I liked them instantly. Soon afterwards, I valued them. Love followed swiftly.

And my parents? Well, they were wonderful. There was no emotional or physical abuse. My father only spanked me once, and unfortunately for him, though not for me as it turned out, it didn't go the way he had planned. In a father-knows-best parental act of love, he put me over his knees, and with his big clear-plastic flat-backed hairbrush, gave my bottom a good whacking. I laughed. It wasn't that I thought it was funny. It was not. It hurt like hell. And I meant no impertinence. It's just that my reaction to the pain and humiliation was to laugh instead of cry. Why, I don't know. However, he never used corporal punishment again. Thinking about it now, I feel sorry for him. I should have cried. We both would have felt better. No, there was no abuse. I was loved and cared for as best they could offer on an often small budget. There was instead a...what? Not an expectation, but more a nurtured assumption of dependency and permanency. A never leaving. While Jessica was always returning, I was never meant to leave.

While Jessica decided to return to her family, I decided to leave mine, and I remember it specifically. It was the summer in-between my junior and senior year in college. During my junior year, my parents moved and, when I came "back home" that summer, I found my mother had, to the best of her ability, recreated my bedroom in the old house. I was both impressed and saddened. It was a loving act, but felt like over-try to me. It felt like a sad attempt. And it wasn't home.

My father, through a member of his congregation, had secured a job for me in a local flower processing plant. It was a good job and I was grateful. However, after a few weeks, a friend from college called me and said the college was looking for students to help paint some of the buildings on campus. He put my name in. We would work about six hours a day, get paid a decent wage, and live in the dorm free. To my shame, I told my father I was going back to the college to work, thus forcing him to have an embarrassing conversation with the man who had gotten me the job. Knowing my dad, he was probably humiliated. However, I knew exactly what I was doing: rejecting both my mother's attempt to make a home for me and rejecting my father's success in finding me a summer job. I packed my bags and left. I never returned home to live again.

It's not unreasonable to ask why I was so determined to leave.

For reasons I'll never recall, when I was in the eighth grade, I told my father I wanted to open a savings account. I had saved money from my allowance and the odd job here and there, and my father took me to the local bank. With his help, I left with an account totaling the grand sum of sixty-eight dollars. One day, Dad came to me and asked if he could borrow sixty-seven dollars. What was a boy to do? I loved my dad. It's family. He apparently needed it. I lent him the money. I never saw it again. That's when I learned that a family loan was a gift.

At the beginning of my junior year in what was then an expensive liberal arts college—expensive as compared to a state university—we all went to the gym to collect various bits of information and our first quarter class schedule. Inside my manila folder, I found a note instructing me to see the dean of students. I, of course, went to the dean's office, where I was told by a very nice man—obviously embarrassed, but caring, sensitive, and honest—that not only had my parents not paid for the first quarter of the school year, which would begin in a few days, they had not paid for the entire last year. That's when I learned I was on my own. Well, kind of.

The dean of students helped me with grants and a job in the cafeteria kitchen. He helped me get a student loan, one that unfortunately my father had to co-sign. Embarrassing for the dean and me, humiliating for my father. The deal included that the money I made in the kitchen went to the college to help pay off my debt. I told my two best friends about the situation and said that our excursions to movies, pizza, etc. were out for me. Without hesitation, they told me that until things were sorted, they would cover my share of the expenses. That's when I learned that family could mean something else.

My mother died three years after the death of my father. My brother, then living with my mother, called to tell me she had died. He then said this to me: he needed money for the funeral, and if I couldn't afford both the cost of the funeral and the cost of the flight to get me to the service, he preferred I send the money. I've never fully clarified within myself what that taught me, but teach me it did.

My mother saved my life when I was very young. I mentioned the dyslexia earlier. Thing is, I just couldn't learn the way the teachers expected me to. So, lots of black stars for me. Once a teacher hit me with a ruler and declared I was stupid, in a voice all the class could hear. My mother kept telling me I wasn't stupid, that I was smart, against all the evidence. She would sit with me on my bed reading from the *Little Red Science Books*. She'd read a paragraph, and then I would attempt to read on. She saved me.

Unfortunately, by the time I reached college, she couldn't let go. I remember that, one winter break, my friends and I planned a week away skiing, but I got a call from my mom insisting I come home for the Christmas season. I told her of my plans, but she pleaded with a tearful voice. I can't remember now the reason she was so persistent, and why it was so important that the entire family gather together. Now, sitting here in Paradise, I don't blame her. She was a mother, for God's sake, a good mother, and she wanted her family together one more time, perhaps one last time, for Christmas.

It didn't work out. Everyone was trying too hard, and so everyone was unhappy. My mother became angry. My father did his best to make gentle the turbulence. My mother and I fought like angry beasts, not because we hated each other, but because we loved each other. The truth was, we were much alike. She had wanted an education, but her father said no. She was a girl after all. She wanted to travel, but my father hated the idea. She wanted a career, but she had two boys to raise.

After that fraught Christmas visit, I never returned home again. She wrote me letters—this was way before email—that could run twelve pages long. I did my best to respond. When I went off to war-torn El Salvador, she was frantic, so I called her as soon as I returned to the States. I have often wondered what our relationship would have been, what my family relationships would have been, if she had only let me go.

I want to make this point. The fact that I never returned was not an indication of my lack of love for my family, but rather a vague awareness, not yet articulated in my mind and heart, that my survival as a distinct and mature human being depended on distancing myself from them. After college, I moved two thousand miles from the home hearth. Then it was three thousand miles. Finally, I settled in a foreign country. I became the distant sheep. The traveler who returned only sporadically. Perhaps rightfully, I was sometimes judged harshly for my wandering. I know I will never be forgiven. Such is life. I not only survived, but I did okay, if I do say so myself. Would I do it all again? Yes.

# 14

# Michael Andrew Walker Johnson and the Poetry

BOY SOPRANO:
   I am the daylight
   and I am the hours;
   I am of this name
   this hallowed night:
   Seasons pass from day to age
   in the palm of my hand;
   As in the sound of silence
   from a falling leaf;
   I am of the green moss
   the down-spun stones

     in the well,

   As well as of the silver salmon
   a sunlit pool under ancient oaks.
   On my thin forehead
   the veil rests in-between,
   Through which emerge
   the vast embraces.
   Breathe
   and desire is good.
   Breathe

and the unseen touches skin.
Breathe
and all living things are healed
by unspoken words.
When I whisper
meet me under the moon.

# 15

# The Palimpsest, the Girl, and the Aliens

A FACE HAS JUST COME to me from out of nowhere. If I were an artist, I think I could sketch it on my yellow pad. It is of a girl around, maybe, fourteen years old. We are sitting at night on some kind of wall because our feet are hanging down. We are sitting close enough that our shoulders are touching, but though we are both in the midst of an awakening puberty, our relationship is not burdened with sexual desire or romantic tensions. We are simply good friends. How delightful that is.

We are looking up at the stars in the night sky and discussing the possibility that there are other intelligent species on other planets looking up at their night sky discussing the possibility that there are other intelligent species on other planets looking up at their night sky. Actually, we aren't discussing possibilities. We both believe with an impressive certainty that there are indeed other species in the universe wondering about us.

What a friendship we had. She was from a Catholic family and I from a Protestant family. In those days, Catholics didn't break bread with us Protestants, which we both thought was rather stupid and, furthermore, a challenge to our friendship. So we pledged that she would worship in my church and I in hers. I'm sure it never happened, but I applaud our defiant desire. Many would have called us naïve, but it was a youthful declaration that relationship is more important than ecclesiology.

Perhaps I'm making way too much of this memory. Perhaps on this day, sitting at my sanctuary table, I'm wanting something she gave me. Who knows? The remembrance of her and that night is worthwhile, comforting, and surprising.

It saddens me that I will not be alive when we human beings finally discover that life exists on some body that is not planet Earth. I'm not thinking of contact with another intelligent species somewhere in the galaxy. No; I'd settle for some tiny bug of a thing that lives, reproduces, and dies on some planet or asteroid or moon that has absolutely nothing to do with us. Sadly, if we find it, there's a good chance we will kill it. It's our way, is it not? But still, it would be good for us to learn we are not the center of the universe. Even a tiny bug could dislodge that delusion.

It would be nice, however, if we did find an intelligent species somewhere in the galaxy. We human beings are such an incredibly stupid intelligent species, I have always hoped we are not the pinnacle of self-awareness. That would truly be sad.

I was sitting by the window in the upper deck of a London bus one day. We had stopped at a red light, and I watched as a man striding with pace while fiddling with his cell phone walked right into a streetlamp. It was humorous and distressing at the same time. He ended up on his ass on the sidewalk. While he was not a contender for a Darwin Award, he looked as dumb as a bag of rocks sitting there holding his head.

I don't remember her name, but as I said, I can see her face, and a nice face it is. She was slender with brown hair almost touching her shoulders. She was wearing a short-sleeved shirt and jeans. She was so sincere. She smiled a lot. I wonder what happened to her. I wonder if she is still alive. I wonder...I wonder if she remembers me and our night talk about aliens. Wouldn't it be absolutely wonderful if she did, if she were at this very moment thinking about a fourteen-year-old me? A me with fears and hopes, not yet too damaged to dream?

As I remember this moment, I am filled with warmth toward this intelligent, sweet, imaginative girl. She is engaging. She is endearing.

God, I miss her.

Abigail?

Abby?

Abby Susan Webster!

# 16
# Megan Margaret Williams, the Mothers, and the Perfect Day

I HAVE MY HEAD DOWN. My pen in hand. My yellow legal pad before me. As always, the weather is perfect. My head is down because I'm trying to think. And write, of course. My head is down close to the yellow pad because today I should be thinking about Jessica or Walker or myself. That's the whole point of seeking sanctuary and undertaking the palimpsest. My head is down closer still to the pad to avoid distractions from the waiters and the people on Hearst Food Court slurping, talking, chewing, walking, laughing. But mostly my head is down, now almost touching the yellow pad, because I can't get Melissa Jennifer Davis and the Brotherhood out of my mind. She can't really be contemplating selling Paradise to fundamentalists! With head now touching the pad, I have decided I must talk to Melissa Jennifer Davis. I must save the café. Save Melissa Jennifer Davis. Save myself. Save my sanctuary. And so, with a sudden thrust of my head upward, determined to tread where I knew I should not, what did I see, but Megan Margaret Williams standing next to my table, very close to my table, with her hand on my table, smiling at me.

The Brotherhood would have to wait. Melissa Jennifer Davis would have to wait. Jessica and Walker would have to wait. The smile would not wait. If I could only believe, the smile might offer peace. It would overwhelm parchment and bleeding and death. Perhaps even the Brotherhood. But, alas, smiles are ephemeral, and so I smiled ephemerally back.

"Hello David," Megan Margaret Williams said.

"Hello Megan," I said. "If you want, you can call me Dave."

"I like David," she said.

"Then you must call me David."

"Hello, I'm Sarah," a voice said.

I looked away from Megan Margaret Williams, and of course, the two women I had met the other day on the sidewalk were standing just behind her. One was stepping forward and putting out her hand. I assumed she was Sarah. I stood up and shook her hand.

"This is my mommy," Megan said.

"And I'm Jill," said the other woman, now standing by Sarah Jane Williams's side with her hand extended.

"This is my mommy," Megan said again.

I shook her hand and said, "Hello Jill. And hello Sarah." And then I just stood there not knowing what to say or do.

"David, you should have lunch with us," Megan said.

"Megan, David looks busy. We shouldn't disturb him," Jill Rosemary Thompson said, with the infant strapped to her chest. Then, looking at me, "David, I'm sorry. Megan can be a bit forward sometimes. We didn't mean to bother you. Megan saw you as we were walking up the court and ran up to say hi."

"It's fine," I said. Looking at Megan Margaret Williams, but speaking to Jill Rosemary Thompson, I said, "If she's forward, she does it with a rather disarming delightfulness."

"Would you like to join us for lunch?" That was Sarah Jane Williams.

I, still standing awkwardly, looked down at the table, my yellow pad, my pen, but mostly at the table. I was loath to leave it. Someone else might get the impression that they could move in and occupy my almost sacred space. It was *my* table.

"We could slide this other table over. I'm sure people wouldn't mind walking around us," Sarah Jane Williams said.

"We should ask the lady if it's okay," Megan Margaret Williams said.

"No, no. I'm sure it's fine. If Melissa minds, I'll take the heat," I said, relieved I would not have to vacate my table.

"Who's Melissa?" Megan Margaret Williams asked.

"She's the lady. She owns Paradise Café. She's a friend," I said, as Sarah Jane Williams began sliding the other table to mine and Jill Rosemary Thompson grabbed chairs.

Melissa Jennifer Davis suddenly came out through the door carrying a tray of food, saw what was happening, hesitated for a moment, smiled at me, and moved to the table behind me.

"Is that Melissa?" Megan Margaret Williams asked.

"Yes, that's Melissa. And everything's okay. She doesn't mind," I said.

"Well, that's a good thing," Megan Margaret Williams said and sat down next to me. Jill Rosemary Thompson and Sarah Jane Williams sat opposite us as I cleared the table of my laptop, pad, and pen, and dropped them all hastily into my bag.

The other day when I was walking to the café and saw the four of them, I assumed the mother of the infant was Jill Rosemary Thompson, simply because the baby was clinging to her, and of course, I was right. Jill Rosemary Thompson gave birth to Eleanor Sandra Thompson, and Sarah Jane Williams gave birth to Megan Margaret Williams. As it turned out, Jill Rosemary Thompson offered little Eleanor Sandra Thompson lunch after finishing hers. Of course, no one minded. The Brotherhood were not present on this perfect day.

Sarah Jane Williams was the shorter of the two mothers, slim with short, dark hair—short like in a boy's cut. She was pretty, her eyes dark and deep. Her hands were slender, actually beautiful. I could tell fairly quickly by our conversation that she was intelligent, probably very intelligent, maybe intimidatingly intelligent. She reminded me of Jessica in attitude, manner, and voice.

Both women exuded a confidence that I have never possessed. They both were kind. Sarah Jane Williams smiled a lot. Jill Rosemary Thompson, stockier, had dishwater blond hair and was as tall as me at about six feet. She was somehow slightly more distant, though that characterization is unfair. It's just that I was naturally drawn to Megan Margaret Williams and Sarah Jane Williams, and less so to Jill Rosemary Thompson. Her hair was thick and fell to her shoulders in waves. Her blue eyes were losing their high density, but they were kind and attentive. I wondered if Megan Margaret Williams, in some way, the way of a small child, knew Sarah Jane Williams as her biological mother and Jill Rosemary Thompson as her relational mother. Or was the distinction completely irrelevant to her?

I guessed both women were in their mid-thirties, but I should also confess that I'm not terribly good at judging people's ages. They met after Megan Margaret Williams was born, but just. They are now married. I have no idea where they got the sperm, and it certainly was none of my business, though I was curious. They seemed good together, comfortable. They had a natural ease with each other with no hint of a boring complacency. They loved and parented Megan Margaret Williams and her sister, Eleanor Sandra Thompson, without distinction or favoritism. If they hadn't told me who the biological mother of each child was, I would not have known by their behavior. On this perfect day, they were an ideal US American family. Well, not ideal for *Fox News*, nor for the Brotherhood, but you understand. And I'm sure I have overemphasized their reality. I'm sure the three of them fought with each other from time to time, were sometimes melancholy, and on occasion downright unpleasant. But on this day, I preferred to see only the good.

Jill Rosemary Thompson was a teacher in what my generation called junior high school. I thought her brave, though she seemed fairly calm about it. Sarah Jane Williams was, was what? A blogger, a writer of nonfiction, and an influencer. I had never given much thought to the "influencers" of our internet age, but when I did, I dismissed them. Thus, it was interesting to learn that Sarah Jane Williams was not an influencer of product sales, a reviewer of perfume or plastic wrap, nor a YouTube celebrity who showed you how to apply makeup properly or wrap a gift. She was an influencer in ideas. This both intrigued me and, ever so slightly, disturbed me. Jessica was a journalist and a damn good one. I'd go so far as to say she did a fair bit of influencing herself. She was the reason we moved to Great Britain. For just a moment, a very fleeting moment, I began to conflate Sarah Jane Williams and Jessica, but killed that puppy in the toilet without mercy or guilt. I was tempted to ask Sarah Jane Williams how on earth she made a living by blogging and influencing ideas, when I remembered reading about a nine-year-old boy who made three million dollars on YouTube reviewing toys. Three million dollars!

To my surprise, given my desired avoidance of distractions, my reluctance to embark even superficially on even one new relationship, let alone four, Jill Rosemary Thompson and Sarah Jane Williams got quite a bit out of me. I talked about Jessica and the fact that she had died, steering clear of details—she died of cancer was the long and short of it. I talked about living in the UK, the move back to the States, and settling in Castine, Maine. When Sarah Jane Williams asked about what was happening on the yellow pad, I did a politician on her and expertly, if I do say so myself, answered any number of questions, imagined and real, but not the one she had asked. There was no need for them to know I had traveled all the way across the country from Castine to Berkeley for the explicit purpose of exposing myself to myself, to the point, if necessary, of bloodletting. If I had said so, I'd have had to explain why I was doing such a thing, that peace had eluded me all my life and that my time to find it was running out, that I am really not sure why I sit day after day writing on a yellow pad (I mean, why the hell don't I use my laptop; it would all go much faster, and I'd be done with parchment scraping), and that my anxiety about all this was growing.

I did not mention Walker. Why, I'm not sure.

Throughout the three-way adult conversation over sandwiches, iced tea for Sarah Jane Williams and Megan Margaret Williams, and red wine for Jill Rosemary Thompson and me, Megan Margaret Williams mostly sat quietly, seemingly paying attention to what was being said, looking to one speaker, then another. But on occasion, she jumped in with a thought that might or might not have had anything to do with what was actually being discussed. And then, in the middle of a deepening give-and-take about the merits of Instagram as a means of communication among early teens as against the established danger to young girls, Megan Margaret Williams said, "David, I think you should come to the park tomorrow with me and mommy."

"That would be Sarah," Jill Rosemary Thompson said. "I have to work. Even though it's summer..."

"No, no. No need to explain," I interrupted. "I've known more than a few teachers in my life, and they never seemed to stop working." I looked at Megan Margaret Williams and said, "Well, I don't know. I will have to check with your mom."

"Mom says it's okay with us," Sarah Jane Williams said. "I was thinking tomorrow about three in the afternoon. Would that work?"

"Yes, that would be good. So, Megan, I'll see you tomorrow, and thanks for the invitation," I said.

With that, Jill Rosemary Thompson got up and said, "Come on, Megan. Let's let David get back to work." Megan jumped off her chair, and before I knew it, was walking hand and hand with Jill

Rosemary Thompson toward the busy street. As Sarah Jane Williams began to turn to follow, I grabbed her arm and said, "Is this really okay with you? I don't want to interfere, and I obviously don't know how to say no to Megan."

"David, Megan has taken a real liking to you. She's been talking about you since we met the other day," Sarah Jane Williams said.

"Isn't that a bit strange, or I should say, unusual? I'm an old man after all," I said.

"Not to Megan, you're not. To Megan, for whatever reason, you're a new friend. And I like it, we like it. You bring something to her life she doesn't have. So, it's up to you. But if you do befriend her, don't underestimate her, and don't set her up. Be straight with her. We live here. You live in Maine. I trust you to do it right," Sarah Jane Williams said.

As I was assuring Sarah Jane Williams that I would indeed "do it right," with a damn good feeling inside, a startling feeling that new friendships might actually be a good thing for me, I saw Barry Patrick Olds and his Christian posse turn off Hearst Avenue, come up the stairs onto Hearst Food Court, and walk confidently toward the café and my perfect day.

# 17

# The Palimpsest, the Old Man, the Village, and the Grave

I ONCE KNEW AN OLD man—his name was Laurie James Skerritt. He lived in the same very small village of Castle Carrock his entire life—no doubt born in Carlisle and brought home to the village in a matter of days. He lived in the same house all those years and eventually brought his wife there. He attended the village school. He attended the same small Anglican church most every Sunday, only ill health keeping him away. He visited the Duke of Cumberland pub five evenings every week—the Duke was the only pub in the village—but he never entered its doors on Saturdays or Sundays. The only time he left the village for any length of time was to fight in World War II. In the end, he was buried in the church graveyard facing the village green, next to the small schoolhouse, and not more than a hundred paces or so from the Duke of Cumberland. Laurie James Skerritt was a good man.

I drove up from London for Laurie James Skerritt's funeral by myself; Jessica was too busy. Perhaps it was a bit eccentric of me. After all, Laurie James Skerritt and I weren't that close, but there was something fascinating to me about a man who never left home. We often use the cliché about "having roots," but in Laurie James Skerritt's case, there were large, long, old, deep roots. A lifetime of roots. The service in the small church, which was damp and chilly even in the summer, was nothing to remember, but when we went outside and into the church graveyard, I was spellbound. Of course, the hole had already been dug. As I watched Laurie James Skerritt being lowered into the ground, into the soil of his church, his village, his people, I was deeply moved. Laurie James Skerritt was being planted in the only home he had ever known. He would never leave. The entire village came out to watch his permanence confirmed.

I have absolutely no idea what it would mean to live a life of such permanence. I imagine lifelong relationships, some wonderful, some horrible, some neither here nor there. I imagine a depth of familiarity that must be profound. Surely sometimes it was boring, but on the other hand, to know one's home so utterly well must be overpowering. I have never experienced anything like it and obviously never will. Never.

Don't get me wrong. Even as I felt envious of Laurie James Skerritt as he was being lowered into the ground, I didn't regret, and have never regretted, the way my life turned out. I've traveled more than some and less than others, but I've spent time in some seventy-five countries—I have no idea how many cities, towns, villages, and hamlets I have had the privilege of knowing. I've had good friends in Taipei, Harari, and Prague. It's been exciting, and what I lost in depth of time, I've made up for in experiences and people.

Still, because I left home and kept moving, there is nowhere to bury me, or at least, nowhere of meaning. There is nowhere to scatter my ashes. Jessica requested her ashes be scattered in a redwood forest, and so they were. There will be no big gathering of people for me, if indeed there is a service at all. With both Jessica and Walker gone, who the hell would plan it? And even as these blue-ink words on a yellow piece of paper look back at me and, yes, sadden me a little, it was the life I chose.

Oh God, I sound like Frank Sinatra! God forbid. I did it my fucking way. No! I don't mean that. I don't mean that US American macho individualism. I was not and am not an island. I was never alone. I never would have made it without people. And now that I really am alone, I've lost touch with...well, me. All hail the palimpsest —My savior for reading truth and emptiness. My last-chance saloon. Who knows? It might work.

# 18

# Michael Andrew Walker Johnson and the Poetry

CREDO

    Let us be in love with all our intentions
    Trans-sex all our relations
    Ride the thrust of every release
    Take the world's impulses within,
    Then glance away
    Into cardboard alleys to
    Give birth to a new
    Anything-yet-to-be-dreamed,
    And crossing over into the unknown
    Raise it to the sun
    With goddamn you bloody hands
    And say
    We are! I am! Everything is!

# 19

# The Palimpsest and the Father

MY FATHER, PATRICK Daniel Bainbridge, was a university professor and a Joycean scholar, his second career, as I have mentioned before. You will recall he gave up Jesus for Joyce. Who would have thought? He loved *Ulysses*. If you have succeeded in reading *Ulysses*, you are either a Joycean academician or one of only half a dozen planetary citizens who have accomplished this near impossible task. The only people who read *Ulysses* are Joycean scholars who make biblical exegetes look like simple-minded, good-natured children discussing Sunday school lessons on a bright summer Sunday morning.

Because my father was a Joycean exegete, I tried and failed on several occasions to read *Ulysses*. In an effort to justify its unreadability, the editor of my edition explains that there are textual faults due to accident, the "misplacement of interlineated readings," imperfect transcription, and Joyce's "omissions in creatively copying out of a protodraft." The editor points out that the "isotext" is the book as Joyce himself actually wrote it, but that it does not make for a good reading text. However, "insofar as it is based on documents within the main line of transmission it is *exactly* the text in Joyce's handwriting (in the main) from which the edition of *Ulysses* published in 1922 and all subsequent editions ultimately derive." Indeed. My father loved this stuff.

To get a feel for how bad things can get, read –or try to read– the editor's helpful merging of an isotext edition of *Ulysses* and his reader's edition: "It is more extensive, engrossing as it does the two prototextual versions of the text that lie behind the (missing) typist's copy," and is, therefore, a synchronic and contextual deconstruction of the said isotext edition. An example:

And {And] mx [matrix] 3; and 0-1} ^[that scholar] $^{(2}$[this scholar] the learning knight {learning knight] mx 3; learning knight mx R } $^{2)}$^ let pour for { for] 0, mx 1, 3, and Rl to r1; $^{(2}$[him] $^{Γ3+}$[the traveler] Childe Leopold$^{+3}$]$^{2)}$ a draught of fellowship { of fellowship] 0, 1; absent3 and R } ^>and $^{V}$a { a] 0; absent 1 }$^{V}$help thereto$^{<}$ the which { which]0-1; while mx 3 and R } >all$^{<}$ they { all they] r0;...

My father read this stuff for hours. He was forever indulging in violent journalistic exchanges with other Joycean disciples who disagreed, for example, on the exact amount Leopold Bloom spent on one square of soda bread as noted in his budget for 16 June 1904. Apparently, their disagreement was caused by Joyce's omissions in creatively copying out of a protodraft or by misplacement of interlineated readings. This kind of nonsense was breath-taking to my father. Academic blood was often shed.

Even if you can survive long enough to read about Bloom's ontological and ethical crisis—which I'm sure he must have had, though it was nowhere in sight when I stopped reading on page 293 with the words, "From the belfries far and near the funereal death-bell tolled unceasingly, while all around the gloomy precincts rolled the ominous warning of a hundred muffled drums punctuated by the hollow booming of pieces of ordnance"—there is every possibility you will not recognize it when you get there. But if you do realize your arrival through some mysterious discernment, you will in all likelihood be unable to understand what you are reading. It might help if you read Homer's *Odyssey* first, but I sincerely doubt it. Leopold Bloom should just be left wandering through Dublin with his free-flowing poetic streams of consciousness.

My father so loved *Ulysses* that he actually went to Dublin and visited the Davy Byrnes pub at 21 Duke Street. As he sat in the pub with his tattered but much-loved edition of *Ulysses*, he copied these words into his journal.

> He entered Davy Byrnes. Moral pub. He doesn't chat. Stands a drink now and then. But in a leap year once in four. Cashed a cheque for me once.
>
> What will I take now? He drew his watch. Let me see now. Shandygaff?
>
> - Hello, Bloom, Nosey Flynn said from his nook.
>
> - Hello, Flynn.
>
> - How's things?
>
> - Tiptop...Let me see. I'll take a glass of burgundy and... let me see.
>
> Davy Byrne came forward from the hindbar in tuckstitched shirtsleeves, cleaning his lips with two wipes of his napkin. Herrings blush. Whose smile upon each feature plays with such and such replete. Too much fat on the parsnips.

- And here's himself and pepper on him, Nosey Flynn said. Can you give us a good one for the Gold Cup?

- I'm off that, Mr. Flynn, Davy Byrne answered. I never put anything on a horse.

- You're right there, Nosey Flynn said.

Mr Bloom ate his strips of sandwich, fresh clean bread, with relish of disgust, pungent mustard, the feety savour of green cheese. Sips of his wine soothed his palate. Not logwood that. Tastes fuller this weather with the chill off.

Nice quiet bar. Nice piece of wood in that counter. Nicely planed. Like the way it curves there.

I have never known why these particular words were what he chose to write in his journal, but I do know the strips of sandwich were, for some inexplicable reason, important to him. When he returned home from Ireland on a cold and wet night, with the desk lamp throwing shadows across the study, he settled into his leather chair and sat me on his lap—I was very young at the time. He described the pub in detail, paused for a moment, and then read the above words. They didn't mean a thing to me, but it was a rare moment, sitting in my father's lap in his favorite chair. It is a night I will never forget, perhaps our most intimate moment. When he finished reading, he closed his journal and placed it on the small wooden table by the chair. He sat silently for a moment and then said, "Tomorrow, I will give you your own copy of *Ulysses*." He loved me that much.

The next day, I sat at the window in my bedroom upstairs at the front of the house, waiting for him to ride up on his bicycle. Sure enough, the left saddlebag was pregnant with a big, fat copy of *Ulysses*. As I said, I have never finished the book, but I have been unable to rid myself of my father's gift. I keep it as a concrete reminder of that night.

He always rode a bicycle to and from the university or any place else in town he wanted to go. He gave up driving completely after he drove his three-year-old car into a three-hundred-year-old oak tree, almost killing a friend in the passenger's seat. Perhaps the bicycle thing was a bit extreme, and even the thought of harming another, let alone killing them, was enough for him to hang up his keys. If you think about it, it was kind of noble. In any event, after the accident, Mary Anne Bainbridge, my mother, did all the driving.

Patrick Daniel Bainbridge died while visiting Jessica and me when we lived in Britain. We had rented a house up in Cumbria as a nice vacation for my parents. The plan was one week up north near the Lake District and then three weeks at home in London. We picked them up at the airport, spent two days in London, and then hit the road to the North. Truth is, Patrick Daniel Bainbridge never felt at ease since arriving at Heathrow. He had never wanted to travel, while Mary Anne Bainbridge always had. Years ago, when I was a boy, he was offered a gig at the University of Hawai'i at Mānoa in Honolulu, and without even telling my mother, he turned it down. She was furious. She never forgot it.

Anyway, on the drive north up the M6, he was nervous, and when we got to the house I had rented, he never settled in. Mary Anne Bainbridge woke me late at night because my father was having terrible pain in his jaws and teeth. He was frightened and had been pacing back and forth in their room for hours holding his jaws in his hands. I called for medical assistance, and when the doctor arrived, she asked him to lie on the bed. As he lay down and she began riffling through her clichéd black bag, he suddenly grew quiet, held his right hand up in front of his face, looked at the back of it intently, and then said quietly, "Here I go." That was all. That was it.

His body started to convulse and the doctor, holding my father to the bed, told me to run out to her car parked in front of the house for a breathing tube in a box in the trunk. She threw me her keys, and, as I ran through the house, out the door, into the street, I was panicking because I didn't know what a breathing tube looked like. Thankfully, when I opened the trunk and found the box, despite the dark, it was obvious. I ran back into the house and gave her the tube, which she placed into his mouth and down his throat. She told me to breathe into it as she administered cardiopulmonary resuscitation. It didn't matter. He was dead. His heart had had enough.

The doctor started making phone calls, and eventually an ambulance arrived to take him away. Two policemen also arrived and began filling in what I assumed were the appropriate forms. I made coffee and invited them into the kitchen. We sat at the kitchen table while they explained each form for me to read and sign. Everything was calm, peaceful. We drank coffee and talked, and I signed forms that to this day I do not understand. When I had completed my task, one of the police asked me if the man were a visitor, and I explained that he was my father. They both seemed surprised, and the one who had spoken simply said he was sorry. It was clear they were both startled by my calmness and almost detachment, but how could I explain that I was in crisis mode? This was not the time to break down in emotional angst. There were things that needed to be done, and one of them was offering coffee to the police.

The days that followed were like living in a bubble. My job was to support my mother. Jessica's job was to support my mother and me. At one point, Mary Anne Bainbridge was sitting in a chair in the living room and started to say, through tears, that the death of her husband was her fault, that for years she had caused him stress, a stress that led to a heart attack and his death. I leaned over her with my hands on the chair arms and told her that she was at a crucial moment in her life, that what she decided at that moment would direct her down one path or another. She had to choose: "My husband's death is my fault," or "My husband died of a heart attack." Seven years later, Mary Anne Bainbridge died in a lounge chair in her living room sitting in her own urine. It was no way for a wonderful woman to leave.

I remained calm and detached for two more days until on the third day, coming down the stairs of the rental house, I inexplicably stopped midway, sat on a stair, and began to cry. Jessica rushed up and sat with me, her arms around my shoulders. I said to her, "I don't know how to do this. The son-grieving-the-father thing. I've never done it before."

The answer to the "how to do it" question is simple. You live.

# 20

# Michael Andrew Walker Johnson, the Scottish Castle, and the Japanese Tourists

WHEN JESSICA AND I had been living in Great Britain for a couple of years, Walker came calling. He had a plan, so I took time off work. The plan was to trace, or attempt to trace, his Scottish ancestry. So, after a few days in London for Walker to catch his breath and put aside the jetlag, we climbed into the car and headed north.

The main route north, at seventy-plus miles per hour, is the M6 motorway. After we had been on the road for a few hours, we stopped in a service area for lunch. We got coffee and sandwiches, and as we sat at a table by the huge window with a view of nothing worth remembering, Walker turned to me and said quietly, "What are they doing?"

I had no idea what he was talking about until he nodded his head toward a table just to our right. At the table sat what I assumed was a father and his approximately fifteen-year-old son. They both were eating hamburgers with knives and forks. Walker looked comically dumbfounded. I smiled and said, "They're eating hamburgers."

"With a knife and fork?" he asked. "I guess they must think we're barbarians." He just laughed and then continued, "I read Britain was having a big crisis over horse meat. I wonder if they're eating horse meat." He laughed again.

Somebody had found horse meat in some ground beef being sold in grocery stores. Or at least, I think that was the case. It was a long time ago. But I do remember it was a big deal.

"I grew up eating horse meat. We were relatively poor. Buying a horse heart and stuffing it with vegetables, corn meal, et cetera, made for a nutritious dinner. You get through with what you have. We also ate calf brains for breakfast. But we didn't have to lie about it. It was available in grocery stores. Some years ago, there was a big stink in California about eating horse meat, and it was banned. So much for other available protein," Walker said, while watching father and son delicately cut their buns and hamburger meat and politely bring the forks to their mouths. He laughed again, finding the whole scene amusing.

Actually, Walker laughed a lot, and he smiled more.

"I didn't know you ate horse meat," I said. "Didn't know you were poor growing up. So were we. Hell, my mom couldn't afford to buy me a popsicle. But we didn't eat horse meat and calf brains."

Now that I'm writing this, I'm thinking, the Brits probably don't eat hamburgers with a knife and fork anymore, or maybe just the old folks do, old folks like me. Or maybe it was just that father and son. As I said, it was a long time ago.

Sitting here at Paradise Café, all this food remembrance takes me back to India. Didn't use knives and forks there. It always took me a few days to get used to eating with my hands. On one visit, a colleague and her husband took me to a really nice restaurant with pristine white tablecloths, wine glasses, beautiful dishes and bowls, but no cutlery. She noticed that I hesitated dipping into dinner and asked if I was okay.

I had already been in India for over a week, so was as comfortable as I was going to get eating with my hands, but the restaurant was so upmarket and wonderful and immaculate. As a result, I hesitated. I said to her, "Eating with our hands is not the norm where I come from, as I'm sure you know. Yes, some foods—hamburgers, sandwiches, that sort of thing. But not a nice meal like this. My mom would give me a good talking to if she saw me now!" My friend smiled, picked up some sloppy rice with her fingers, and brought them to her mouth. I joined her. But I've drifted, of course, from my story. Where was I?

We didn't have much luck finding his family tree at any of the planned destinations. He had done his homework, mapped everything out, but no luck. He was disappointed more than I would have guessed. I just didn't know it meant that much to him. Walker insisted we go back to the hotel before heading to our last stop, a small ruin of a castle that he thought might be an ancestral link. He wanted to change. I waited on a bench in the small garden of the hotel. When Walker appeared, he was completely decked out in his formal kilt.

He walked up to the bench and posed before me with complete confidence. There he stood—kilt shirt, argyle jacket, sporran, belt and buckle, kilt hose, ghillie brogues, kilt pin, flashes, and, of course, his sgian-dubh tucked in his right sock. He said, "Well, come on!" and strode off toward the car. I couldn't decide whether to play it serious or chuckle. In the end, I decided to trust him and played it with sober dignity. After all, the boy could act.

I don't remember much about the castle, though it was clearly a tourist attraction. We walked slowly around the grounds, and at one point a group of six, seven, maybe it was eight, Japanese tourists came up to us. They were kids between fourteen and sixteen years old, or there abouts, all with impressive cameras, all dressed well, and all very beautiful. A girl stepped forward and, in an accented English, asked if they could take Walker's picture. I looked quickly at Walker and said, "For God's sake, don't speak. If they hear your American accent, they'll be shattered."

I turned to the girl and told her Walker would be honored. We found a spot with the castle in the background, and Walker took a noble pose with a friendly yet thoughtful expression. If the kids hadn't been so thrilled and serious, the whole thing would have been comical. When they had each taken a photo, they asked to have their photos taken one by one with Walker, at which point the pretense of thoughtfulness was replaced with big smiles. When they had all posed beside him, I told them to gather around Walker, took their cameras, and took a group shot for each of them.

The whole experience lifted Walker's mood, and the next day, we hit the road for London. I've often thought about those kids from Japan who believed they had met a real live Scottish native, with photographs to prove it. Walker never said a word. And I have to confess, he was quite handsome in the kilt.

# 21

# Jessica Margaret Phillips, Jessica Fletcher, and Cabot Cove

WHEN JESSICA AND I decided to move back to the United States, I asked her where in the United States she would like to go. In truth, there wasn't a particular place we instinctively thought of as "home," at least not in the US. We moved around a lot during our marriage, including to a foreign country. I figured a lot of the country was up for grabs, but I did declare, as a non-negotiable condition, that it had to be a blue spot in a blue state. Jessica responded without hesitation, "Cabot Cove, Maine." I kid you not.

I trust you know that Cabot Cove, Maine, doesn't exist. It's a fictional town where the fictional character Jessica Fletcher writes murder mysteries and the congenial Sheriff Amos Tupper polices with less than competent skill but with, nonetheless, good, humored grace.

Jessica, my Jessica, not Ms. Fletcher, was one of the most intelligent, professional, driven people I've ever known. She had class. She was dignified and yet unembarrassed to play. She was young, she was old. She was perfect—well, that's not true. No one is perfect, and Jessica had many faults. It's only that after her death, most of those faults and all the things that annoyed the hell out of me have become endearing. But one of those things—and here I'm talking about faults—was her never-ending love for the TV show *Murder, She Wrote*. I was not a fan.

The series comprised 264 episodes over twelve seasons. Jessica bought both the US and the UK versions of the DVDs. My fear was that she would want to upgrade to Blu-ray. Fortunately, she did not. Kindly and patiently, I told her that the fictional town was actually a screen set in Montecito, California, and the harbor scenes existed only in the Universal Studios theme park. And if that weren't enough, I emphasized that Cabot Cove was the deadliest fictional town of them all, with 149 murders for every 100,000 people. In case she was not impressed by that statistic, I told her that Inspector Morse's Oxford only had 3.2 murders per 100,000 people. However, she was undeterred, insisting there had to be a Cabot Cove somewhere in Maine. As it turned out, it was the town of Castine in Hancock County that fit the bill.

In all the years we had together, I had never known Jessica to have any interest at all in Maine. It's tempting to pull out a few clichés about how we can never know a person, and aren't we all mysterious; however, I'll resist. It's obvious that we cannot know a person completely and that most of what they think is never revealed. I'm assuming that some of it is unrevealed, rather than concealed –life is less about secrets and more...well, mundane, boring, private, protected– for whatever reasons a person may have. It is interesting, however, that when I first told Walker how surprised I was that Jessica wanted to move to Maine, he said, "Yeah, of course, she was always talking about Maine." Well, there you go.

Once we were fairly sure Castine was the place we wanted, we flew over and stayed in the Sail Loft, a nice three-bedroomed rental home on the water. Downtown Castine was almost ideal in Jessica's mind with its shops, guest houses, cafés, bookstore, restaurants, and dock area. While walking down main street, looking in windows, stopping for a coffee, it was easy to imagine you actually could see Angela Lansbury and Tom Bosley standing on the sidewalk. If you have a cozy idea in your head of what a coastal town in Maine should look like, I'm betting Castine will match quite nicely.

We found a small but nice house to buy about a mile outside of town. It didn't have a view of the water. We couldn't afford that. But it was surrounded by trees and green grass with a back yard that got the sun. Once we signed the papers and paid the money, we headed back to London to pack up our lives. Much of what we had we left behind, partly because it is expensive to move things across the planet, and partly because in the US voltage is 120V and in the UK it is 220V.

The plan was simple. I was to retire and start living off my less-than-impressive pensions. Jessica was going to continue working, mostly from home, and keep some money coming in. Not having children, we had saved a fair amount through the years, so we were not looking at hardship, just a slight tightening of our metaphorical belts.

Jessica's journalistic focus had become, almost by accident, political coverage, and with the US electing a man whose incompetency and mendacity were utterly breathtaking, she thought it was a good time for a political journalist to return home. I did not. But foremost in her mind, in her plan, was to write *the* book on the interplay between politics, multinational corporations, the oligarchy, and the internet. Through the years she had written two books and, of course, numerous articles. The books did okay, meaning they were well received among her colleagues and the critics but didn't make us a lot of money. But this was going to be the big book, the career-defining book, the book that could only be written after a lifetime of work and international travel. Jessica was one smart human being. Unfortunately, she never completed the book, though I have a boatload of research on a thumb drive and in a filing cabinet and a half-completed first draft.

We had just over two years in our pleasant home in almost picture-poster-perfect Castine. Sitting in comfortable and stylish cafés with our books or laptops. Browsing in the bookshop. Nice meals and bottles of red wine in a friendly restaurant. Walking along the docks looking at the boats. You get the picture—almost ideal. Or so it seems to me now sitting in Berkeley, California, six years later.

The acute panmyelosis with myelofibrosis appeared on a sunny warm day in July. I have to say, our doctor—Dr. Barbara Emma Frosch—was great. She laid it all out with an open, professional caring that impressed me. I guess she'd done it before, probably many times, but still, I've known some doctors who were better kept away from patients who were awake. And Jessica, after the initial shock, followed by the tremendous sorrow, did pretty well herself. Yes, she did plug into life with more intensity, but it wasn't one of those cases where birdsong suddenly became more beautiful and colors brighter and deeper. Once the word got out, whenever we were in public, she seemed stoic and beautifully resolved, lacking in bitterness or anger. At home, especially in the dark, there was a lot of depression and weeping. There was also a lot of love and holding on to what could be relied on. I did my best to remain reliable until the last.

She continued working on the book as long as she could while knowing it would never be completed. I could not have done that. But mostly she spent time with me, keeping life as normal as could be expected. We still watched TV together (I endured *Murder, She Wrote* without complaint), read quietly together, and shared meals, of course. And we talked, a lot of talking time. Many years ago, I had a friend whose wife died of cancer. She had become so depressed and withdrawn that one day my friend went to her and told her if she was not willing to live until she died, he would have to leave. Jessica never stopped living, and that was a great gift to me.

I'm thinking about selling the house in Castine. Truth is, neither the house nor the town is as ideal as I have painted them. Perhaps it is a combination of remembering those last two years with Jessica and the fact that sitting at Paradise Café puts three thousand miles between me and the place. I've always believed geography actually does have impact, sometimes significantly, on our attitudes and memories; which means, I guess, that I won't be able to decide whether to sell up until I'm once again sitting in the house.

There is good news, however. Jessica never did follow through on her threat to haunt me. The house is filled with memories but not her ghost.

## 22

# Michael Andrew Walker Johnson and the Poetry

O! BE!
  Be and be again!
  Yet, again!
  Eternally born!
  Everyday after everyday
  Placing our soft pads callouses feet
  On the earth wood carpet floor
  Saying Thank You:

  The trees nevertheless forever green While drinking water
  Stolen into private ownership
  The children nevertheless forever fed Despite beliefs in
  the usefulness
  Of poverty and famine:

The men forever tenders
Of the hearth
Bearing the weight
Of swords and stories
The women forever powerful
On the land
Bearing herbs and philosophies
The communities forever gracious

Making poetry, dance, and ecstasy
The children forever-born-to-morning
Greeting the wombs of dusk
The teachers forever catching raindrops
With open mouths
And our great forever aging elders
Forever playing drums
In our consciousness.
O! Be and be known!
What the elders and the children
And the true teachers forever know:
We are born creating

As is the Eternal Forever Watcher seeing us from within our

everyday after everyday hearts

As the forever children are equal adventurers with the elders, in whom within all

the egg is always awakening.

O! Be!
Be and be again!
Yet, again!

# 23

# The Palimpsest, Václav Havel, and the Russian Tank

YEARS AGO, JESSICA and I visited Czechoslovakia—before the Great Divorce—almost immediately after the Velvet Revolution. Prague still had the atmosphere of a communist state, but there was something in the air. Our hotel on 28. Října was a block from Wenceslas Square, which is actually a huge boulevard. We left the hotel and turned right toward the Square. As the road opened up onto Wenceslas, we were confronted by a crowd of 300,000 people. They had come to listen to President Václav Havel give a speech about the changes that were needed to create a just and moral society. Imagine that. The dissident president talking about politics and morality. There he was, at the end of the boulevard, standing on the steps of Národní Muzem, addressing his people.

Don't get me wrong. We didn't actually see him or hear him. We were at the other end of Wenceslas Square with 300,000 people between us. Nonetheless, we started making our way through the crowd toward the museum. We encountered an overturned Soviet tank, and for the life of me, I could not figure out how they turned the damn thing over. There were a few people standing on the side of the tank, so I began climbing up and was quickly assisted. I did this partly because I thought it would be a great idea to stand on an overturned Soviet tank on Wenceslas Square, and partly because I thought I might get a view of Havel giving his speech. It was great standing on the tank, but I could only pretend to myself that I could see Havel. It was the anniversary of the Soviet invasion of a Prague past, the first anniversary in freedom, with 220 volts running through the city's veins.

We went to the Magic Lantern where he had directed and acted in one of his plays. We went to the Café Salvia, I with a copy of the *Lidove Noviny* under my arm. I could not and still cannot read Czech. We stood looking up at Havel's family apartment in Prague for far too long. And, perhaps most important, we went to the local pub near his flat for drinks and a meal. I imagined I was sitting at his table, drinking his favorite beer.

I was told on good authority that the dissident playwright sat in this pub with others talking about society, spirit, ethics, and freedom, the very things he would be responsible for providing in the unbelievable future. The story goes that when he was arrested, the cook was also imprisoned as a dissident, for she too spoke of the impossible possibilities of dreams. When the prisoner became president, his first official act was to free the cook and give her back her job. Was it true? I don't know, but that's what they told me over Czech beer. I can only hope it was true. When I met her, she was fat, happy, and very busy.

I've never had what it takes to be anyone's groupie. Yes, of course, I greatly admire some public figures, but too much fawning just feels embarrassing. Nor have I been prone to exaggerated expressions of mourning when a person of note or a celebrity dies. Again, yes, there have been exceptions. The assassination of John F. Kennedy in my youth was traumatic because it was the first attack on my innocence regarding my home country. Many more attacks followed. The assassination of Harvey Milk left me furious, and the candlelight vigil in San Francisco didn't soothe me. The death of Kurt Vonnegut left me feeling empty. His particular way of looking at and talking about the world was intoxicating. How could there be no more novels? This is all to say, I was somewhat surprised by my almost-infatuation with Václav Havel and even more surprised by how deeply I was moved when he died.

When we returned to London, I read everything of his I could get my hands on—*Toward a Civil Society, Letters to Olga, Living in Truth, Open Letters, Disturbing the Peace, Summer Meditations,* and *The Art of the Impossible.* I read his plays: *Audience, Protest, Unveiling, Redevelopment or Slum Clearance, The Garden Party, The Memorandum, The Increased Difficulty of Concentration, Mistake, Temptation,* and *Largo Desolato.*

I turned to other Czech writers—Skvorecky, Kundera, Klíma, Hrabal. I was so taken by Hrabal's *Too Loud a Solitude* that, when I returned to Prague, I bought a copy of the novel in Czech. *Příliš hlučná samota.* As I said, I can't read or speak Czech. Why did I do such a silly thing? I have no idea, but I have the book still.

Prague became one of my most frequently visited cities. I watched it move from communism to capitalism. I watched the Velvet Revolution become the Great Divorce. And then one day, Václav Havel died.

I remember returning when the first blushes of capitalism hit the city. I stayed in the same hotel on 28. Října, only the street was no longer quiet because there was a very loud disco and bar next door. In the evening, I went to Wenceslas Square, and along the way saw graffiti covered buildings. When I turned the corner onto the Square, a young woman stopped me in front of the Dobrá čajovna and asked if I wanted "pleasure." I looked past her into the bar, which was full of men and women having much pleasure. I looked at her and said, "No, thank you," but an older woman standing next to her said, "She will give you pleasure." I realized she was the young woman's mother. I walked toward Národní Muzem and then back down the other side of the boulevard. As I passed the Svatého Václava, I saw a young woman sitting by herself at a table in the front window. She was dressed well, legs crossed, smoking a cigarette. She looked up, saw me, and smiled. Not a sexy come-get-me smile, but a shy can-you-help-me smile. She was pretty. I just smiled back. The evening was warm, so I made the loop one more time, and there she still was, only this time her smile was pleading. I shook my head no; she looked sad, let down. I walked on.

Welcome to the fresh blossom of capitalism.

I have not yet discerned why some memories end up on my yellow pad and others do not. Well, yes, I know, I'm diving deep into my life, as the cliché goes. But there are—there must be—many memories deeply relevant that aren't surfacing. Perhaps it just takes time. Maybe if I sat here at the café indefinitely, eventually everything worth remembering would appear, leading to my complete self-awareness and the final peace I desire. It seems, at least to me, that these experiences should matter. Oh, I don't mean matter in the sense of being important in the course of human history. I am not under the illusion that I have contributed much to the arc of morality and justice in the universe. I am no Václav Havel. But still.

The Prague experience is on the list of encounters which, I tell myself and sadly, too often, tell others, signify that I'm more than the average brown bear. After all, I stood on the Berlin Wall at the turn of a decade when the Soviet Union collapsed, celebrating with 500,000 others. At the first truly democratic election in South Africa, I stood in line for eight hours with black Africans who had marched out of the townships in their millions—no one had ever counted them before. I walked both sides of the Peace Wall in Belfast, talking to people in small cafés and pubs with caged windows at the signing of the Good Friday Agreement. I joined hands with two million people, forming a human chain stretching the length of Taiwan, from Keelung Harbor to Eluanbi, on the 28 February Peace Memorial Day remembering the 228 massacre—February 28, or 228, is Taiwan's 9/11.

Surely these experiences mattered. If not, what the hell? But sitting in the sun at Paradise Café, I have to confess, beyond being interesting and perhaps building my ego, what was the point? When the end of the journey is near, the point of things is important.

Trust me, I'm not moaning. I've had a fortunate life. I'm just curious. What matters?

I read in one of Havel's books that the Soviet Union's sudden collapse was due to the accumulation of small, seemingly insignificant actions by unknown people. One man writes an essay, makes ten carbon copies, shares it on the samizdat, and so his thoughts are read by ten other people. According to Havel, that man—invisible—and that essay—insignificant—brought down the mighty Soviet empire. I must embrace my invisibility and insignificance. If Havel said both are profoundly important, then I must believe. At least today, in the sun, I must believe. They matter. But true confession time. I actually do wish they mattered more.

# 24

# The Palimpsest and the George W. Bush Emotional Strategy for Coping with Dis-Ease

CANCER HAS NO INHERENT value, and I see no value in having cancer. If there are lessons to be learned, I would rather learn them in another way. If there is something to be gained, I would rather gain it through some other means. I, unlike cancer, do have value and live not to destroy but to create, though admittedly I do not always succeed in this fundamental ambition. The only good thing that can be said about cancer is that the killing of its host (that would be me) is a suicidal act. If I were to die of cancer, at least I would have the pleasure of knowing it would go with me to the grave. I am not glad I have cancer. It is neither a gift from God nor Fate nor the Force. It quite simply sucks.

I am not at war with my cancer. I am not a warrior by nature, though like everyone else, sometimes circumstances demanded that I must fight. However, this doesn't seem like one of those times. Keeping positive, to me, is not a form of warfare. Nor is living healthily. Nor drinking pomegranate juice or eating broccoli. I realize that if I die of cancer, as opposed to taking my own life before cancer kills me, people will say things like, "he fought to the end," and "he was such a fighter." But, honestly, I'm not sure that would be the case.

In truth, having cancer and seeking treatment is about handing your body, and perhaps your life, over to others, to experts with exotic knowledge and remarkable skills. It is handing yourself over to numerous powerful drugs and hard technologies made of steel and plastic. It is about making yourself radically vulnerable. These are the acts of a person hoping someone else will kill their enemy before it kills them. Yes, I can help, but the real theater is the operating theater or the radiotherapy theater or the chemotherapy theater. My job is to lie down and either go to sleep or keep very still. Those are not the acts of a warrior.

Some days before my radical prostatectomy, Jessica asked me if I had cried yet. I said, no; however, it was not an unfair question. I'm not embarrassed to say I am a fairly emotional person. I should have had a career on the stage because all too often I wring every amount of emotion out of a situation. However, in this case, I felt I couldn't afford to let the emotions of fear have their way for even a moment, for to do so would render me unable to face what so many others have faced with dignity.

To deal with my fears, and there were many, I had a strategy I called it my George W. Bush Emotional Strategy. Do you remember when George W, in his flight jacket that had never seen combat, told the bad guys in Iraq to "bring it on!"? (Yes, I know, ancient history, but try and find the mental image.) Well, that was my strategy too, but my pumped-up machismo was not directed at bad guys or at my cancer. No, this macho outcry was directed at the technology and chemistry that was about to assault my body in order to save my life.

Well, you get the idea. No vulnerability until the moment of complete vulnerability. Admittedly, my strategy had its limits, but it did get me to that small room lying on my back, with a cannula in my wrist and sensors on my forehead, falling into a deep sleep without having to hide behind my metaphorical mother's metaphorical skirt.

It must be said, Jessica was not completely convinced by my George W. Bush Emotional Strategy, so instead gave me some new-age crap about tears releasing toxins. I didn't buy it, but I did google tears and toxins when she wasn't looking. This is what I found. Emotional tears (as against tears caused, say, by hitting your thumb with a hammer) were found to contain approximately 24% more protein than reflex tears and had increased concentrations of prolactin, manganese, potassium, and serotonin. Furthermore, tears help you see better (not really important in my preparation for surgery), kill bacteria (could be useful), elevate mood (that would be good), lower stress (also good), release feelings (not good at all), and, yes, remove toxins (though some think the toxin thing is debatable). Having absorbed all this, I went back to my wife and said something like this: I can't afford to cry before the surgery, but, and you can probably take this to the bank, sometime after the surgery, after I've returned home and the stress, pain, and drugs kick in, I will no doubt release a seeming lifetime of toxins.

After two and a half days in the hospital, I returned home. It was a Monday evening. I went straight to bed. The dam burst the next morning. I hadn't taken a shower since Friday morning. We put a chair in the bathroom so I could steady myself as I stepped into the tub. I couldn't touch my abdomen, it was so sore, swollen, and bruised. Even the water from the shower was unpleasant against my stomach. When I had finished washing, I turned off the shower and stood while Jessica handed me a towel. I could see my body in the mirror. I dried my upper body and stepped out of the tub, leaning on the chair. Jessica began to dry my legs, and I began to cry quietly. I wasn't upset because I needed help drying my legs. I accepted that I needed help and would for the next week. It was the sight of my body in the mirror. It was ugly and left me feeling extremely fragile. There were the wounds, and there was a catheter in my penis attached to a wet leg bag. And I was in pain. I started to cry harder. I shuffled to the bed and sat down. The crying became weeping and the weeping wailing. Just couldn't stop it. I cried like a baby.

To Jessica, and to the entire universe if it cared to listen, I shouted, "I can't do this! I can't do this! I can't do this!" But while I was saying those words aloud, in my mind I was saying, "They cut me! They cut me! They cut me!" And then I fell silent. The weeping became crying, and the crying stopped as suddenly as it had begun.

The words are interesting. Even as I said, "I can't do this," I knew very well that I could, that indeed, I had no choice but to do it. I would live with the catheter, take pain medication, and avoid touching my abdomen (and avoid mirrors). And yet I couldn't help saying it. Perhaps I was asking Jessica for help, though I knew she had been nothing but helpful and would be until I was okay again. Or perhaps after the waiting, the surgery, the drugs, the horrible taxi ride home, the sleeplessness, and the pain, I was just soul weary and body exhausted and had to protest. As for the "They cut me!" well, of course they did cut me, I told them to cut me. I could have told them to radiate me, but I didn't. They did what I asked them to do and apparently did it quite well. But still, to be cut, to look at your body, to see seven sutured and bruised incisions was, at least for me, difficult.

But why the tears at that precise moment? I guess my George W. Bush Emotional Strategy had run its course that morning as I stood dripping wet in front of a mirror. What I saw, dramatically speaking, was a wounded man in pain who looked older than his years, utterly vulnerable to the pressures and knocks the universe would throw at him. A man too damn naked, and not a pretty sight, I can tell you. He looked as if the slightest whisk of air, undetected by the most delicate of instruments, would knock him over. The stress, fear, and drugs had had their way.

Perhaps it wasn't clever of me, the one who claims not to be a warrior, to choose a rich-boy fraud of a warrior to be the inspiration of my emotional strategy. After I released all that protein, prolactin, manganese, potassium, and serotonin, I can't say I felt less stressed or enjoyed elevated moods, though perhaps I did see better. But it seemed pretty clear that with all those toxins also went the last vestige of Bring-It-On macho posturing. My George W. Bush Emotional Strategy went bankrupt as the last tear dried. What followed were weeks of mood swings. It wasn't the medication schedule or the pain that never quite disappeared. It wasn't the sleeplessness. It wasn't the dealing with the catheter, trying to avoid pulling or jerking the tube, any mistakes being very unpleasant. It wasn't the emptying of the leg or night bag of urine or even the awkwardness of sitting on the toilet trying to defecate without pulling the catheter tube and stretching the opening of my offended penis. It was the having been run over by a train, the time it took to heal, the worry that something might yet go wrong. That's what challenged my moods.

I've concluded that the George W. Bush Emotional Strategy is not the best way forward. Walker emailed saying he might instead have imagined a beautiful, peaceful, pastoral place where he could sit quietly and calm himself. This strategy might have had more staying power, and given my experience of a rather limited strategy, I am now recommending the Beautiful Peaceful Pastoral Emotional Strategy for Coping with Dis-Ease.

In his email he said:

*I've thought periodically, with you in mind, how would I feel if a medical professional said to me, "You have cancer." It's enough to be told I am HIV+, even though not diagnosed with AIDS according to some Center for Disease Control and Prevention criterion. I still occasionally feel dirty, unwashable, if not also unwanted, and that shrinks my dick. And you know what, if I were there and you asked me to be*

*with you when you cried, Jeez, I would be so fucking honored*
*to share that moment with you. Funny about Jesus having*
*the hem of his garment touched by an "unclean" woman,*
*and the disciples not seeing the honor in it. So where's the*
*healing one for us? I want/need some guy's garment to touch.*
*Then I want him to turn around and make it all okay for*
*you and me. I wouldn't mind kneeling in the dust to reach*
*his hem with everyone shrinking away from me like the dirty*
*wretch I imagine myself, if only he lifted me up because of*
*my faith, and I rose on a breath so distinctive I couldn't even*
*hear the murmuring throngs.*

Well, I never stumbled across some guy's garment, but I did find
this from Sharon Olds:

*Even as we speak, the work is being done, within. You were*
*born to heal.*

And so I have.

# 25

# Michael Andrew Walker Johnson, the Empty House, and the Presence

COULD IT BE TRUE THAT houses collect things on their own? Walker said once that he believed it. I always dread moving, and I've done it lot. I sometimes would look around me and feel shocked by how many things Jessica and I had accumulated. I admit, some of the stuff was and still is precious to me, but much was not. When we moved to the UK, we got rid of almost everything we owned. Felt good and bad, liberating and debilitating, at the same time. The times I have stood in an empty house have been poignant, sad, scary, and exciting. For Walker, an empty house meant a lot more than that.

Jessica and I had already moved to Great Britain by the time Walker was standing in his empty house in Eureka, California. He thought he might be falling in love with a man by the name of Gregory, always called Greg. Thing is, Gregory Stuart Peel lived in New York City. Thus, the empty house in Eureka.

He emptied the house of most of his possessions for *"complicated reasons,"* one of which was very mundane—it is less expensive ridding yourself of possessions than moving them across the country. He would talk about the impact the state of the economy had on senior citizens in Amerka (he always wrote "America" as "Amerka"). That impact drove his whole decision about what to send to New York—creating a *"not his choice zone."* He talked about how Amerka challenged his determination to find the way to live in a *"choice zone."*

He was vividly aware that people on this planet do not have the option of moving from a "no choice zone" to a "choice zone." But through the years, he had often said that, before he died, he wanted to utterly change how he lived his life. Standing in the empty Eureka house, he wondered if the time had come to make the change. He emailed, *"Maybe I will learn to be a humble human being before I slip over to the other side."*

I confess, at first, I struggled to understand what exactly he meant by "living in a choice zone." At one level, it was simple. He simply wanted to be free to make his own choices without the economic, cultural, political constraints of Amerka. However, at another level, a deeper level, all this pondering about emptying his house ultimately led to what he recognized as the real reason, the big reason—his need for a *"spiritual shift,"* a shift that demanded he answer a simple question: What is an unencumbered life? Which led to two more questions: What would happen if he really did get rid of everything that hung around his neck? What would a spiritual shift mean, look like, feel like, in his *"Amerka, Amerka, the beauteeful"*?

He never stopped wondering whether he was doing the right thing. When he emailed me, his anxiety about the move was at an all-time high. Why? I'm not sure. It wasn't Gregory Stuart Peel. The relationship seemed fine and firm. No; it was not the relationship. Walker kept saying that he had fucked up, that he was running out on people, though in truth he wasn't. He thought he was an unstable and unreliable son of a bitch who couldn't be pinned down to anything. Or, that he was waiting for something to go horribly wrong; in his words, *"See! You shouldn't have done it, you piece of no-good shit."* And then he would go on about the *"maniacal crap"* that he was fed by the church, how it came on *"three flying screaming banshee fates to nail me to my insecurities and hoist me into the crowds chanting, 'Give us Barabbas!'"*

Give him one detail that was not quite right, and he could build it into an empire of wrongness slowly zeroing in on what he called his *"home base."* It wasn't that he was paranoid. He never thought the world was out to get him, which is something, given that he was a left of center radical gay dyslexic. He said that he had been damaged by growing up in the Army. Seventy-five percent of military dependents turn out clinically neurotic or depressed, he would say, and to make his point, he would claim that this military neurosis *"teased his wellbeing with the notion of pushing him off a cliff."* On some days, I was not sure if the push and the cliff were metaphorical or real. Living in a *"choice zone"* was at times difficult.

Whatever the case, the empty house was real. Gregory Stuart Peel was real. New York was real. The hope of love was real. All these things were real to the point that he seemed compelled, as if it were out of his hands, to move on, no looking back. If he allowed himself to stop the flow of events, that would be more significant than the decision to start the move in the first place. The unknown stretched before him, while some dark angel kept wiping the past clear with its wings, as if to say, *"there is no turning back now."*

He went through a period of night terrors, and when they stopped, he had strange dreams of people and situations he had not known before. He wondered if it was some kind of weirdness from his childhood, and thus, if he was having a child's reaction to significant change in his life. He wasn't sure who he was.

Of course, he could have changed his mind and stayed put, though it wouldn't have been easy. He had discharged all his commitments in Eureka, the house was rented, the date was set. However, and this is interesting, he did not sell the house, and one bedroom was designated as his in the rental contract, while the attic was reserved for the belongings he had not jettisoned. Cut the tether, but not quite yet.

He wrote in an email, "*The house sounds hollow. The loudest sound is the clock ticking in the kitchen, measuring the time.*"

When most of the tasks were completed, the details checked and checked again, he stood in the hollow house and realized yet again how big a decision it was to move to New York. Ah, the things we do for love. But not love in this case. The things we do for the *chance* of love. We all know love can fail. Walker was courageous, even in his fear.

When he got to New York, he planned on renting an apartment, not yet ready to move in with Gregory Stuart Peel, but the decision threw him into a tailspin. Still in Eureka, he emailed me saying he was experiencing "*demons*," in the sense that his mind was overflowing with doubts and anxieties, and he couldn't sleep. When I asked if he was all right, he answered, "*No, not all right. I don't know if I ever will be all right.*"

I emailed back saying I wished he would call me during his "*nights of demons*," as he described them. I tried to put myself in his relational shoes. I wrote that as a straight man, I could see the appeal of having a place of his own in New York, but also as a straight man, or at least as this straight man, I saw such a choice as fundamentally defining the nature of the relationship. His willingness to move to New York spoke to the truth of his commitment and the decision to have his own place, at least for a while, the essence of the relationship—though I stressed that I was straight and thus might, probably would, see these things differently. I wrote, "*It's not that such an arrangement can't work or wouldn't be great, but that it says something about the nature of your relationship. However, at this point, not knowing Greg, and loving you, I am aching to know that you will be happy getting a flat in NY with all the relational and practical issues in mind. What I want for you is love and joy, so don't let my straight perspective get in the way.*"

In my mind, Walker's questions about how he had gotten to that particular place and what he had become seemed deeper than issues about living arrangements. When I have asked those questions of myself it has meant that I was uneasy or unhappy about who or what I perceived myself to be. So I wanted to reassure Walker; indeed, set him straight. I wrote, *"What you have become is an amazing, beautiful, intelligent, compassionate, battered, oppressed, often-marginalized person. But it's important to separate the 'what you did' and 'what they did to you.' How you got there is, for me, a perhaps interesting historical exploration, but not significant, unless that exploration is important in influencing who you are becoming. I'm not dismissing the past journey! It's just that you and I have less time on the planet than we did, so make sure that the questions are vital. We can't undo the how. We can influence the future what."*

His reply, *"Your email actually was helpful in a confirming sort of way that I'm neither crazy nor alone in my perceptions. I am glad you wrote it. I think I'll copy it off and put it in my journal as a reminder. You said a mouthful!!"*

Later, in a much-needed moment of rest, he stood in the empty house and sensed a Presence. With no anxiety, no fears, nothing but his intuition of the Presence, by which he meant the flow of life in the house, he asked one last time if he was doing the right thing. He said that he could not recall having felt such a thing before. He sensed its sensuality, its imperturbability, its vastness, and his humility and humanity in it, and he responded by singing to it. What pure Walker! How could I not love him? He sang love songs, songs of joining and union, songs of awakening. He sang because *"the wisdom arising from nature within is illuminated by sound and melody and given body by the singing."* It was for him a source of great joy. The song, received into the Presence and returned to him, amplified his ecstasy.

As he was packing up his life in California, he, of course, missed Gregory Stuart Peel. He wished they could be packing up his life together. And then, surprise of surprises, Gregory Stuart Peel called in the middle of the Presence, and Walker was so speechless because of the experience he was having singing to, in, the Presence, he could hardly talk to Gregory Stuart Peel. Ah, the things we can't do for joy.

However, as he said, that kind of speechless joy doesn't come that often and doesn't last that long, and he ended his email with these words, *"If only I could smile when I go to sleep and sleep peacefully through the night. That would be lovely! I'm leaving so much behind to do this—belongings, home, community of friends....and old patterns, the way I used to cope with life. I am so excited, but I am now tired."*

As to what all this said about the person Walker was—the child, the boy, the young man, the middle-aged man, the old man he was, all at the same time—well, I'm not sure. However, I would bet my fortune that his decision to move three thousand miles across the country, radically changing his life on the hope of love, was not fundamentally disconnected to decisions he made as a child, boy, youth, and old man.

Many years ago, I sat at my desk late one night; well, actually, early in the morning, and I replayed my life in wonderful and painful detail. By the time I was done, I realized the obvious: while I had always assumed that the decisions I made were isolated, distinct, independent realities, they were actually small parts of a large pattern which I was creating and which can be called My Life. That's not to say that some decisions weren't good and others bad, some right and some wrong. They were simply, authentically, organically, me. I had been making myself all my life, decision after decision, without ever being aware of that fact. I had made me, and from that, there was no escape. Scrape the parchment all you want. There is no escape from what I have created.

# 26

# The Palimpsest and the Necessity for Windows

LAST NIGHT, AFTER THE dark had settled in, I left my small and temporary apartment to take a short walk—"take the air," as they used to say in a less brutal time. As I was walking, I saw soft light through a window in a small house. I stopped and just looked. I could see the lamp, a bookshelf on the far wall, a large comfortable chair, and an open book lying face down on a small table beside the chair. There was nobody in the room.

The view, so soft and inviting, reminded me of a time I was coming home in London after a long trip to who knows where. Night had fallen over the city, and as I approached our house, I saw our front room as if for the first time. The view was very similar—soft light, bookshelf and books, comfortable chair. Only looking in that London window, I saw Jessica sitting in the chair reading a book. As God is my witness, I fell in love all over again. I thanked God for the view that was calling me in to a place of safety and love.

I love looking in people's windows. Windows have always intrigued me. A glimpse into a softly lit room while passing by on a dark night will caress my imagination and longings, life seeming somehow securer, or better, or more inviting inside than outside, though perhaps it seems so because it is an inside I can only experience through frames and panes.

There is a Czech proverb that describes people who wander and browse their way through life, which I have done quite a bit myself. It says that such people are "gazing at God's windows." I confess I was drawn to the words, which is paradoxical since my relationship to even the notion of a god is tenuous to say the least. And also, the words are awkward. We don't gaze at windows; we look through them.

As I thought about that awkwardness, I wondered if God's windows have windowpanes or are "open," without the glass. With glass there is a separation, something between us and what's on the other side. Without glass, no separation. And was I supposed to assume that God Windows offer a view of the divine, or of things with divine quality, or of things framed by the divine?

In principle, that is to say from a position of belief, if indeed one has belief, there should be continuity between the worlds on each side of the window, nothing getting in the way to distort the view. We should be able to walk right through a God Window. If not, then what's the point? But my heart and my experiences tell me that it is not so. A proper window always has a windowpane. You can't just step through to the divine.

There is another book that talks about windows, *The Ruin of Kasch* by Roberto Calasso. What a great book. You should read it. In a section entitled "Behind the Windowpane," Calasso quotes the film maker Max Ophüls:

> *The person who looks in through an open window never sees all the things that are seen by someone who looks in through a closed window. There is no object more profound, more mysterious, more fertile, more tenebrous, more dazzling than a window illuminated by a candle. What one sees in the sunlight is always less interesting than what happens behind a windowpane.*

The idea of looking into a window illumined by a candle touches something deep inside me. That touch results in a sense of a painful beauty, which becomes a deep longing to embrace the things of divine quality, to see the world with godly eyes, and to see through the window as if it weren't there. This feeling or desire never lasts. It exists for only a moment. It is as unique and beautiful as a snowflake settling on a windowpane. And then it melts away.

I am aware that a metaphor denies literalism, and to attempt to read it literally will distort it beyond all recognition. I am aware too that a metaphor laid out, dissected, and analyzed will die. We wind up standing in the ruins of literalism—as Paul Ricoeur would say—and meanings are sacrificed. So I always try and avoid both literalism and reductionism.

I am aware that there is no window view removed from the reality of me as the viewer. It is impossible to approach a window view in a historical, cultural, anthropological, political, theological vacuum. I am unruffled by this knowledge. No window offering a view of life can exist outside or divorced from my personal experience, identity, sexuality, and culture. Nor is it possible to gaze through a window without my individual and shared religious, political, social, and economic realities influencing the gazing—and the window itself. It is impossible because no such experience or window exists. From the moment I see through the window, that window, its pane, and what it frames are affected by my individual and corporate being, even as the window and what it frames impact, perhaps define, my individual and corporate being. In fact, to speak metaphorically of *God's* Window reverses, if only for a moment, the traditional notion that only God can be the knower and I must always be the known. The metaphor itself demands that I am the one seeking knowledge, and because I look through the window, I finally see. The point of looking and seeing is to become the knower, at which point, God disappears, as God always does.

But that night, coming home to London exhausted from my travels, seeing Jessica peacefully reading by a soft light, well, it felt divine. To lose that love like the snowflake on the windowpane is beyond difficult. And yet, the experience and the memory are mine. They have enormous value, do they not?

# 27

# Michael Andrew Walker Johnson and the Poetry

MOUNTAIN SONG HAS A Path to the Snows
Mountain song has a path to the snows
High over ice floes
Birds in hollows below
Warning in the leafy surround
Up here is peace
After you grunt through
Storms and streams
To this cabin at the peak
Snow otters greet you around your feet
White goose carries food to table
Snow owl harvests herbs with its beak
Sunrise glistens on the beams
Now I am singing
I am saying
Many tears water the climb
To the summit
And the dead lie scattered
Irretrievable
Frozen in the crevasses

# 28

# The Palimpsest and the Fear

I'M AFRAID OF THE DARK. That's right, David Robert Bainbridge, seventy-four years old, is frightened by the dark. I assume it's some kind of species-specific genetic inheritance from way back when being afraid of the dark was a survival mechanism. Still, it's embarrassing.

I sometimes purposely enter a dark room and just stand there feeling the darkness, experiencing the fear, forcing myself to count to ten before turning on the light. I once stayed in a farmhouse B & B on the Isle of Mull. The farm was just outside Fionnphort, where I was going to catch a ferry to Iona. I had arrived late and missed the last ferry so had to find a room or sleep in my car. Back in those days, Fionnphort wasn't much to talk about, size-wise I mean, and the only room I could find was in the farmhouse. The owners of the farm were a couple in their mid-sixties, both as nice as you could want. As I say, I arrived late, but the woman still fixed me a light meal. Wish I could remember their names. After I ate, the man invited me to go with him and his dog for their evening walk. I could barely keep up with him, and I was around forty at the time.

However, the reason I'm telling you this is that when it got late, I went to my room, got ready for bed, and turned off the light. The light switch was across the room, but there was a light outside the window, so I had no problem getting to the bed. I fell asleep quickly, which was unusual for me, but woke hours later. I opened my eyes but could see nothing. The light outside the window was off, there was no moon, and I was in *complete* blackness. I lay there for a couple of minutes, assuming that my eyes would adjust and that eventually, I would be able to make out the features of the room. The adjustment never came. The complete blackness frightened the crap out of me. It was a kind of existential despair. I got up and slowly made my way to where I thought the light switch should be. After sliding my hands over the walls for what seemed like an eternity, I found it and was saved by blessed light.

I'm not afraid of the dark when I'm outside, of course. I guess the moon is there most nights, and there are the stars. But mostly, it's that the outside is open and big. In dark houses, in dark rooms, I'm frightened. Obviously, I'm not afraid of a lion or a bear or a baboon or whatever, coming at me in the dark. So, what am I afraid of?

I should also confess that I'm scared of ghosts. I don't believe in ghosts, but I am quick to repeat the ageless cliché, *I don't believe in ghosts, but they scare the shit out of me.* Jessica used to tell me that when she died, she was going to come back and haunt me. This was before the acute panmyelosis with myelofibrosis, of course. After the diagnosis, we didn't kid about death. But before that, she knew my fears, including of ghosts, and teased me often. I pleaded with her to stop, saying that if there were such things as ghosts, she would be doing me a great disservice to come back and stand at the end of my bed at night, in the dark. After she died, I slept, or tried to sleep, for weeks with the light on. Actually, I left lights on all over the house. She has never appeared, and now I am just a little disappointed. I would love to see her one more time, even if it frightened me.

Once, when I was young, I went to a sleepover at my cousin's house. We watched some scary ghost movie that, now that I think about it, probably should have been banned by his mother. My cousin loved the film and slept like a baby, but I was literally up all night. The next night at home, my father saw the light was on in my bedroom well after I should have been asleep. He came in, sat on the bed, and asked what was up. I told him everything—the movie, my fears, not being able to turn off the light. Even as a child, I could see that the depth of my fear over a silly film disturbed him. Hell, it disturbed me. He sat with me for over an hour until I fell asleep, and to his credit, he left the light on. My father was a good man.

The next day, I wandered through the hours as if in a bubble of some alternative reality, but before night and darkness came, I had found a solution. I reasoned that, for me to be in danger, the exact circumstances of the movie would need to be replicated in my life. The same island, the same house, the same people. Of course, none of it had anything to do with me, so problem solved. I had nothing to fear. You could hardly call it rational, but I resist labeling it irrational either. Perhaps it was nonrational—not able to be explained by reason, or any reason any reasonable person would use. Or perhaps it was faith-based reason, the faith lying in my rather clever filmic determinism. Whatever, it got me through the night; though, I should add, my father was on the alert thereafter.

When I was a freshman in college, the 1963 film *The Haunting* with Claire Bloom and Julie Harris was shown on campus. The film was based on Shirley Jackson's novel, *The Haunting of Hill House*, and it scared the living daylights out of me, out of us all. Julie Harris was utterly convincing, as was the house.

Decades later, I decided to read the book, go back to the source as it were, thinking it would be a good way to address some of my fears—look them in the face and all that. It was a bad idea. The book is *frightening*. I mean, who would not be afraid at the end of Part V, Chapter 5? Theodora and Eleanor, frightened because of the event of the night before, decide to sleep together holding hands. They leave the lights on. But later Eleanor awakes in the dark! She wonders what has happened to the lights. She hears a "little gurgling" sound and eventually realizes it is the sound of a child in misery.

The child is frightened and being tortured, pleading to go home. Eleanor is frightened. She is "lying sideways on the bed in the black darkness, holding with both hands Theodora's hand, holding so tight she could feel the fine bones of Theodora's fingers..." But she cannot endure the House hurting a child, and eventually she shouts, "STOP IT!" The sound ceases. The lights come on. And Eleanor realizes that Theodora is on the other side of the room just awakening. Eleanor screams, "Good God—whose hand was I holding?"

Tell me you're not scared shitless? I had to reemploy my childhood everything-must-be-the-same determinism to stop from selling our house. I also deleted the damn book from my Kindle.

Fear: dread, fright, alarm, panic, terror, trepidation, anxiety, painful agitation, presence or anticipation of danger, loss of courage. I think that covers it.

# 29

# Sarah Jane Williams and the Divorce

I EXPERIENCED A BIT of a surprise mid-afternoon yesterday. I was sitting at my table with a glass of red wine, my yellow pad and pen, writing what I'm sure was a profoundly significant, if not life-changing, entry in my palimpsest, an entry that would, no doubt, result in my finally becoming the best possible version of myself, when I sensed someone standing in front of the table. It was Sarah Jane Williams and Megan Margaret Williams.

"David, do you mind if we join you?" Sarah Jane Williams asked.

"No, not at all. Pull up another chair," I said.

"Are you sure? I see you're writing again," Sarah Jane Williams said.

"No, no, really, it's fine. I would enjoy the distraction."

Sarah Jane Williams stole a chair from an empty table for Megan Margaret Williams. As they sat down, they both smiled, but each in her own way lacked the brightness I had become accustomed to.

"Can I get something for the both of you?" I asked.

"To be honest, I could use a glass of that wine, if you don't mind," Sarah Jane Williams said to me. She turned to Megan Margaret Williams and said, "Honey, what would you like? David's treating."

Megan Margaret Williams looked at her mother as though thinking deeply, but it was clearly a subterfuge. She obviously knew what she wanted. Sarah Jane Williams said to her, "It's okay, Sweetie.

Let's let our hair down today. I'm having wine, so why don't you have a Coke?" With that came a more genuine smile.

I went into the café and placed the order, and in no time, the drinks were on the table.

"David, I've asked you this before, so forgive me, but what are you writing day in and day out on that yellow pad of yours?" Sarah Jane Williams asked.

This presented me with a dilemma. I had grown to like Sarah Jane Williams. That thought, with the accompanying feeling, surprised me. Yes, we had spent time together, but we didn't know that much about each other. Not by a long shot. Still, we human beings sometimes can sense the possibility of friendship before it fully blossoms, and it was, I concluded, that possibility I was reacting to. It seemed somehow less than right to withhold information from her. On the other hand, how in the name of sanity would I explain what I was writing? And why? I thought, *Ah, well, funny you should ask. The people in my life whom I have loved are all dead. I am alone. I am on the brink. I am in my third and final act. I thought if I came back to this café,* Paradise Café *for God's sake, and claimed sanctuary and sat down and, with brutal self-truthfulness, remembered my life, I might be saved. Saved from what, I don't know. Saved for what? I also don't know. But saved, nonetheless.*

No, that wouldn't do. Not with a woman in her mid-thirties with a sad smile.

"It's silly, really," I said. "I'm just writing down some of my memories. I used to come to this café years ago when my wife and I lived in Berkeley, and I thought it would be, I don't know, nice or comforting or something, to visit for a while and, well, as I said, recall some of my life."

"Is your laptop broken?" she asked with a smile.

"Oh!" I forced a laugh. "The legal yellow pad. Quite. No, the computer is fine. I just thought it would be interesting to actually *write* the memories instead of *typing* them. I don't know why, and trust me, on some days I regret my decision. But, you know, mostly it's kind of fun. And interesting. There is a difference between writing and typing. It's a different experience, a different physical endeavor which may, perhaps, affect the words that come out. Or maybe not."

"Boy, I wouldn't know. I do all my writing on my desktop or my laptop. I barely write longhand at all," Sarah Jane Williams said.

"Well, you may have noticed, but I'm a bit older than you. Different generation."

A silence settled over the table for a moment. Megan Margaret Williams was watching a small bird in the latticework over a table behind me. Sarah Jane Williams and I were looking at the table, our glasses of wine, our hands, anything, everything, but each other. I wondered where the awkwardness had come from. Well, in truthfulness, I knew about mine. I had just concealed a truth that I certainly wasn't obligated to share, but something felt wrong about disclosing it, nonetheless.

"I hope you don't mind me asking," Sarah Jane Williams began.

She paused, and I said, "What? What do you want to ask?"

"When we had lunch here that day, the four of us, you said you lived in Castine, Maine, and your wife had died there. I was wondering how long ago that was."

"Oh, Jessica died six years ago. Some damn rare cancer."

"I'm sorry. I shouldn't have asked," she said.

"No, it's all right. It's fine. I'm glad you asked. I'm glad I told you," I said.

Once again, quiet, which didn't feel comfortable to me. I'm not afraid of silence, but it wasn't right at that moment of all moments. "Megan, you're unusually quiet today. Are you okay?" I said.

"My mommies are getting a divorce," she said, and nothing more.

I looked at Sarah Jane Williams, and instead of avoiding my gaze, she looked me straight in the eyes and let the tears come.

"Sarah, I'm so sorry. Do you want to talk about it?" I asked, while looking at Megan Margaret Williams.

"Oh, it's okay. I've told Megan everything. Haven't I, Sweetie?" she said looking at her daughter. She simply nodded in agreement.

"Is it actually divorce or some kind of separation? A cooling down period or something?" I asked.

"No, it's divorce. Jill has already talked to a lawyer and got the process going. I need to get a lawyer too, I guess."

"Is it a..." I wasn't sure how to continue. Sarah Jane Williams had just said that Megan Margaret Williams had been told everything, but I didn't really believe that. How could that be true? "Is it a challenging split? A lawyer-difficult split?" I asked.

"No, not in the way you mean. We agreed mutually it was time to go our separate ways. No, no fight. But, of course, difficult and challenging to end a marriage and leave someone you've loved," she said.

"Listen, I know you don't really know me that well, but I'm okay, an okay person. If I can help in any way, let me know. I've grown fond of you and Megan, and if there is something I can do, I'll do it," I said.

Sarah Jane Williams looked into my eyes and then buried her face in her hands and cried. Megan Margaret Williams turned to her mother and put her hand on her mother's arm. "It's okay, Mommy. You don't have to cry," she said.

"Sarah, give me your cell," I said to Sarah Jane Williams. "I'll give you my number. You call anytime, night or day. And you too, Megan. If you need a friend to talk to, you call. And we can get together. We can have lunch. We can go to the park. Or not. Whatever you need. Do you need help finding a lawyer? Is there some immediate need? Do you need money? I've got a little money."

At that Sarah Jane Williams dropped her hands to the table and laughed through the tears and said, "The biggest practical problem is the house. Jill and Eleanor have moved out already. They have their own place. I can't afford the house on my own. But I do have a little time. And thanks for offering! You're being a good friend."

I guess I was, though I did think it might be easier to give her money rather than emotional support. I am hardly the shoulder to cry on, given that I am in the act of tearing my life apart in a Berkeley café three thousand miles from my home.

"I'll do my best," I said to Sarah Jane Williams and took her young hands in my old hands.

# 30

# The Palimpsest and the Hatred from Others

I AM PROUD TO SAY—I'M aware that pride can quickly slip-slide into a quality best avoided, but I'm sticking to it anyway—that in my life I have been hated by a number of people. When I say, "a number," I should clarify that I haven't actually counted how many people have hated me and hate me still, but trust me when I say it is much more than a few. And why am I proud of this fact, you ask? Because what would my life have been if I had never demonstrated the courage and conviction to offend even one oppressor, racist, misogynist, gay bigot, woman-beating, fascist, bastard?

# 31

# Michael Andrew Walker Johnson and the Poetry

THERE IS A SLEEP
    There are some, who
    Having struggled against the sun,
    Have by absolutes
    Repealed all variety in nature
    from their senses.
    Creatures of infinite variation—
    Their tasseled tails and dappled hues
    Flung carelessly against the moon
    To cause their wild beauty to be given away
    Extravagantly—even against these
    There are some whose motto often repeats
    in the air:
    *Reducio ad absurdum*, which always means
    "Nothing outside my own limitations
    Can be thought to have substance."
    These (and they have Generations
    and populations)
    These have all gone to sleep,
    While the melodious shimmer of God's hand
    Plays lightly in the night.
    There is a sleep from which some

By cultured acquiescence
Have taken oars against the tide
of their own nature
And, grimacing, held their place
in the swirling stream
By anchors to any doctrine
Crying, "Out! tidal demons!" and therewith

Curse every joy that watches
in puzzled wonderment
of this struggle from the shore.

Then they speak harshly to the lovely grass,
calling it "You vanity!"
Then, beholding all the lovely creatures
that beckon them in
Cry out against the invitation,
And would sooner drown than be
Thought less a warrior by quitting their tirade
against the flow.
[Water was not meant to vanquish our energies
(though often enough some of our brothers
sleep in her depths)
But to quench thirst and fire, to provide
And be nourishing blood
Through veins in the earth.]
Those tired strugglers,
like blood borne diseases,
Shall all be washed away,
Because they would not unanchor,
Would not row to waiting tribes of earth,
And dance.
There is a sleep

To which some are eternally consumed.
But you, my lovely family,
who have so often beckoned to the dance of life,

Who have yourselves walked healing paths

through nettles that blistered every footfall,

Who have sufficient beauty to hallow your

stories and make of them a new language,

You, you, you, be outrageous, and taking all in, be the inclusive world you yearn for.

Leave no one out, even those asleep, for they most deserve your grace and your love,

Being, as they are, insufficiently kind
To receive their own wounds.

Remark only that the sun is shining,
the rain falls, all is good,
and everything is Yes.

# 32

# The Palimpsest, Jeffrey Karl Becker, and the Discovery of Dinosaur Tracks

THE OTHER DAY, I WATCHED Megan Margaret Williams playing in the sand. Sarah Jane Williams picked me up at the café late morning, and the three of us went off for a picnic. Our destination, which Megan Margaret Williams refused to tell me because it was going to be "a huge surprise," was the beach at Crissy Field. I had never been, and it was quite nice, so yes, kind of a surprise. The pleasantly sandy beach gently slopes down to the bay. To the right, you can see the Golden Gate Bridge. To the left, the City. Megan Margaret Williams explained to me that we would have to leave by late afternoon "because it always gets windy then."

Sarah Jane Williams had made a picnic lunch, brought a blanket, and even a bottle of wine, which she drank from only once and I, well, more than once. I was again impressed by this person, and there is much to tell about the outing, but that will have to wait. For now, I want to note one simple thing. As Sarah Jane Williams and I ate sandwiches and drank very small glasses of red wine, I watched Megan Margaret Williams playing in the sand on the beach. What she was playing was not important to me, though if I had asked her, she would have told me in fascinating detail. No, what caught my attention was her focus, as if she were creating a reality all her own, and so she was. She was *making believe* and making it well.

Watching her, I suddenly remembered Jeffrey Karl Becker and the summer roadworks near his home. I remembered dinosaur tracks. I had taken my leather bag with me to Crissy Field—couldn't have left it at Paradise Café—and I pulled out my yellow legal pad and began to write. Was I being rude? I guess a little. But Sarah Jane Williams didn't seem to mind. When I began to write on my yellow pad, she gave me a pleasant and knowing smile, which I found ever so slightly moving, and then went down to the beach to play with her daughter.

When I was growing up, I spent a lot of summers with my cousin Jeffrey Karl Becker. He was three years older than I, and I looked up to him. He was also more streetwise, which wasn't difficult because I had no street knowledge at all. But truth is, we were more friends than cousins.

I remember one summer when my family was staying at the Beckers'. There was a lot of road development in their area—trees torn from the ground, earth leveled and piled up, and dirt tracks laid, eventually to be covered in asphalt. To two small boys, it seemed that there were hundreds of bulldozed mountains. They were high, and they were great, and for us they served many purposes. One was hiding while we threw large hunks of dirt at passing cars making their slow way through the construction. But what I really remember was the search for dinosaur footprints.

Like a lot of kids back then, we were into dinosaurs, and that particular summer, for reasons I cannot remember, we decided to study dinosaur tracks. Somewhere we got hold of a book that had pictures of dinosaur footprints. Jeffrey Karl Becker was convinced that dinosaurs had roamed the very area where he now lived. He reasoned that all the bulldozing and digging must surely have exposed some dinosaur footprints. And so we made a simple plan. After dinner, we studied pictures of dinosaur footprints, and the next day, we headed to the mountains of overturned dirt where we were certain to find what we already knew was there.

Given the nature of our expedition, our first task in the morning was to make snake killers. A snake killer is a simple device made of two pieces of wood—one long board that functions as the handle with a shorter board nailed across it. We drove large nails along and through the cross boards and then attached them to the handles. Simple but elegant. We went to the garden to test the snake killers' effectiveness. We had seen small garden or garter snakes there, inoffensive and of no harm to anyone. Our snake killers proved lethal. We were pleased. We set out on our quest.

Jeffrey Karl Becker wisely decided we should split up to optimize our chances of discovery. With clear pictures of dinosaur footprints in my head, I went off on my own, climbing over one earth mountain after another. I can't remember how long I looked; I do remember feeling a bit skeptical that we would find tracks on top of a bulldozed heap of dirt. But Jeffrey Karl Becker thought we would, so I looked, and, in short order, I heard him calling excitedly that he had found a dinosaur track. I followed the sound of his voice, and there he was on the top of a mountain, his snake killer in his right hand, standing over a single dinosaur footprint. I got on my knees for a closer look. There was no doubt about it. The footprint he had found looked just like the ones we had seen in the book. I congratulated him and reached for a marker. We had tied small pieces of cloth to twigs and tucked them into the back pockets of our jeans. We stuck one of these twigs into the ground next to the dinosaur footprint so we could find it later. We continued our search.

To my surprise, not long after his first discovery, Jeffrey Karl Becker was calling out again. As sure as the sun was hot that day, he had found another dinosaur footprint, this time from a different species. I was very impressed with his ability to find dinosaur tracks. However, as I walked away to continue my search, thoughts intruded and refused to be silenced. For one thing, the footprints he had found were in soil. The pictures in the book were indentations in hard rock. And for another thing, given that the footprints were so fresh and fragile, how did they survive the bulldozing and turning over of the earth?

I pondered these matters as I climbed to the top of a mountain by the side of a dirt road. I stopped, put down my snake killer, and fashioned out of the soil a dinosaur footprint. I pulled a twig with a small piece of red cloth tied to the end from my jeans and marked my find. I then called to my cousin that I had indeed found a dinosaur footprint. In no time at all, he was at my side praising my find. I have to say, it felt damn good. And that was only the beginning. I became quite accomplished in finding dinosaur tracks that day.

Apparently, playing make-believe is fairly universal in children, and that was what we were doing. And as a first-rate palimpsest like myself knows, when children make believe, they do know the difference between play and reality. Jeffrey Karl Becker and I certainly did.

We knew it was all pretend. But what fascinates me is that at no time during our hunt for dinosaur footprints, or any time afterwards, did we blow each other's cover. The first rule of dinosaur footprint hunting is that you do not talk about how you found your footprints. We pretended that each of our discoveries was real. No smirks, no giggles, no challenges. From the moment he called me over to look at his first discovery and I accepted the find as authentic, we "agreed" without words to continue to play. If I had challenged him, pointing out that the footprint was so fresh that it was simply impossible that it could have survived a bulldozer, we would have forgotten about dinosaurs and gone looking for snakes to kill. Game over. Instead, we marked the find with a twig and moved on. Crucially, however, we never found a dinosaur footprint together. To do so would have pushed our willing suspension of disbelief beyond tolerance. I mean, we were willing to dig footprints in the dirt but certainly not in front of each other.

At some point in our lives, however, the willingness to participate in mutually agreed pretenses ends. Or at least, I used to believe it did. Unfortunately, I now live in a country of alternative facts and a mendacity that runs so deep it's breathtaking. Either millions of my neighbors are childlike great pretenders, or they are delusional, or perhaps just stupid. For now, they agree that the sun is shining as they stand in the rain. They believe drinking bleach and their own urine cures disease. They believe Jews have laser weapons in space. They believe almost anything. The Flat Earth Society membership is growing. If the right person were to tell them, they would profess with great enthusiasm that Jeffrey Karl Becker and I had found dinosaur footprints in recently turned over earth. It sort of takes the fun out of a kid's memory of playtime.

When we returned home after a busy morning of dinosaur footprint hunting, we did, to our surprise, find a dried up, hard, very old looking footprint of another kind. We surmised that it was the print of an ancient species of wolf. We carefully dug it from the earth, wrapped it in newspaper, and placed it in a box. We took the box to our mothers and instructed them to send it to the Smithsonian Institute. Confident that our mothers would never let us down, we proceeded to explore for the rest of the summer, the prehistoric wolf print forgotten. Until now.

# 33

# Michael Andrew Walker Johnson, Old Compton Street, and the Package Tour Group

IT IS NO SURPRISE THAT on Walker's first visit to London, I took him to Old Compton Street and the Admiral Duncan pub in Soho. We headed for the underground after dinner on a Friday night and surfaced at Leicester Square. We worked our way over to Shaftsbury Avenue, hung a right onto Greek Street, walked up to Old Compton, and then left to the pub.

The old street is a center for the lesbian, gay, bisexual and trans communities, and if you're looking for a gay pub, that's where you go. It is lined with restaurants, bistros, and cafes. Every place is gay friendly. Look a little closer and you'll find what might be called specialist gay shops. If you wander off Old Compton and walk the warren of Soho streets, you can find specialist straight-people shops too. One of my favorite restaurants is Balans, not far from the Admiral Duncan and always alive, crowded, and noisy. I would go there between breakfast and lunch for eggs benedict.

The Admiral Duncan is gay as gay can be. In 1999, it was bombed by some neo-Nazi who will remain nameless. Three people were killed and over a dozen injured. Before the bombing, the front of the pub was painted in neutral colors, but when it was re-opened after the attack, it was painted in ostentatious pink and purple with a large rainbow flag flying over the entrance. As far as I know, that flag flies there still. And when the pub was re-opened, hundreds of us gathered in solidarity to listen to speeches to honor and remember the dead and to sing together.

Walker and I went into the pub partly for a couple of pints and partly so Walker could go home saying he had been in the Admiral Duncan on Old Compton Street in famous Soho. It was good and interesting for me to see him in his natural habitat. He was not as flamboyant as the paint job, but neither was he shy. He's a flirt, and he's good at it. I thought a couple times I might be going home alone. I'm proud to say I was hit on twice. But we know where that went.

We left the pub sometime before midnight and headed up Old Compton toward Frith Street. About halfway between Dean and Frith, we saw two guys, obviously drunk, really getting into it, throwing punches like there was no tomorrow. There was more than a little blood. Walker immediately said to me, "Come on," and ran toward them. I followed with less enthusiasm. He edged his way in between the two men, so I did the same. We pushed them apart. All the time, Walker was talking to them in a soft and almost gentle voice while using his considerable body strength to keep them separated. The contrast between his gentle voice and the force of his body was striking, and it did the trick. We left them sitting on the curb talking.

But here's the thing. Just as we were approaching Greek Street, a package tour came around the corner onto Old Compton and headed past us. A young man leading the group held up a pole with a yellow sun on the top. The people following him looked like they were from the United States, middle-class tourists on an adventure tour. They sure as hell didn't look gay. Walker looked at me and just started laughing. He wanted to join the tour, but I refused. I was dumbfounded. I couldn't believe it. It was an actual package tour, the kind that takes people to castles and museums, but this was a tour to gaze upon the LBGTQ+ people on Old Compton Street, Soho, London, England late at night. I squinted at the bright yellow sun at the top of the pole, looking for the name of the tour company but could see none. The group, almost twenty strong, obediently followed their guide, looking amazed with pretentions of courage. They wore yellow baseball caps, but again, no name, just the sun logo. I could imagine the puffed-up chests of the men once home in Iowa or North Dakota telling of their Soho experience.

Walker continued to laugh while the tourists stopped outside G-A-Y Bar to take photos. He dragged me into Wun's Tea Room and Bar on the corner of Old Compton and Greek Streets. We found a small, round table toward the back of the bar. Walker still had a big, shit-eating grin on his face. I thought he'd be offended and angry, and perhaps on a different night, and without the alcohol, he would have been. But not that night. He put his hand on mine and told me to relax. "It's funny," he said. "It's surreal. It's Amerka!"

I looked at him, and something like a Joycean flow of consciousness spilled out of my mouth. "I have been fighting for gay rights and dignity and full inclusion for most of my adult life. I have been close to gay men and lesbians. However, I'm straight, and thus I can only know your struggle second hand. The price I have had to pay for my part in the struggle has been minor compared to what you go through. Actually, what am I saying? It's been nothing. Selfishly, however, your being gay has given me, and I'm sure others, so damn much. Without you and other gay men, but especially you, I would not be the person I am. I'm so grateful that you are gay. If I believed in a god, I would thank him/her/it that you are gay. I know. Easy for me to say! But fuck all, I am saying it. Thank you for being my friend and for the bonus of your being gay. I get it. I am an educated, straight white male in a Western country. So I don't know what you have been through—well a little, since I have stood by you—but... Well, I know I have only an idea of your oppression. But you really don't need a fucking package tour group observing you like you're an animal in a zoo!"

His smile was gone, but his face was loving. He leaned forward and kissed me on the lips for a second time in our lives. "David, it will never end," he said. "Your naivete is sweet, but I know you know."

"I want a world where it is not an issue. I want a world that rejoices in a celebration of human diversity. If I had the magic wand that could change everything, there would always be gay people," I said, feeling self-conscious. I sounded like some Johnny Sunshine who believed that the world is actually good and not a nonstop struggle. I sounded like I had just fallen off the proverbial truck from the sticks. I'm intelligent and articulate, but that night I sounded like a *Leave it to Beaver* rapture of universal harmony. Joycean flow of consciousness, my ass. What a damn embarrassment I can be. And I bet what I've just written from memory isn't half as bad as I must have sounded that night. How absurd that the straight guy was angry and the gay guy was laughing.

"I know," Walker said. "I want that celebration too. But what I really want is for you to be gay. David, don't you get it? You need to laugh. Laughing is a prophetic act."

# 34

# Jessica Margaret Phillips and the Corduroy Jacket

OH MY GOD, IT WAS A long time ago. Corduroy jackets were in. Mine was a light brown, soft, slightly worn, possessing a comfortable look that enhanced its integrity and handsomeness. I loved it and wore it all the time. Jessica was of a different mind. I'm not sure why she loathed it so. I mean, it didn't have those swede patches on the elbows or anything. It was just a really nice, comfortable corduroy jacket.

We had a friend who lived in Heidelberg—Stefan Günter Müller. We had met in those Berkeley days when I was in seminary and Jessica was in journalism at Cal Berkeley. Stefan Günter Müller had been working on a PhD which he ended up completing in Germany. After Jessica and I moved to Britain, we made a point of visiting him in Heidelberg during our first summer.

We had a great time. Stefan Günter Müller showed us the Heidelberg rarely seen by tourists. We were there in July, and the city was packed with visitors. I asked him how he coped. I was bracing myself for a multilayered complaint about the intrusions of the tourist industry, but what he said was certainly a glass-half-full perspective. He said the tourists just reminded him of his good fortune living in such a beautiful city and region of Germany.

I, of course, wore my corduroy jacket. Stefan Günter Müller admired it. At the end of our visit, the car packed, I was sitting behind the wheel ready to go, when Jessica opened the rear door, reached in, grabbed my jacket off the back seat, thrust it into the hands of Stefan Günter Müller, and told him with a firm and commanding voice to give it to the German equivalent of Goodwill. Stefan Günter Müller looked genuinely confused, not knowing what to do. Jessica jumped into the front seat. I started to unfasten my seatbelt to get out, but she grabbed my arm and said softly, "If you get out of the car, I will break your legs. I'm done with that damn jacket." I was so struck by her belligerent tone that, to my shame, I didn't protest. Stefan Günter Müller came around to my side of the car and looked in the window at me. I told him to go ahead, keep the jacket, do whatever he wanted with it. He protested that he already had a corduroy jacket and certainly didn't need another. I simply shook my head, said goodbye, and drove off. I'm not sure why I didn't get out of the car and get my damn coat. Perhaps I was just fed up with our never-ending arguing about it. To say the least, it was not my proudest moment. I abandoned an old friendship that I'm sure had many years of good service left.

I was furious and didn't speak to Jessica for the entire trip home, which took over nine hours. She, on the other hand, was a damn chatterbox. She made no effort to hide her glee. In fact, she flaunted it. Who the hell did she think she was? My damn mother? It was clear to me there had to be repercussions. Actions had consequences. Even the most extreme, divorce, was considered. Fortunately, by the time we pulled into the driveway in London, I was physically and emotionally exhausted. Before we got out of the car, I turned to her and said, "We will never speak of this, ever." She could tell by the look in my eyes that I was serious. And we never did.

Well, that's not quite true.

A couple of years passed, and one day I received a package in the post. I couldn't believe it. It was the corduroy jacket! With it was a handwritten note by Stefan Günter Müller saying he could never bring himself to get rid of the jacket and thought I might like it back.

It was an emotional moment. I shook the coat out and put it on. It was tighter than I remembered. I went to the full-length mirror in the bedroom to have a look. The coat was wrinkled badly because of the journey from Heidelberg. It looked smaller. To be honest, it looked terrible. Without a thought, I put my hands in the pockets, and in the right-side pocket was a pair of beautiful, lacy, skimpy women's underwear.

I hadn't noticed, but Jessica had come into the room. I saw her in the mirror quietly looking at me as I stood there in the horribly wrinkled old corduroy jacket with a sexy pair of women's underwear in my right hand. She laughed, turned, and left the room.

The corduroy jacket ended up in the British equivalent of Goodwill. I never did ask Stefan Günter Müller about the women's underwear. What I did with the underwear, well, I don't remember.

# 35

# Michael Andrew Walker Johnson and the Poetry

## There is More than One Diaspora

THERE IS MORE THAN one diaspora on this planet,
    More than one people
    who want their homeland back
    With guaranteed return passage
    to their heritage
    To restore what once was stolen
    and never lent:
    The land that gives them shape,
    where ancestors speak in trees.
    There is more than one sage of old,
    ancient Moshes and Siegfrieds
    Or great grandmothers in solitary huts
    beside the sea,
    And others in their forests
    leaning on their knees,
    Remembering prophecies
    of sacred soul relationships,
    Reaching along paths of peace.
    This is their song:
    My hair is flying in the wind

Full of sparks and flames
Razor shreds of lightning
flashing in the sun's heat
Showering every shadow with revealing light.
For I am a wild horse
Snorting through unkempt forests
and apple trees
Prancing out onto battlefields
with harp and song
Laying down arms by the glow
of my ancestors' hearts
Flush to my skin and in my voice.
My hair has grown children
of songs and circles
My silver hair has gardened
all my heirs and grandmothers
My hallowed hair has gone
from whispers to shouts
Against all blandness, and in canyon winds,
Mountain winds, meadow winds,
desert winds,
Ocean winds, river winds, winds of red spires,
Winds of thundering trees,
snow winds and icy fingernails
Scratching along icebergs,
wind to wind to wind:
My hair has become the earth the stars
the moon
My hair has weeping
of children and elders' stories
My hair has howling of wolves and waterfalls
My hair has cumulus clouds before rain

My hair has the patter of mice in summertime
Hiding in stalks of wild corn
Where in its shade is heard
the sharpening of the scythe,
For a thousand thousand harvests
and firelights
Glisten in my hair
where colors dazzle the flanks of trout.
Come, dive into my hair
of blue mud for scrying
And fly in the wind
and sing the eternal chants.
My hair and my heart are fragrant
with fire of roses in the wind,
The dense smell of a spice market on Iona
among the sheep.
I am the wind. Did I tell you?
Blowing sparks over the landscape.
Did I tell you? And my teeth
Are rockets of words
Singing on the ocean floor
where luminescent night creatures
Pulse into existence and pulse out,
Delicate threads of antique forms
Yet to be known, and this my teeth are singing
My tongue licking the salt and waves
and sail winds
North winds, west winds, south winds,
east winds, trade winds,
Catching the breeze wind
that fans my hair into
Long long long ribbons upon the rolling sea,

Swimming in front of the eye of a whale.
I am the eye of the whale. Are you seen?
And my sonorous humming
Is in the waves.
I am the waves.
Swim in me.
My hair is the waves and the wind
and the whale.
I am the quite ordinary human heart
Beating deep, deep, deeper than before
Reaching back, back, back farther than before
Into the soil,
Every day birthing again the vital earth.

# 36

# The Palimpsest, the Oneness, the Terror, and the Old Man

BEFORE MY BERKELEY seminary days, I got an MA degree in anthropology, specialty in archaeology, at the University of Montana in Missoula. Jessica was studying journalism and landed a part-time job at a local radio station reporting the evening news. During the summer of our third year in Missoula, Jessica went off on an internship to Washington DC, and I spent the three months doing an archaeological survey along the Continental Divide. I distinctly remember two things about that summer...well, no, actually three. Let me start with the third.

My home base was Wisdom, Montana, a very small town surrounded by farms and ranches, but mainly farms. I was given a forest ranger flatbed truck for the summer and would go up into the mountains for a week or two and then return to Wisdom for a long shower, a halfway decent bed, and a good burger and beer in the restaurant.

I always ate at the same restaurant and always sat at the counter—breakfast, lunch, and dinner. To call it a restaurant may be a bit enthusiastic, but nor was it a café. It existed somewhere in that in-between place. Often behind the counter was a waitress I'd guess was two or three years younger than I was at the time. She had bright blond hair and clear blue eyes. She was slender with alabaster skin as if she had just arrived from England. While you might not describe her as a typical beauty, she was attractive and did have something about her. And she liked me. After three months, I liked her too. It did occur to me that if I hadn't been with Jessica, I'd have asked her out, though what it meant to "go out" in Wisdom was beyond me. And it was more than a certainty that she had a father and at least one brother who owned big guns. So who knows what I would have done? Probably nothing. Nonetheless, I do remember her. When my summer ended, she asked me to meet her around the back of the restaurant, and indeed, I did. She came out the back door of the kitchen, handed me a coffee mug from the restaurant, and gave me a very pleasant kiss on the lips. She then turned and walked back in through the kitchen without saying a word. I never laid eyes on her again.

When I went up into the mountains, I more than not slept in forest ranger cabins, though I did sometimes sleep in the flatbed of the truck. I remember one early evening after a day of walking more miles than I can guess surveying along the Divide. I set up in the cabin—sleeping bag and food—and then went out to sit on the edge of a high bluff looking down into a valley. In the distance, I watched two wolves running down an antelope. The smell of sage was everywhere. There was birdsong. The sound and feel of a gentle breeze. Suddenly, somehow, I felt connected to it all. The wolves and the antelope. The birds. The breeze. The insects by my feet. The sun setting quickly. The appearing stars. I leaned forward and dug my hand into the earth, scooping up a handful of soil, and then I rubbed my hands together as if washing them with water. I felt the cleanness of the dirt. For a moment, I was part of everything, as if I belonged. I was home. And so I sat there as the sunlight faded and the Milky Way appeared, gloriously. The huge, very close canopy of stars, planets, and interstellar gas shielded me from all harm. I had never felt, experienced, anything like that before and never did again. But I experienced it, and I remember.

Two nights later the opposite happened. After my day of surveying, taking photos, filling in forms of sites found, and jotting notes, I found what I thought was a nice place to park for the night. There were no cabins close enough to where I had finished that day or close enough to where I wanted to start the next, so I was happy to get the camping equipment out, cook myself a meal, then climb into my sleeping bag in the back of the truck, hoping to fall asleep looking at the stars.

As darkness fell, I found it difficult to settle. I told myself to relax. I sure as hell needed the sleep, given the miles I would have to put in the next day. But I couldn't. My unease became anxiety, anxiety became fear, and, though I cannot explain it, fear became a kind of terror. The only thing I thought about was getting the hell away from where I was. I got out of my sleeping bag and stood in the flatbed ready to jump to the ground, get into the cab, and drive away. But I couldn't. The thought of touching the ground, for even a couple steps to the truck door, was unbearable. And so—you won't believe this—I reached around the side of the cab and opened the driver seat door and then climbed from the flatbed into the cab without touching the ground. I turned the engine over and started to drive away. I wanted to floor it, but racing along the Continental Divide on a dark night would not be the smart call. I did my best to take my time to be safe.

I don't know how long I drove, but I finally stopped and sat in the cab for some time. I felt okay. I opened the door. I still felt okay. I stepped out of the truck, and everything really was fine. I climbed into the back of the truck, settled into my sleeping bag, and slept peacefully for the rest of the night.

I'm almost too embarrassed to tell you what happened next, but I am exposing memories and truth, so here it goes. In the morning, I drove to the area for the day's survey. I felt great, and since I wasn't finding much of anything, the work was easy. I found a pleasant place to stop for lunch by what was a mere trickle of water. Before breaking out my meal, I walked up the incline, following the trickle to its source, which was just some moist earth. I looked at my map and figured I was more than likely standing atop the Divide, one foot in the east and one in the west. I knew that the moisture by my foot, moving eastward and downward, became a trickle, and the trickle a flow, and the flow a creek, and the creek a river, until it joined something greater.

I walked back to where I had left my pack, pulled out my lunch, and took off my cowboy hat, placing it on the ground to my right. Sitting there peeling an orange, I realized someone was approaching me from behind. In all the weeks surveying along the Divide, I had never met anyone, so I must confess I was more than a little nervous. I turned and got up at the same time and saw an elderly gentleman walking toward me. He was wearing faded jeans, a blue work shirt, and cowboy boots. He had a blue bandana around his neck and a cowboy hat shading his eyes. His face had deep wrinkles. His hair was braided. He raised his right hand as he approached and said hello. He was Native American.

I walked up to him, said hi, and we shook hands. He said he had seen my forest ranger truck a way back. I asked him if he needed a ride somewhere. I was in the middle of nowhere and couldn't fathom where he had come from. He had no pack, and I didn't hear a vehicle in the distance. He laughed and said no.

"Where did you come from?" I asked with a smile.

"Oh, just over the hill there," he said, turning to his right and pointing.

I invited him to sit with me and share some of my food, and he seemed genuinely pleased to do so.

We sat down next to the trickle of water. He took off his hat, dipped his bandana in the trickle, and wiped his face and hands. I couldn't guess his age, but he was an old-timer for sure. We got to talking, almost as though we were old friends, or at least good acquaintances. I learned that he was a member of the Siksika Nation, which is part of the Siksikaitsitapi, what I called the Blackfeet Confederacy. I got some more water and oranges from the truck, and we continued to talk.

I found myself so at ease with him that I ended up telling him of my experience the night before, about how I became so frightened, that I had to drive away. I told him I was so terrified that I couldn't even put my feet on the ground.

He listened and then rather nonchalantly said, "Oh, it was Wakan."

I told him I knew a little about Wakan but had always understood it as something good or at least neutral.

"Yes, you are right. Wakȟáŋ Tȟáŋka means many things. It can mean the Great Spirit or the Great Mystery. It can mean sacred or divine. It is everywhere and in everything. It can mean the creators. They are never born and never die. The Wakanpi are spirits and have power over everything on earth. They control everything. The Wakanpi are good, benevolent, and can grant the wishes of human beings. But the Wakanpi can also be evil, and wise people fear them. Last night you invaded the ground of evil Wakanpi. It is very good that you left. It is that simple."

We talked for some time more, and finally he said his goodbye and walked off over the hill to the right. I never got his name. I never saw him again. After he left and I continued my day, I promised myself I would forever more take seriously my inner feelings, especially feelings of anxiety and fear. I kept that promise for a number of years, until I did no longer.

Soon I will be seventy-five years old. As I write this story down on my yellow pad, I feel embarrassed. Not so much about the experience of oneness on the bluff, but certainly about the story of terror in the truck. Do I believe in Wakan Tanka, or as my old friend said, Wakȟáŋ Tȟáŋka? No, I don't. Do I believe in the supernatural? Again, that would be a no. How could I have believed in the unbelievable for so many years, just because some old man told me an ancient story? I simply cannot believe in the unbelievable anymore.

It's too late for that now, and I'm not going to succumb to my old man's fear of getting Pascal's wager wrong.

# 37

# The Palimpsest, the Teacher, the Father, and Science Fiction

MANY YEARS AGO, MEREDITH Gwen Murphy made an important and shocking discovery. She discovered that I couldn't read worth a damn, that I had made it all the way to the fifth grade with only very rudimentary reading skills. Meredith Gwen Murphy then saved my life.

Up until then, my teachers either didn't care or actually humiliated me in front of my peers by mocking me while I was reading aloud during lessons. (Do teachers still make kids read out loud in class?) But not Meredith Gwen Murphy. She asked me to stay after class within the first week of the new school year. She sat with me, looked me in the eyes, and simply asked, "Can you read?" There was something about the way she asked—tone of voice, sincerity, and most importantly lack of judgment. There was something about the way she looked at me—kindly, caring, focused, interested. To my surprise, I responded, "No."

"How did you get this far?" Meredith Gwen Murphy asked.

"I pretend," I said.

"How did you do book reports?"

"My mother did them for me."

"Ah..."

"What happened to your finger?" I asked. The index finger on her right hand was permanently bent at the first knuckle.

"Playing basketball when I was young."

"Oh."

Meredith Gwen Murphy had me come to her home on Saturday mornings. I'm sure that would not be allowed today, but then it was. She and her daughter, younger than I was, taught me how to read. She quickly established that phonics was a waste of time. She discovered, however, that I'm very good at memorizing. So she and her daughter would hold up flashcards while feeding me tapioca pudding.

The realization that memorizing was easy-peasy for me also helped me with spelling tests. For whatever reason, my dyslexia reverses linguistic voicings. For example, the sound we make for a "c" and a "g" are very similar. If you put your hand on your throat when making the sounds, you can feel the difference. As God's little joke on young David Robert Bainbridge, his brain often reversed the sounds. So, instead of writing or saying, "It would be good if you could come by at nine," I'd write, "It would be could if you good come by at nine." See, reversed voicing. I know, fascinating, but also a real pain in the ass. Thanks to my Saturday sessions with Meredith Gwen Murphy and her daughter, I stopped trying to "sound out" the words and simply memorized them. I went from black stars to gold stars on those weekly tests.

Before Meredith Gwen Murphy saved my life, I hated reading, to the point of having a rather unpleasant physical reaction when picking up a book. After Meredith Gwen Murphy, I learned to love books.

The first book I ever read cover to cover was *Powder Keg: A Story of The Bermuda Gunpowder Mystery* by Donald E. Cooke. I had promised myself that I would read every single word in that book, and I mean *every* word. To skip one word would have meant failure. A few years ago, I searched the internet for a copy and, to my delight, found one. It is now a prized possession.

This story of young Tom Rawlins helping to bring gunpowder from Bermuda to Boston to fight the evil Brits in the revolutionary war was the first book I read. But it was the discovery of science fiction that ignited my love for reading. I devoured sci-fi, sometimes reading until four in the morning. Since we didn't have much money, it was difficult to satiate my desires. When the library failed me, I would use my meager allowance to buy sci-fi paperbacks. I even considered turning to a life of crime. One day, I took a fat hardback book—I don't remember where I got it—and cut a hole in the pages the size of a typical mass-market paperback. I planned to go to the bookstore, discretely place my chosen sci-fi adventure in the hole, and then nonchalantly leave with the hardback under my arm. In the end, I couldn't do it, perhaps more out of the fear of being caught than any concern for my moral integrity.

Nonetheless, I read so many science fiction books that one day my father, concerned, sat me down. He feared that reading so many fanciful narratives written by so many questionable characters would warp my understanding of reality and could be, in some way he never explained, detrimental to my wellbeing. I remember saying to him, "But Dad, I'm reading!" And with that, looking rather sad, he got up and left my bedroom. So I kept reading, though I never have gotten through *Ulysses*, so lovingly given to me by my father.

My study back home in Maine is filled with books. There are books in the living room. Books in a small downstairs reading room. I have books in closets. Every once in a while, I think I should count them. I doubt I ever will, but it would be interesting. And when I die, if I die without warning, some poor sod is going to have to get rid of them all. It will be good I'm not there to watch.

# 38

# The Palimpsest, Sarah Jane Williams, and the Drunken Boat

SARAH JANE WILLIAMS got a babysitter and invited me to dinner. Who would have thought? We went to Le Bateau Ivre—the Drunken Boat in English—on Telegraph Avenue. To be honest, I was surprised it still existed. Jonathan Randal Davies and I used to go to Le Bateau Ivre when we were in seminary way back when. In those days, there were two comfy chairs in a corner, and we'd go later in the evening when it was quiet, drink Irish Coffee, and flirt with the waitress. In those days, Jonathan Randal Davies was pretty damn active sexually, so I know for a fact that the lovely waitress went home with him more than once.

Le Bateau Ivre is very atmospheric, and the food is good. Sarah Jane Williams and I sat at a round table by a large window looking out onto the patio. Given it was summer in Berkeley, there were people sitting outside enjoying both the weather and their meals. But I liked sitting inside with the exposed bricks and stones and soft lighting. Natural wooden floor, wooden table, large fireplace—no fire, of course. It was a very pleasant place to sit, converse, and enjoy the food and drink. My memory tells me there was a more formal room—white tablecloths, off-white painted walls, waiters with white napkins hanging on their arms, that sort of thing. Maybe I'm wrong, maybe not, but it was nice being back.

Sarah Jane Williams insisted she pay, so I convinced her I'd cover the wine. I was torn between two cabernets, Born of Fire and Freakshow, not because I was seduced by their bouquet or flavor. I had never tasted either one, and I'm a long way from being a wine expert—I do know wine comes in red, white, and rosé, but that's about it. No, I was just intrigued by their names. I went with Born of Fire.

It was awkward at first, so we did the small talk thing. We were both pleased about how beautiful the weather had been but also acknowledged that California almost always needed rain. We were both disappointed and more than a little concerned that the new virus out of China had found its way to the Seattle area but assumed that even a Republican federal government would introduce a prevention program very soon.

I asked if Sarah Jane Williams had found a roommate yet to help cover the costs of her house since Jill Rosemary Thompson and Eleanor Sandra Thompson had moved out. She said no, she still had time, and she wasn't sure what she would do. And finally she said this: "The other day at the café, I was sorry to hear your wife had died, but to be honest, I kind of thought she might have. I had never seen her, and you never talk about her. I should have just asked."

"That's all right. Her name was Jessica, though I called her Jess and Jessie too. She died a couple years after we came back from living in Britain."

"You must miss her," she said.

"Yes, you have no idea. I used to try and imagine what it would be like if she died first, and, well, I had no idea," I said.

"I'm really sorry," she said, and then paused. I took a sip of wine and decided Born of Fire was very good. I placed my wine glass back on the table and watched a small dog run past the window. Sarah Jane Williams said, "Were you ever unfaithful?"

That took me by surprise. She was looking right at me when she asked. Her tone wasn't aggressive or accusatory in any way. In fact, it was kind of sad. I looked at her and said, "No, I don't think so."

"You don't think so? Either you were or you weren't, and you should know."

I chuckled and said, "Well, it depends upon how you define faithfulness and unfaithfulness. I never had an affair, but I was kissed by two women while I was married to Jessica. One was a waitress in a café in Wisdom, Montana. I had spent three months in the area and ate in the café, well, a small restaurant really, numerous times, and she was almost always there. When I told her my time was up and I was leaving, she asked me to meet her behind the restaurant. We didn't say anything. She just kissed me and walked away."

"Well, that was kind of romantic," Sarah Jane Williams said, with a slight smile.

"Thing is, I didn't stop her."

"Okay, but it's hardly a huge infidelity. What about the other kiss?"

"Ah, that's a little more complicated. Her name was Samantha Esther Cunningham—I never learned the name of the woman in Wisdom. Samantha invited me to dinner, again because I was leaving my job and moving on. Thing is, she wore a suggestive black dress, and she wore stilettos. I asked her why she wore such harmful shoes, and she said because they made her feel sexy. And then, when we were saying goodnight in her car, she kissed me. Sarah, there was tongue! And before you say anything, no, again, I didn't stop her. In fact, I kind of joined in. And to be honest with you, with her dressed like that and her comment about feeling sexy, I'm thinking she was, well, interested in me. Right? So, even more reason to stop her."

"Oh, I'd say she was into you all right. And you're right, that's a little more complicated."

"There's more. Through the years, I have thought about her from time to time. Not very often. I mean, she wasn't on my mind every week or anything like that. But when I did think of her, I thought of her almost constantly for days. I wondered what it would be like seeing her again, what we would talk about, having sex with her. That kind of thing. And just a couple of weeks ago, I wrote about her on my yellow pad," I said. "But why are you asking me this? Is it your divorce?"

"Not directly," Sarah Jane Williams began. "I'm heartbroken. I thought this marriage was good and the right thing to do, but I guess if I'm honest, we both knew it was ending. How can people get things so wrong? I mean, how can we be so sure of the rightness of something and be so wrong? But the breakup has got me thinking about the past, the first time I was heartbroken. That first time was devastating. When she ended it, everything turned gray. Color just disappeared from my life, and what frightened me was that I thought it would never come back. I'm not sure how to describe it, explain it. Everything was just gray and broken."

She took a big sip of wine, put the glass back on the table, and just looked out the window. I really didn't know what to say, so I said the first thing that came to me. "I'm sorry, but you don't strike me as gray now. How did you get through it?"

"In part, time, of course, and I had a good friend who helped me. She told me over and over again that the color would come back, that it would be different, but that it would come back. The color would be different, light would be different, life would be different, but I would see my way through. It really helped. But the reason I asked you about your marriage was because she, the heartbreaker, not the friend, was married when I met her. We fell crazy in love with each. And David, for almost a year! I contributed to her unfaithfulness. I almost aided in breaking up her marriage. We talked about her leaving him. We would take walks in the park, sit at a picnic table, and talk about ending her marriage. He found out."

"They almost always do," I said.

"And now I know what he felt like, what he went through," she said.

"What do you mean?" I said.

"Jill left me for someone else. And he is a man, for fuck's sake!" Sarah Jane Williams said, taking her glass of wine in her right hand, throwing her head back, and emptying the glass. She almost slammed the glass down on the table and said, "Fill it up! I'll tell you when to stop!" I did. I thought we might try the Freakshow cab for the next bottle, assuming that Le Bateau Ivre would order us a taxi when the time was right.

I started to speak, and she interrupted, "I made choices, and I knew I was making choices. I was rational."

"But if you were rational, as you say, and you knew you were being unfaithful, then why did you continue? I was blind-sided by Samantha, but it sounds like you went into it with your eyes open."

"Well, first, I doubt you were quite the innocent victim regarding Samantha's black dress and stilettos, unless you're saying she was a whore, and I'm pretty damn sure you're not. A woman doesn't just invite a man to dinner, wear a suggestive dress, and put on fuck-me shoes out of the blue. But your question is, of course, legitimate. Why did I continue?"

She offered no answer. I said, "I'm wondering why you're telling me all this."

As she looked at me, I saw her eyes begin to fill with tears. "I'm not sure," she said. "But I think you are a kind man, and I think you are my friend, or perhaps I think we will be friends. And I do need a friend. You're here, you're safe, and my daughter adores you."

I didn't know what to think. How the hell was I going to respond to that? I'd told her in the café that I'd help in any way I could, but all I could think sitting there in the Drunken Boat was that I wasn't good friend material for a young woman in turmoil. I was an inch away from the rabbit hole myself.

"Sarah," I said hesitantly. "I'm not sure what to say. I don't live in Berkeley, and one of these days I'll have to return to Maine. And to be honest, I'm not in much better shape than you. I'm not here on a vacation."

"No, that's obvious. You and your yellow pad," she said. "So, tell me why the hell you are here. What the hell are you writing?"

"I'm writing my life," I said. "Or rather bits of it, the bits I remember and think are worth taking the time to write down. Longhand! But you don't want to hear my sad story, certainly not when you're dealing with the end of your marriage and painful memories of the past."

"Yes, I do! David, I need someone to confide in me. I need someone to confess to me. I need someone to trust me. I need someone to do the things friends do with each other."

All I could do was look at her for the longest time. She held my gaze. She didn't disappear. So, I began.

"I've only really been in love with two people in my life. Yes, of course, I've loved many people, but only two have touched me so deeply that the love, the relationships, defined me. I mean, it's hard for me to know who I am without them. Does that make sense?" She simply nodded.

"Obviously, one of those people was Jessica, but the other is a person I've not mentioned. By the way, he was also responsible for my third kiss, also complicated. His name was Michael Andrew Walker Johnson, but I always called him Walker. I was in love with him. It was with him that I learned I'm really not bisexual. As God is my witness, I'm straight as straight can be."

I took a big bite of my salmon—yes, we did have food in front of us, though it was going stone cold—and then emptied my glass. I caught the waitress's eye and ordered a bottle of Freakshow. Neither of us spoke. It was like an invisible witness or confessor was with us at the table and silently told us to take a breath, to eat some of our not-cheap meal, and to let things season. I wasn't about to tell Sarah Jane Williams in graphic detail about my physical relationship with Walker. Besides, she's no idiot. I'm sure she had already figured some things out by the time the bottle of Freakshow arrived. I'm also sure she knew that answer I'd given to her question about my fidelity in marriage was disingenuous because I had not mentioned Walker.

I poured some more wine in our glasses and said, "Thank the gods for taxis. Are you sure you want to hear this?"

"Yes, if you want to tell me," she said. "You know, I'm not shocked to hear you were in love with your friend Walker."

"I'm sure you're not shocked, and even if you were, it wouldn't matter to me. I don't turn to others to receive validation for my relationships, and I certainly don't seek permission. Here's the thing. Three weeks ago, when I was still in Castine, I got a call from Walker's partner, Greg. Greg told me that Walker had been missing for two weeks. I was annoyed he had not told me, but I wasn't panicking, because it wasn't unheard of for Walker to absent himself, isolate himself, from time to time. He spent time in the Pacific Northwest. He went to Peru to study with a shaman for over a month. There were times he was gone and times he didn't communicate with others. But what Greg was really calling to tell me was that Walker's remains had been found in the wilderness in upstate New York, in the Adirondacks. He called to tell me that Walker was dead."

I could see by the look on Sarah Jane Williams's face that she was not surprised. She simply said, "I'm really sorry."

"Yeah, so was I," I said. "When Greg first called me with the news, he had very few details, except that Walker's *remains* had been found in the Adirondacks. He had no idea what Walker was doing out there or how he had died. Just remains. Thing is, as soon as Greg told me Walker was found in the wilderness, I had a pretty good idea what might have happened. Walker used to talk about the benefits of choosing the time of his own death, that he had a right to choose. He told me he would walk out into a forest one day, find the perfect tree, sit down, lean his back against its trunk, and eventually die. As I was talking to Greg, I assumed Walker had shared his thoughts with his partner, but nothing Greg said to me on the phone indicated that.

"However, here's the thing. For a week after that phone call, I kept picturing Walker sitting against a tree peacefully dying. But he had never told me why he would do such a thing, what would be going on inside his mind and heart to justify the act to himself, the taking of his own life. Knowing he was dead, but not knowing why he was dead, precisely what he was thinking that took him to the wilderness, was breaking me down. Why now, why this particular time? Had something happened? Had nothing happened? And why the fuck didn't he tell me?

"I was furious. I was broken. I barely survived Jessica's death. I feared, I still fear, I won't survive Walker's. I was alone in Castine, Maine, a place of no natural or historical connection for me, because Jessica wanted to live there."

I stopped talking. The Freakshow was almost dead. Neither of us was in the mood for dessert. It felt like it was getting late. But Sarah Jane Williams still wanted more.

"So, this writing on the yellow pad? It's about Jessica and Walker?" she said.

"No. As I said, it is me remembering me. Okay, obviously in part, it's about them because they were so important to me. Sarah, I don't know who I am without them."

"I think I can understand that. You..."

"No, I doubt you can. I'm seventy-four years old, and Jessica and Walker have been there the whole of my adult life. I loved them. I was in love with them. I breathed them. It's not that I feel lost like some college kid wanting to find himself meditating in the mountains of India! There is nothing. There is a black hole where there is supposed to be something. Hell, I would welcome grayness. I see no point to it all.

"After the phone call I got another email from Greg with an attachment. The attachment was a scanned letter Walker had written to me. Greg found it in Walker's desk drawer in an envelope addressed to me with instructions that it should be mailed to me after his body was found. I was livid with Greg for opening the letter and scanning it to me. He said he thought it best for me to receive the letter immediately. But it wasn't his right! Walker specifically told him to mail it to me. It was private!

"But when I read the letter, Walker's death finally hit me. I couldn't...I couldn't...I don't know. I decided I had to come to Paradise Café. It's where Walker and I first met. I know, it was irrational. And I decided when I got here and sat down at that table, I would just start writing thoughts that came to me, any thoughts in no particular order, until something filled the black hole that I had become. I thought somehow the café would be my safe place. I know, it's crazy, but I had to come. And I decided to sit there until I was done writing whatever I was writing."

"Walker's letter drove you from Castine, Maine, to Berkeley, California?" she asked.

"Yes, it did," I said.

"What did he say?" she asked.

"It was his reason for dying," I said.

She looked at me and put her hand on mine. "David, what did he say?"

I was exhausted. Yes, I know talking is supposed to be cathartic, but all I wanted to do was cry. If we had been at her house or in my apartment, I might have. I simply said, "No, not tonight. I'm done."

# 39

# Michael Andrew Walker Johnson and the Poetry

A GOOD DEATH

>   When she comes,
>   Death delivers my last pulse—
>   My limbs cooling, all energy closing in;
>   Unspeakable knowing
>   Kissing my terminal breath
>   Combing my matted hair,
>   Sweated into dark pillows,
>   Returning me to the vast, perturbable realms
>   Of new creation.
>   *Requiem aeternam dona eis, domine*
>   *Et lux perpetua luceat eis.*
>   I shall be birdsong, burrow the bark of trees,
>   Share soil with dampness and beetles, and
>   With the shroud's worm sail on green fusion,
>   Singing my bones
>   Into rusting cannons of our last war.
>   In my good death I forego my distinction.
>   I go interred to mud, into the eternal song,
>   My ancestors invoking my sweet trouble
>   into their midst
>   Of which there is no end, no beginning,

no flush of separation.
May the name of this be spoken
from my forehead: Amen.
*Requiem aeternam dona eis, domine*
*Et lux perpetua luceat eis.*

# 40

# Jessica Margaret Phillips, the Journalist, and the Queen

WHEN JESSICA AND I moved to Great Britain, it took us some time to settle into our jobs and our new home in London. Being finished with the local church, I had landed a job working in international relations—educational programs, partnerships, exposure visits for individuals and small groups, that sort of thing. Jessica had a job working for a news outfit, primarily online, which was the reason we moved to the UK in the first place. We weren't being paid a lot, but it was enough.

It must have been nine months after moving that we finally were able to take some time off. We decided to head north to Cumbria, with no destination in mind, a let's-drive-and-see-what-we-see trip. We stumbled upon a small town called Brampton, which we liked immediately. We wanted to stay for a few days but couldn't find a hotel room or B & B anywhere. We went to a small tourist office, and they told us to go to Talkin Village and ask for a room at the Hare and Hounds. The directions were simple. Drive out of town, and just after the level crossing, turn left onto a one-lane road. That would take us straight into Talkin. The Hare and Hounds would be in the village square on our right as we entered. It was all clear, except we had no idea what a level crossing was. When we bumped over the railroad track, it became obvious, and sure enough, shortly afterwards, we saw the single track to the village.

The inn was run by Lesley Brandon Stewart and Joan Emily Steward. Lesley Brandon Steward was a character and Joan Emily Steward an intelligent beauty. For a middle-class, US American boy, the pub and inn were ideal. Joan Emily Steward asked if we wanted to reserve a table for dinner in the pub, which we did. She said we would have to share the table with another couple. When we went down for dinner, the pub was already packed. Joan Emily Steward sat us at a table for four near the bar, and within twenty minutes, Ian Jamie Breach and Jackie Pauline Breach arrived. Ian Jamie Breach was not happy having to share a table. Jackie Pauline Breach told him to relax, and when they realized we were from the US, things changed for the better. We were something new.

To make a long story short, we all became good friends and remained so for the years we lived in the UK. But what was really interesting was the fact that Ian Jamie Breach was a freelance journalist and documentary filmmaker. Ian Jamie Breach and Jessica really hit it off, and within a week or two, he was introducing her to colleagues in the BBC. She shadowed him while he was working on a documentary, and years later they ended up in Iraq reporting on the burning of close to seven hundred oil wells.

Sitting here in Paradise, latte and croissant to my right, yellow pad in front of me, missing her like hell—no, really, it is hell—I can still remember seeing Jessica on the TV screen. She is standing in the desert in front of numerous blazing oil wells spewing black smoke into the crystal-clear sky or next to oil lakes or fire trenches. It would look like something out of an end-of-days apocalyptic film. That was my beloved doing her thing. I was both proud of her and frightened for her.

Our first night in Talkin Village was great. A crowded lively pub, good food, great beer, wonderful and interesting conversation, and the beginning of new friendships. We talked and talked, but Ian Jamie Breach and Jackie Pauline Breach had a long drive back home, so they bugged out before closing time. However, before they left, we exchanged addresses and phone numbers, and they invited us to come by their house when we were ready to leave the Hare and Hounds.

They left and we went up to our room. We were both sitting on the bed, and for reasons I can't remember now, I emptied my wallet of cash and laid it on the blanket. I picked up a five-pound note and looked at the picture of the Queen. Jessica asked me what I was doing, and I told her I was just looking at the Queen. I then turned the note over and said, "Damn, I thought I'd see the back of her head." It was a stupid thing to say. I wasn't particularly trying to be funny. It just came out. Jessica paused for a moment but then started to laugh, and she didn't stop. She rolled over on the bed and laughed until she cried. Her laugh was so utterly beautiful. She was beautiful.

It's interesting how we remember someone we love. Today I'm remembering her fierceness and intelligence in front of a burning world. I'm remembering her face as she laughed. I'm remembering the sound of her laughter. People like to say, perhaps need to say—hell, I've said it enough times—that we keep our loved ones alive in our memories. The intention is, I'm sure, metaphorical, but it has often seemed to me that people believe it as literal truth. Of course, it is not. Jessica is dead. My imperfect, oftentimes hazy remembrances, my mental constructs of her and our time together, are not Jessica. They are me hanging on to fading images and sounds. They are a mirage. But they are all I have, so hang on I do.

I am sorry you didn't know her. I am sorry you didn't see her face brighten in laughter. I am sorry you didn't hear the sound of her beauty. So, I need you to trust me on this. She was everything. Her death has taken the air out of me. For a moment, her death caused the entire world to become silent.

# 41

# The Palimpsest, the Mushrooms, and the Window

ONCE WHEN I WAS IN Amsterdam with Jonathan Randal Davies, we went into a nondescript café, and along with our cheese sandwiches and beers, we ordered mushrooms.

Jonathan Randal Davies worked out of New York, so he had first flown into London to spend a few days with Jessica and me. He was an old friend from seminary days, the one I went to Le Bateau Ivre with to drink Irish Coffees and flirt with the waitress. We did our best to keep in touch.

After those three, or was it four, days in London relaxing, going to pubs, and sharing great meals, the two of us flew off to Amsterdam for a conference on...well, I don' t remember what it was on. I've been to hundreds of international conferences, programs, workshops, and I can't remember them all. I guess when I leave this café sanctuary and return to Maine and begin the task of transferring these yellow legal pad scattered ruminations into digital ones and zeros, I could look it up in my journals. I always wrote in journals when I traveled—real journals, not computer note-takers. But I digress.

We had arranged to spend a couple more days in the city to play after the conference ended. I believe that was my third visit to Amsterdam, but Jonathan Randal Davies had been there on many occasions and so knew the lay of the land much better than I did.

In those days, the Oude Kerk (the Old Church) on Oudekerksplein was surrounded by sex workers in shopfront windows. I imagine it still is. In fact, the church is a short walk from the Belle statue, installed in 2007 as a symbol of respect for sex workers all over the world. On our first free day, Jonathan Randal Davies took me past Belle to the Oude Kerk, down a narrow alleyway to the sidewalk in front of a sex worker's window, which was actually a clear glass door. A curtain was drawn over the window, meaning the woman behind the window was with a client. Where I had picked up this bit of street knowledge is a mystery to me, but then again, so much knowledge seems to come through the cultural ether. Eventually the curtain was pulled aside, the door opened, and out stepped a man — a tourist, I was sure, because he did his best to hide his face. As the woman behind the window was about to close the door, she stopped, seeing us sitting on the sidewalk with our backs up against the wall of the building opposite. I had to admit to myself she was very attractive. She was dressed for the bedroom. Jonathan Randal Davies stood up and took the few steps to the door-window. It was clear that she recognized him as they said hello. Jonathan Randal Davies looked back at me, gave me a slight nod of the head, and then disappeared into the small room.

I tell you all this, not to titillate your imagination, though titillate I may have. If so, apologies. No, I tell you this to establish my success or failure, my courage or cowardice, depending upon who you are and where you stand.

However, back to the café, which was nothing to write home about. I doubt I even noticed its name. We went in for a quick lunch and a beer. On one side of the laminated menu were listed sandwiches, salads, drinks, and so on. On the other side were various kinds of marijuana and magic mushrooms. We ate our sandwiches in the café and took the mushrooms back to the hotel. Before long, we were giggling like children or laughing like drunken sailors, depending on what struck us as funny, and most everything was funny if not hilarious. Then, suddenly, Jonathan Randal Davies's mood changed. His face went from huge smile to concentrated thought to overwhelming sadness. He left the hotel with hardly a word, just saying he had to go somewhere. I didn't see him again for hours, and he never told me where he went or what he did.

Things in the hotel weren't quite as funny on my own, so I decided to go for a walkabout. Before long, without thinking about where I was going, I found myself—as if I were not responsible for my own actions—standing in front of the window a stone's throw from the Oude Kirk, staring at the mushroom-enhanced vision of an utterly beautiful woman. She opened the door and leaned out, asking if I wanted to come in. Indeed I did. Inside the small room was a single bed, a sink, and, believe it or not, a coatrack. The room's lighting was surreal and somehow made her dark skin glow. After quickly agreeing on the financial arrangement, she put her arms around me and kissed me on the cheek. She started to unbuckle my belt, and I stepped away from her. I rather shyly told her I could not continue, paid her the money anyway, and left.

As I walked along one of the many canals of Amsterdam, with the mushrooms wearing off, I contemplated my nobility or lack thereof. I did, after all, go into the room. However, I also left before anything untoward happened, and I wondered why.

First, of course, was my marriage. When Jessica and I married after some years together, we made an agreement. Part was explicit and part was simply assumed. Fidelity was assumed, as it is in almost all Western marriages. Most everyone would agree that being faithful to your partner and relationship is right and moral, despite the fact that somewhere up to 70 percent of people admit to having been unfaithful at least once in their marriage. Still, the arrangement between Jessica and me was less contractual and more covenantal. If the distinction confuses you, google it. Having sex with a sex

worker in Amsterdam would not just be breaking our covenant, it
would be betraying Jessica the person. The covenant was words and
assumptions. The person is the physical incarnation of those words
and assumptions, an incarnation that laughs, weeps, and bleeds.
Jessica was more real than words, and certainly more real than
assumptions. It's one thing betraying words and quite another flesh.

And yet...as I sat on a bench looking at the canal, I also thought,
*"I'm always the Good Boy. Always."* I wondered why. Perhaps simply
because I am a good person. But now, sitting here in the Berkeley
sun, desperately attempting to be honest with myself, intuiting that
now finally, at this moment, it is very important for me to be
truthful, or all is lost, I think my supposed goodness may not be
grounded in virtue. It was not nobility, honor, loyalty, love, that
made me leave that small room with the weird light. It was fear. I
have never been bold. I have never risked it all. I have never been the
Bad Boy. Not once. And now, at seventy-four years old, sitting in the
sun, what the hell did it get me? Where the hell did it get me? It
got me here and alone. Truth? Scrape the parchment until it hurts?
I wish I had had sex with that woman behind the window in the
shadow of the Oude Kerk.

What a damn bore I am. Could it be that the worst thing I've
ever done in my life was let my older cousins teach me to swear on
a New Jersey boardwalk? The greatest sin of my life is the occasional
use of the word "fuck" and its many derivatives. Okay, yes, there
was that one-time kiss with Samantha Esther Cunningham. And yes,
of course, the one-time kiss with Walker. Oh wait! I forgot. There
was also that one-time kiss with the waitress in Wisdom, Montana.
While I may have enjoyed those kisses, I didn't initiate them. And for
God's sake, they were only kisses!

How can you be fully human and not have sinned boldly?

# 42

# Michael Andrew Walker Johnson and the Poetry

THERE'S A FOREST IN My Blood
>    There's a forest in my blood
>    The ancestors come to talk to me
>    It's a place I often like to sit
>    While sheltered in a board-leafed tree.
>    We've walked on deep to other worlds:
>    We've gone to bring back healing songs
>    We're coming back with worlds to sing
>    To help us all along, along.
>    I don't know why this path winds on so long
>    I don't require the verse to every song
>    I don't know where the shadows go
>    when gone
>    But knowing you are waiting keeps me strong.

# 43

# The Palimpsest, the Dead Plants, and the Ghost

JESSICA AND I USED to kill plants. We killed them in both the United States and the United Kingdom. It's not that we wanted to kill them. We didn't purposely deprive them of water or place them in extreme heat or extreme cold. We didn't hit them with sticks or anything. It's just that every plant we ever owned died, and in a rather short timeframe. Our house was a death sentence for plants.

Once, early in my ministry, when we were living in a parsonage near the church I was serving, we had a *Monstera deliciosa*—otherwise known as a Swiss cheese plant. It had grown almost as high as the ceiling. Obviously, it wouldn't have grown that tall under our care. No, a journalist friend of Jessica's was moving to Taiwan, and she gave it to us. We tried to dissuade her, explaining that plants died simply from being around us. She didn't believe us, pointing to a number of plants in our home. I said, "Yes, that's because we keep throwing the dead ones on the compost and buying new ones to replace them. In fact, we're waiting for the social services to come to the house and take all the live ones away and forbid us ever to own a plant again."

She went off to Taiwan—what was her name?—and the Swiss cheese plant ended up in our living room. It came in a big pot with a large, tall stake to climb. We placed it in the corner of the room near, but not directly in front of, a window. What's-Her-Name had told us that the Monstera deliciosa liked indirect light and that it needed watering weekly. That seemed simple enough, and if truth be told, it did look pretty good in the room. A real conversation starter. It was a little over eight feet tall. I know because I measured it.

It only took three weeks. The plant started looking sad and then, well, less green. Brown started to appear. I just shook my head and told Jessica to do something about it. What's-Her-Name was her friend, after all, not mine.

That house had a sunroom in the back off the dining room. We had a couple of comfortable chairs out there, each with a small table, plus a bookshelf and a small desk. The view out the windows was actually quite nice. There were trees, bushes, and green grass, but nothing to stop the sunlight from coming in. In the winter, it was a great place to sit and still be warm. In the summer, we opened the windows, but it could get hot.

One day, I came home, and Jessica had moved the Swiss cheese plant out to the sunroom, placing it against the interior wall, not the windows. When I saw the plant out there, I immediately protested, reminding Jessica what What's-Her-Name had said about indirect light. Jessica on her part said she thought the plant needed more warmth, to which I said, "Well, it's going to get plenty of that. It's fucking August!" I was a tad angry, though why, I'm not sure. Perhaps I just liked the plant. It was noble in its way and must have lived for some time to grow so tall.

Within another month the Monstera deliciosa with its Swiss cheese leaves was dead.

One evening a couple of months after the plant's demise, some of the church members came around for a meeting. Over coffee and cookies afterwards, I told a woman how we had killed the Monstera—her name might have been Joyce something-or-other. Why I told her that I cannot recollect, but there must have been a good reason. I didn't go around telling people how Jessica and I killed plants. However, the woman told me in a voice as calm and natural as could be, as if she were telling me the bus schedule, that Jessica and I had not killed the plant, the house had. I, of course, asked her to explain, which she did at some length.

Apparently, that parsonage was a very sad house, and everyone knew it, had known it for years. There was no debate, no discussion. What was less clear, and led to much debate, was exactly why the house was sad. By now, the others who had attended the meeting, who were drinking my coffee and eating my cookies, had gathered around and began offering interpretations for why the house was so sad—it was unhappy, miserable, gloomy, wretched, dejected, despondent, desolate, forlorn, sorrowful, or melancholy.

I had remained quiet while the thesaurus-heavy conversation was going on, but finally I had to ask, "You're not telling me you think the house itself 'feels' these emotions, are you? Do you think wood, brick, concrete, plastic, glass, and whatever else can feel emotions, that the house is sentient?"

For a moment, the living room was silent as people either looked at the floor or the ceiling or each other, pretending to be deep in thought. The room had become so serious, it was as if even the angels in heaven, assuming for the moment there are angels and a heaven, had also stopped their sacred singing to contemplate my patently ridiculous questions.

Opinion was split. About a quarter of those present indeed did think the house itself "felt" and could affect living things inside—thus the dead Monstera deliciosa. George So-and-So asked dramatically if any of us had read *The Haunting of Hill House* by Shirley Somebody, to which only I nodded in the affirmative. "Well then," he said, "why are you asking such a silly question? No disrespect intended."

"None taken," I assured him, "and it's Shirley Jackson. Jackson."

The rest of the people disagreed. They said it was silly to think that a house could be sentient and feel anything, notwithstanding *The Haunting of Hill House*. After all, *The Haunting of Hill House* was just a novel, a work of *fiction*. But this house, the house we were all gathered in, was *real*. This majority believed that the house itself was not actually sad, but it felt sad to us because a sad ghost was in residence. When I asked why no one had ever bothered to tell me this, they said everyone had assumed I knew. After all, *everybody* knew, and I actually lived in the house—where plants died.

As people were saying their goodbyes and heading home, Joyce Something-or-Other waited so she would be the last to leave. Slipping out the door, she turned to me and said, "I bet you can't sleep." She was right. I hadn't slept well for a long time. Then she said, "The ghost prefers the sunroom. She is less sad there."

"She?" I asked.

"Yes. She."

"Does she have a name?"

"I suppose she does. Everyone has a name. But I don't know it." And with that, Joyce Something-or-Other finally left.

Interestingly, though I had just had a roomful of people who thought the house was sad or occupied by a sad ghost, not one of them seemed frightened at all. They all were quite at home, relaxed, casual, enjoying the cookies. I, on the other hand, turning my back on the front door and looking through the living room and beyond the dining room to the sunroom, felt decidedly uneasy. Jessica was on assignment in Israel/Palestine. She had left the previous week and would be gone for two more. I was alone.

I cleaned up the coffee cups and plates and ate the last three cookies. I watched a little television but couldn't concentrate, so I decided to go to bed. The house was ranch style, and the bedroom was off the living room. I took comfort in the fact that it was as far from the sunroom as you could get.

I lay uneasy in the dark. I am a very rational person. As I'm sure you have surmised by now, I don't believe in many of the things people assume I should believe in. I hadn't just fall off the turnup truck either. Nonetheless, I got up and turned on a light in the living room, then went back to bed. I turned on the small lamp on the bedside table. I turned on the radio and listened to some all-night call-in program. God, a lot of people have sad lives. A lot of people have boring lives. The level of banality I heard was soul destroying.

Suddenly I experienced what felt like a sharp, strong kick to my leg, and I jerked up in bed. I was confused. The radio was on, as were the lights in the bedroom and living room. I realized I had fallen asleep. I must have awoken when my leg jerked to the side. That sort of thing happens sometimes when you sleep. And then, suddenly, there she was. I saw her standing by the side of the bed. She looked about fifty years old. Her face was thin, drawn, and grayish. She had large, dark brown eyes, stringy, unwashed brown hair down to her shoulders, and bangs that hung down to her eyebrows. And yes, she was sad, very sad. I didn't get a sense of anger or hostility from her. She was not threatening. She embraced all of the thesaurus-like descriptive words spoken earlier. She didn't say a word.

Obviously, it was a dream suggested by the discussion in the living room. A vivid and unsettling dream, but a dream, nonetheless. I lay back down but left the lights and radio on. I didn't sleep anymore that night.

Her name was Harriet Claudia Burrows.

# 44

# Michael Andrew Walker Johnson, Peru, and Shapeshifting

JESSICA AND I HAD BEEN living in Britain for maybe five years when I got a long email from Walker describing his experiences in Peru where he had gone to study with a shaman. The email came to me in the morning on a day when I was off to Zimbabwe and Mozambique, so I saved it for the long-haul flight to Harare. I can't sleep on airplanes, so I would often leave emails to read and respond to, and reports to write during long flights. I would settle in with a rum and coke, plug in my laptop, and get to work.

I read his email over four times, and when I finally settled back into my seat, I wondered if now was the time, the time when Walker and I would select paths so divergent that we would lose what we had—profound respect, friendship, and love. But before I tell you about the email, I need to go back, way back in time to when I was young and would have been more receptive to Walker's email.

It was the early 1970's. I was just out of college when I discovered Carlos Castaneda. I say "discovered" as if Castaneda was a hidden gem to be found. In fact, he was everywhere. By the time the Castaneda phenomenon was over, he had written twelve books, the first being *The Teachings of Don Juan*, followed by *A Separate Reality* and *Journey to Ixtlan*. I read those three and then stopped. While the details of the books have now drifted off to where books read many years ago reside, I do remember quite a lot about the whole affair because, at the time, I wanted to be a true believer.

Castaneda's writings were about his training with a shaman by the name of don Juan Matus, which means "Man of Knowledge." He claimed don Juan Matus was a Yaqui, and as a Yaqui, descended from the Toltecs. He also reported that don Juan Matus was a *nagual*, that is a leader among seers in his ancestry, and that he, don Juan Matus, recognized Castaneda also as a nagual. But here's the important part. Naguals are also a kind of shaman who claim they can change into an animal, or "shift" into another form, with the aid of, for example, mescalito. Castaneda wrote that he witnessed don Juan Matus actually go through a transformation into an animal. He implied that the shift was not metaphorical, not an illusion caused by the use of psychoactive drugs, but it was a literal, biological change.

Castaneda's writings were presented as anthropological ethnographies, and his observations were received as factual. The University of California believed him, granting him bachelor and doctoral degrees. Eventually, it all fell apart. His descriptions of the Yaqui and his very veracity were challenged, and the university took back its degrees. Still, he sold, indeed sells, a lot of books and is still believed by lots of people.

As I said, I wanted to believe and argued at the time that shifting might be possible. Now, writing this, that young David Robert Bainbridge seems like a stranger to me. He's an embarrassment. I think I wanted to believe in at least the possibility of mystery, that there might be more out there than the reality proclaimed by Western culture and its interpretation of what is true and possible. I wanted to encounter the unexpected.

I no longer expect the unexpected. Human beings don't biologically, literally, turn themselves into other animal forms. Sounds in the night, together with everything else supernatural, metaphysical, and other-worldly, are mysteries only because we lack the knowledge to explain them. And when we gain that knowledge...poof, they are gone.

Halfway between London and Harare, on my second rum and coke, I was remembering all this—Carlos Castaneda, don Juan Matus, and me. And of course, Walker.

He had left behind much of Christianity's interpretation of reality some years before. He had severed his relationship with the church, though he insisted that his ordination was "still good," and that his monthly pension should still arrive in his bank account, which was not unimportant. He wrote to me about his changing perspectives and understandings. *"I wouldn't know how to write a Christian 'faith statement,' being an animist. For me, god is the luminous background to creation, but not a monotheistic luminosity. Maybe it's closer to the Star Wars myth and the Force....use the Force, Luke...meaning that it's accessible. I can't imagine how that would lead to Christology or anything else defined as 'Christian.'"*

Obviously, his spirituality had taken new paths, but which paths were unclear to me. He had told me he was heading to Peru to work with a shaman, but he had not elaborated. The email he sent me, the one I read on the plane, began with these words, *"Peru was all-out spectacular."*

He *"drank the medicine"* three times that week, and from what I read, I could only guess how profound and profoundly important the experience was. He wrote, *"In the first ceremony, I saw all the people who had hurt me, from the most pernicious to the merely political (such as church leaders). They all were fucks, but some clung with more damage. I saw them with their broken spirits, their shattered souls, their splintered integrity, one after another. They just showed up, and when they didn't come spontaneously, I brought them into my space and could almost see them as if they were in the room with me. And I no longer felt like a victim, nor that I had to seek explanations or justice. I just saw them as they were and accepted that that is who they are. I just looked at them and saw what is true. And I wept."*

I have tried to imagine him sitting somewhere, drinking medicine and eventually weeping. All that came to mind were films I had seen, or imagined I had seen, of the white man sitting with "natives" in some jungle or desert. A kind of *Altered States*, but with Walker in the lead. So instead of William Hurt sitting around a fire, drinking the medicine and tripping to who-knows-where, it was Walker. The images were crap, of course. I had no idea what the setting was, who the shaman was, what the medicine tasted like. So I did my best to purge my fashioned images and leave it all blank. I just tried to read the damn email.

*"Then I wept a second time just for the weeping. Then I wept a third time, and this time I saw all the people I had hurt, including some in the first group, and I cried it out until I was done. And then some other visions started, and after that, dreams came as I slept in my bed."*

One of Walker's dreams was about a plant. In the dream there were six pots of the same plant in his home. The soil was bone dry, but the plants were not dead, though they obviously needed care. So he watered them and put them in the light on the windowsill in the kitchen. He wrote in his email, *"When I woke up the next morning, I was thinking that that plant must be on the property there in Peru. So I had my friend give me a tour of all the power plants, and Wow, there it was. He told me what that plant was and said that if I wanted to work with it, I would have to come and stay and go out into the jungle for six months."*

His second ceremony was, apparently, good, but *"really really rough. I had a very difficult time in that conversation with the medicine. And so I didn't eat for two days while the ayahuasca was still working on my system."*

Ayahuasca, for the uninitiated, is a South American psychoactive, a psychedelic and entheogenic brew used both socially and as a ceremonial spiritual medicine among indigenous peoples of the Amazon basin, or so says Wikipedia. Walker assumed I knew what it was, but I had to be sure so I looked it up. Details can be important.

The third and final ceremony was also good. "*I asked permission of the shaman to hold some of the leaves of the plant during the ceremony. And he gave me permission. And then, during that ceremony, I got a clear indication to slit open my abdomen with my fingernail and put the spirit of the plant in me, then close up my skin. Which I did. Sort of amazing to feel this plant inside me. I'm now starting to sing. And today, back home in New York, I went for a walk to get out of the apartment, bringing this plant into the light, plus I am drinking a lot of water. So the experience continues to work on me.*"

I'm assuming that Walker did not actually split open his abdomen with his fingernail, place the spirit of the plant inside himself, and then close up his skin. I don't believe that, any more than I believe don Juan Matus actually, factually, biologically shifted into another animal. But now that the years have passed, I'm not quite as sure what is "real." I read that email while flying to a place where people were very different from me and saw the world in different ways from mine. I've never drunk the medicine in a spiritual ceremony. I have no idea what actually happens to a human mind and spirit after drinking ayahuasca. But how about this.

When I was about thirty years old, I was going through a very difficult time. For reasons that are not important now, I felt unloved and lost and unsure where I was going. I had been having grotesque nightmares and even thought about seeking professional help. And then one morning, while lying in bed fully awake, deeply depressed, and with my eyes wide open, it was as if the universe cracked open and I was transported somewhere different. And a message was given to me in words and feelings. The message was, "You know nothing about love," and at that moment and only for that moment, I knew and felt love, what it truly is. It was utterly amazing. When the crack closed, and I was once again lying in bed staring at the ceiling, the knowledge and experience were gone. I couldn't think it or feel it back into existence. However, I did know that for a moment *I had experienced it*, that it had been real, and that the knowledge I had glimpsed was deeply significant. Even though I couldn't remember the true essence of love, I was certain that a love unknown to me did exist.

No psychoactive drugs, just me lying in bed in the morning. The experience is easily explained through psychology, by which, of course, I mean it is easily reinterpreted or dismissed. In time, that is exactly what I did. But approaching Harare that night, I remembered the crack-in-the-universe morning. Carlos Castaneda and don Juan Matus be damned. I'm not reverting to my youth in my old age. No damn second childhood. But I did wonder what it would feel like to have the spirit of a plant inside me.

We flew into Harare in an African storm that shook the plane and bounced us onto the runway. As we were taxiing to the gate, the pilot announced that due to the severity of the storm, the computer had landed the plane. Magic? No. Software. But still kind of magical.

About a year ago, Walker came to visit me in Castine. He was still living in New York and still with Greg. It was a short visit, but wonderful, nonetheless. Now we were two old friends approaching their mid-seventies, not just talking about old times, but also about what was happening in our present, and what we hoped would happen in our future. Jessica had died, and I have to confess I wasn't all that interested in the future. While dealing with her death taught me that I was not suicidal, I wasn't all that enthusiastic about living. Except for Walker. I was interested in him.

During the visit there was laughter, hugs, kisses, seriousness, silences, friendship, and love. But I mention all this while sitting here at Paradise Café because he also told me he was a shapeshifter, and I believed him. I didn't demand he define his terms. I didn't dissect his experience, laying it out on the stainless-steel table to see what bled. No, I did none of that. I just listened.

I wanted to be a true believer.

# 45

# The Palimpsest and the Offense of Offending

I'VE BEEN SITTING HERE at my table thinking, *I'm no fan of Barry Patrick Olds.* He's on my mind because he and his posse just walked into the café, no doubt to harangue Melissa Jennifer Davis. Barry Patrick Olds and I live on different sides of the divide, and I'm not likely to give him a big hug in an attempt to overcome our differences and bring peace to a troubled nation. As he and his boys walked past my table and continued through the front door of the café, he nodded a hello, but with a smile that could never be mistaken for friendliness. It was a smile of superiority, of victory. It was a smirk. I wanted to hurt him, or at least throw my latte at him. But here's the thing, the thing I'm thinking about, the thing that is keeping me from reaching self-actualization on a legal yellow pad this glorious late morning. It's never been my intention to offend people, though offend them I have, and it seems to me inevitable that one day, and probably one day soon, I will offend Barry Patrick Olds and the entire Brotherhood of Christian Businessmen. My intention is not to offend Barry Patrick Olds, but I dare say that when that day comes, I will probably feel pretty damn good about it.

While my purpose is not to affront anyone, it was obvious from the get-go that if I was unwilling or unable to offend people, I could never join in the struggle to overcome injustices. If you're not willing to offend people, don't bother getting in the fight. By definition, fighting for justice means you will offend the unjust. And don't be naïve: it's a battle with casualties.

Being a straight white male, I'm obviously more than privileged, but I have always tried to use my privilege to benefit some and offend all kinds of others—misogynists, rapists, wife beaters, racists, gay bigots, fascists, and oppressors of many kinds. It's a gift, really. It's simple. If you're fighting for women's rights, then having a man stand by your side may help. If you are fighting against racism, then a white guy standing shoulder to shoulder isn't necessarily a bad thing. A straight man standing up for a gay man may make a point. And yes, it's a slippery thing, this privilege. Standing in solidarity with a woman must not mean mansplaining. A white person walking the line with a black person must not mean that the white person runs the show.

Years ago, when I was invited to participate in a commission in Berkeley to study the impact of poverty on people in the greater Bay Area, we started by introducing ourselves and what organization we represented. As it turned out, I was the last person in the process, and after giving my name, I pointed out that no one in the room was poor or represented the poor. Good intentions of the privileged, yes. Solidarity, no. It was embarrassing. I'm sure it wouldn't happen today. Right?

Don't get me wrong. I'm not claiming that I wear a great cloak of nobility—David Robert Bainbridge, the magnificent social justice warrior, bloodied on behalf of others, wearing his red badge of courage with saintly humility. And if being truthful with myself and you is the reason I flew from Castine, Maine, to Berkeley, California—and I continue to declare it is—it's time once again to scrape my ever-thinning parchment skin.

First of all, I haven't paid much of a price for my so-called courage. No red badge of anything. Sure, a lot of bad people hate me. So what? And yes, I've offended even more people. Big deal.

The number of times my "noble" acts of solidarity put me in real danger, or at least in uncomfortable situations, I can count on one hand. There was the time the military stopped me on a dark night on a lonely road in San Salvador. When I was in Angola, the civil war briefly returned to Luanda, and the gunfire was impressive. My hosts in Yangon came to my hotel to whisk me out of the country because they had it on good authority that protests and riots would begin in two days. The police quickly ushered me out of my hotel in Durban two days before the 1994 election because there was a bomb planted somewhere in the building. In each case, I was anything but a warrior for the cause. I did what I was told to do and with speed. Trust me when I say I didn't break into a rendition of *Kumbaya*. If hiding was in order, I hid. If running was best, I ran. If staying was appropriate, I stayed.

Second, you'd think that standing in solidarity with others, fighting the good fight for justice, would come out of deep and meaningful moral, ethical, philosophical, theological contemplation and commitment. But I'm not sure that is true of me. It could be I never really gave it much thought.

Once when we were much younger, Jessica and I stayed with friends for a couple of weeks in Missoula, Montana. Their house was on a corner, and one evening we were all sitting on the front porch drinking beer and talking. Suddenly, we heard a large crashing sound on the other side of the house, which, of course, we could not see. I got up instantly and ran from the porch, and as I turned the corner, I saw a car in flames about a half a block away. I ran toward the car as fast as I could, thinking that if there were still people in the car, they'd be in pretty bad shape, and if there were still people in the car, I would probably end up in pretty bad shape too. But here's the thing. I just ran. There was no thought of doing good. I was not motivated by nobility. I didn't think about it at all. I just ran. I did not think of Kierkegaard or Nietzsche or Arendt or Gutiérrez or

Haack. I didn't ask what prima facie duties might be in play or what virtues were applicable. I didn't wonder if utilitarianism or situation ethics was driving me. I certainly didn't ask myself what would Jesus do? I just ran towards the burning car.

If I search below the hidden text of my living, I suspect that just running towards burning cars is descriptive of my entire life. I mean, did I ever think it through? If you don't contemplate the goodness and evilness of actions, can it be said you are an ethical person? Is just running good enough? Surely your character is not just defined by your actions but must also be created by your intentions. I am not just an agent who acts. I'm also a being who feels and thinks.

And there's one more thing. All my running, fighting, shouting, pleading, never really made a damn bit of difference. Hell, I couldn't even convince Samantha Esther Cunningham that she was really sexy without the stilettos.

So, you tell me. Who am I? Because quite frankly, I'm at a loss. My mom saved my life when I was a small boy. Jessica saved my life for over forty years. Walker saved my life for almost as long. And now, the only one left to do the job is me! Place your bets, people. I'm in the third act of my life, and I'm told there is no encore.

This palimpsest thing is a real drag. It's a fucking burden.

# 46

# The Palimpsest and the End of Days

THE MOMENT JESSICA died, I was sitting there holding her hand. I started to cry but shut the tears down with a sudden brutality. The reason, understood by those who have experienced such a death, was that I was afraid I would lose myself in the weeping and despair and never resurface. I was terrified.

Jessica died at home. That is all I'm going to say about it. Paradise Café. Sanctuary. Palimpsest. All can be damned. I'm not talking about it. I'm simply not going to do it.

Except for this. When Jessica died at home, the angels ceased to sing.

When Walker died in the wilderness, the angels disappeared.

# 47

# Michael Andrew Walker Johnson and the Poetry

WHEN RICHARD DIED
   There are, of course, always
   Angels slipping away at 3 o'clock or 4
   from terminals of departure
   onto a last flight
   before the devil pisses

   on the blackberries

   their work done, no one listening
   to what they must hear alone,
   the final call to board
   Angels departing,
   Lying on sanitized sheets
   Then slipping sideways
   Through another hole in their lungs,
   Exit portals for the soul
   hands relaxing into wax on his chest
   eyes sinking forever

   into bowls too deep to use

anymore, muscles slumped

against face bones

workers who have lost their rights

    to negotiate.

My angel is a musician now,
Whispers rhythmically
To oxygen pumps
And whistling face masks.
In the hallways, behind the curtains
muted speaking, words creeping
on crepe soles down linoleum halls
voices disappearing into kindness.
I ache for a requiem to your going,
O my shriveled angel:
Kyrie! Kyrie! Kyrie!
Even though there's not enough mass
to call your attention this ward,
even your gaze

    having gone soft and waxy.

I hold your bones in silence:
This is my body, you seem to say.
Behold, and do not turn away
from these ascensions into death.
After the last softening grip,
When your fingers tightened
with finality around my skin,
an electric surge shot into my hand
as I was holding you.
Your last breath

pushed through your body into me
as an impetuous shove
from flesh to flesh,
one more intimacy between us,

  as you headed for the drifting clouds, saying:

"Look for me there when you need me."
A last tear rolled down your cheek.
The nurse saw it.
She said so, sweetly leaning in my ear:
"Look, one little tear."
But I,
I had already memorized it and was
already flying

  toward the open window,

a fistful of tubes
limp swords against the lord of life,
a fistful of wilted lightning bolts
hailing upwards

  from outstretched fists,

banging against the ceiling of the sky,
arcing upwards, searching,
wanting to see even one,

  fine etched cloud

and wailing, Wait for me! Wait for me!
flinging my voice

into the hot afternoon sun

until it took flight
a light thing
with bright wings.

# 48

# The Palimpsest, the Prison, and the Murderer

ONCE UPON A TIME, FOR a short while, I was a chaplain in a prison—the California State Prison Solano in Vacaville, California. The inmates call it the Holiday Inn of prisons. The hallways, while larger and dirtier, were painted not unlike the hallways in my high school. While I was there, I pretty much had a free run of the place. I attended chapel services and group therapy sessions, and met with individual prisoners. It was at the Vacaville prison that I met Charles Manson, but that's another story. It's also where I met Luis Jesús Hernández.

Luis Jesús Hernández was in prison for killing a man. One night on alcohol and drugs, he beat a man to death with a pipe. Luis Jesús Hernández was a handsome young man with pleasant, sharp features. He was short, slender, and well-built. He had a great smile and clear eyes. For reasons unclear to me, he took a liking to me and became my main contact among the inmates. I never asked why he was in prison, but he volunteered the information during our first session together.

I welcomed Luis Jesús Hernández' interest in me, partly, perhaps mostly, because he provided a kind of cover for me while I walked the halls, ate in the mess hall, and attended group sessions. He was not interested in the chapel. I felt safer, perhaps naively so, when I was with him. He also introduced me to other inmates, thus enabling me to form other relationships.

One day he invited me to his "house," which was, of course, his cell. I had been told not to enter a prisoner's cell, but if I did, never to enter first. When we arrived at Luis Jesús Hernández's "house," he politely invited me in, and just as politely motioned for me to enter first, which I did. I sat on the edge of his bed as he stood in front of the door to the cell. Of course, I realized that I was now trapped in the cell and could only leave when Luis Jesús Hernández allowed me to. To say the least, I was unhappy with myself and not a little anxious. For his part, Luis Jesús Hernández was a delight. He smiled and talked and almost seemed proud to have a guest. He told me about his family—a wife and one little girl—and his hopes of one day being released. When he was done talking, we left his "house," and he accompanied me to where I exited the main hallway of the prison.

I only visited the prison for a few months, and when I left, I put the experience behind me. It was clear from even that short time that I was not cut out to be a prison chaplain.

A few years passed. One day I attended a friend's wedding in a small church in a small town south of San Francisco. I sat near the back of the almost-full sanctuary and watched the photographer and his assistant set up for the ceremony. The assistant was Hispanic with a round, full face and plump body. While he was working, he caught my eye and hesitated for a moment. He smiled at me. He seemed familiar, but I concluded that I didn't know him. He smiled one more time, and I looked away.

During the reception after the ceremony, I grabbed a small glass of wine and stood under a large, beautiful oak tree in the church patio. Everyone was enjoying the warm sun and the good food and drink, sitting at tables or on benches, or like me, just standing under a tree or near the small creek. As I was looking around at the people,

I noticed the photographer's assistant walking toward me with cameras hanging from each shoulder. He stopped in front of me and said, "Hi, David. It's me, Luis."

I stared at him for what must have seemed to him like an eternity, and suddenly there he was. The handsome lean face inside the puffed-up face before me. The slender strong body engulfed by the fat. It was Luis Jesús Hernández. I didn't know what to say. We just looked at each other and I finally said, "Luis, when did you get out?" I figured he had been free for some time given his weight gain but didn't know what else to say.

Luis Jesús Hernández had been paroled almost a year before. He was with his wife and child and had landed this job shortly after his release. He seemed happy. We exchanged a few words, he more eagerly than I. He gave me his phone number and asked me to call him. He needed a friend now on the outside as I had needed a friend when I entered the prison.

I never called him.

I have never forgotten that I failed him. He seemed well but still adjusting. I got the sense that he wanted to talk about something in particular. However, I never learned if that were true because I never called. I have never known why. He did me no harm; indeed, he helped me when I was in his environment, a place dangerous for me. It was often a frightening place to me. I needed him more than he needed me. And yet, I never contacted him.

I wonder if Luis Jesús Hernández is still alive. He brutally killed another human being but got another chance. I don't begrudge him that and didn't that day in the church courtyard under the oak tree. But I do wonder why I so often almost do the right thing. I wonder why I only sometimes stand up. Am I as frightened by life as my father was? Or am I just selfish and lazy? Is it worth finding out?

# 49

# Megan Margaret Williams and the Dark

I'VE BEEN SPENDING more time with Megan Margaret Williams and Sarah Jane Williams. It may be time for me to refer to them simply as Megan and Sarah, but I'm not sure. Maybe I'm quite ready for that. That might imply more than I'm capable of. However, an endearing episode took place last night that is, I think, worth recording.

The three of us had gone for a late afternoon visit to Tilden Park. Sarah Jane Williams and I were interested in a short walk among the trees, while Megan Margaret Williams was partial to riding on the merry go round. We did both. On the ride home, Megan Margaret Williams told me, as is her way, that I was going to have dinner at their home. This would complete what she thought made a perfect day. I looked at Sarah Jane Williams. She smiled not taking her eyes off the road and said, "It's up to you, but trust me, dinner won't be anything special. It's already getting late, and I'm tired. So you'll get whatever I can find in the kitchen that won't be much work."

"I can help, or I can even cook the whole meal if you want. I'm not bad in the kitchen. Jessica wasn't much for cooking, so I took it over early in our marriage. But whatever, I'll eat most anything. Or we can order out if you want," I said, slightly surprised at my apparent eagerness to continue the visit.

"Well, help would be appreciated. There's no need to order out," she said.

"We can play a game after we eat," Megan Margaret Williams said. "Do you like playing games, David?"

"Not really," I said, turning around to address Megan Margaret Williams in the back seat. "But I think I can make an exception for you."

"That's good, David. Games are fun. You'll really like it."

As it turned out, it was tuna casserole, salad, wine, and juice for the smallest among us. After dinner, Sarah Jane Williams gave Megan Margaret Williams a bath as I did the dishes. Sarah Jane Williams insisted I should not run off, that she would crack open a bottle of brandy that had been sitting in the cupboard for what seemed like years.

Washing the dishes on my own, I had time to think about Megan Margaret Williams. It was clear that she was quite fond of me, and these feelings had developed, in my mind anyway, very quickly. So quickly, in fact, that I confess it was difficult for me to trust them. As you know, I've never had children, so I am not wise in the ways of their affections, loyalties, loves. However, I've never underestimated them either, and I wasn't going to start with Megan Margaret Williams.

After the bath, Sarah Jane Williams told her daughter she could have one game, and only one game, with me, and then it was off to bed. Sitting on the floor, playing some stupid child's game, one I was losing honestly, I looked at Megan Margaret Williams and marveled at her knitted brow concentration, her laughter, her pure joy in victory. After the completion of the game, without protest, she got up, gave me a hug while I was still on the floor, and said, "Goodnight, David. Sweet dreams when you go to bed."

"You too, honey. Sweet dreams," I said.

"David, I don't have sweet dreams in the dark," she said.

I began to say, "Why is..." but Sarah Jane Williams interrupted me and said to Megan Margaret Williams, "Megan, don't start.

There's nothing in the dark. No monsters. Now come on. Time for bed." And with that, she picked up her daughter and carried her to the bedroom.

When Sarah Jane Williams came back into the living room, I asked her what all that was about, and she explained that over the last few weeks Megan Margaret Williams had been saying she was afraid of the dark. She insisted it was nothing, and I figured she would know better than I would, though I did wonder if it had anything to do with the divorce and the breaking up of her family.

Sarah Jane Williams got the brandy down from the cupboard, and we sat in the living room talking about everything and nothing when Megan Margaret Williams came walking into the room, wide-eyed and in her pajamas. She looked at her mother and said, "I don't want to close my eyes."

"Sweetie, you have to close your eyes. You need to get some sleep. We're right out here. If you want, why don't you leave your door cracked open a little bit?" Sarah Jane Williams answered.

"I want David to sit with me."

"Honey, David doesn't want to do that, and besides he will need to get home soon," Sarah Jane Williams said and looked at me with embarrassment.

"Sarah, if it's all right with you, I don't mind," I said. Sarah Jane Williams gave her daughter a stern look and then gave me a nod of approval. I got up from the chair. Megan Margaret Williams took my hand and led me to her bedroom.

Megan Margaret Williams climbed into bed, crawled under the covers, and looked at me standing at the entrance to the room. I entered the room and sat on the edge of her bed and said, "So, what's up? Why can't you close your eyes?"

"If I close my eyes, I can't see what's happening in the dark," she said.

"Do you think something is happening in the dark?" I asked.

"I don't know, because I can't see if I close my eyes," she said. "If something is happening, I have to see it."

"I don't think anything is happening in the dark," I said.

"How do you know?"

I didn't know what to say to that. She was right. If I close my eyes, I can't really know.

"Megan, are you scared?" I finally said.

She looked at me, fragile and vulnerable. "I'm scared of the dark," she whispered. "If I close my eyes, it's worse."

"Ah. Me too. I'm scared of the dark," I said.

She propped herself up on her elbows and said, "You're scared of the dark?!"

"That I am," I said.

"Why?"

"Oh, I don't know. It's silly really. When it's time for sleep, dark is actually a good friend. This I do know. There are no monsters in your room. Nothing is happening in the dark. Trust me."

She lay back down and looked as though she were thinking about what I said. "Can you stay with me tonight?"

"No, I can't. I need to get home and leave your mom in peace."

"She doesn't mind. She likes you. It's okay if you stay."

"Well, that's nice, but I still can't stay. But I can sit with you a little while longer. Honey, you can close your eyes. It will be okay. It won't be long before the sun is shining, and I'll see you then. Close your eyes, Sweetie."

She looked at me for the longest time. Then she laid down on her side facing me. She closed her eyes and said, "I love you, David."

"I love you too, Megan," I said. I closed my eyes to hide the tears.

It's time—she is *Megan*.

# 50

# Michael Andrew Walker Johnson, the Sacred, and Fyodor Dostoevsky's Innocent Child

When we lived in the United Kingdom, Jessica and I returned to the United States once, sometimes twice a year. The visits were mostly to see friends and family, well, Jessica's family, but also to keep in touch with US American culture, both in the sense of "feel" and knowledge. Each year we would discover something new, something that had changed. I remember one year everyone was talking about being hydrated. Before then we drank water when we were thirsty. Suddenly we hydrated. Another year, seemingly every commercial on TV included website addresses. We used to talk romantically about the San Francisco fog, but one year I flew into the marine layer. The romance was gone. But the visit I am thinking of now was void of such minutiae. Rather, it was overflowing with essential meaning.

Walker and I hadn't been in contact for some time, not even via one of our flurries of emails. Jessica and I arrived in San Francisco, checked into a hotel, headed down for a late light dinner, and then went back up to the room to crash. My plan was to surprise Walker—just show up at his door unannounced—so before I fell asleep, I tracked down his address. He was living in Alameda.

The next day, Jessica was up and out early to meet friends. I lingered in bed and then called room service for breakfast. After a shower, I caught a taxi, figuring I'd get to Walker's place by noon. It was a Sunday.

I remembered Alameda from my days living in the Bay Area. The city itself is on Alameda Island and Bay Farm Island. It bumps up onto Oakland on the south and is east of San Francisco across the Bay. It has a lot of houses on canals, and as it turned out, Walker's house was one of them.

It was absurd of me to assume he'd be home, but I did, and thus, as the taxi drove away, I realized I had no plan B. With excitement I rang the doorbell, imagining Walker's face, first expressing confusion, then the expansive look of surprise, followed by an enormous smile. But when he opened the door, he looked shocked.

We just stood looking at each other on opposite sides of the threshold. He looked exhausted. His eyes were red. His face was ashen. His clothes were wrinkled and weary. Neither of us spoke. Tears filled his eyes. He stepped forward, kissed me on the cheek, and hugged me. He started to cry, so I just held him tight. He pulled back and said, "I can't believe you are here. Richard died yesterday."

Richard Eugene Moss was Walker's partner. They had been together for a number of years. He had AIDS. He died at home. When I was flying toward San Francisco, checking into my hotel, eating dinner, and falling asleep, Walker had been watching the man he loved die and sharing grief with Richard Eugene Moss's parents.

Everyone who knew Richard Eugene Moss and knew that he was dying; that is, everyone except me. I swore I would not lose contact with Walker again, though, of course, I would and did. What that says about me is something others can decide. Palimpsest or no, I'm not in the mood to bleed and scrape today. Paradise Café isn't as inviting this morning. The marine layer is still hovering over my head. I'm chilled. The damn Brotherhood just arrived to continue their assault on Melissa Jennifer Davis.

We entered the house, and Walker led me straight to the back patio. For some time we sat in silence looking at the canal. I really don't know how long "some time" was. It was one of those experiences when time loses concreteness and exactitude. Suddenly Walker got up announcing we needed lunch. He went to the kitchen to make sandwiches and grab beers. I didn't follow him.

As we ate, he told me that funeral arrangements had been made with Richard Eugene Moss in anticipation of his death. Lawyers had been paid for the giving of advice and the writing of a will well in advance. Finances had been settled and arranged. Walker got up again, and without speaking, he went back into the house. I sat with my beer and the sunshine. In less than a minute he returned, sat back down at the table, and handed me a check. It was made out to him and was for five hundred thousand dollars. Richard Eugene Moss had money. I hadn't known that.

"Richard's parents are okay with this," Walker said, looking at the check in my hands. "They've been great. But I need your help. Come to the bank with me. I need to set up an account and get this damn thing out of the house. I really don't want to do that by myself. I can't believe you're here."

We spent the day talking about the things you talk about when the one you love dies. I called Jessica and told her what had happened, and we agreed that she would check out of the hotel and head north the next day to connect with her family, and that I would follow when it was appropriate. She put my suitcase in a taxi with the Alameda address. I made dinner for Walker and me with what I found in the kitchen. We cracked open a bottle of red wine and then another. By nine in the evening, Walker was falling asleep on the couch, so I got him into bed and then settled myself into the guest bedroom. With jetlag and emotional exhaustion both hitting me hard, I wasn't far behind him in sleep.

Walker slept until after eleven the next day, but when he walked into the kitchen, he was showered, shaved, and looking somewhat refreshed. We sat over coffee for an hour doing our best to "catch up" as if this were a normal visit. That's what people do.

With the check in his wallet, we went to the bank. We walked up to a teller. Walker handed her the check for five hundred thousand dollars and said, "I'd like to open an account."

The teller didn't blink. She said, "Of course, Mr. Johnson. Would you and your... friend...come with me please?" I could see in the instant she made eye contact with me that she was trying to decide if I were a "friend" or a "partner." No marriage back then.

She led us into a small but very pleasant room and asked us to take a seat. Walker and I looked at each other with eyebrows raised ever so slightly.

"Mr. Johnson, there are forms to be filled out. We will do that for you, of course. While you're waiting, you might like some refreshments. Can I get you and your companion some coffee, or something cold?"

"I'd love a cup of coffee," I said. She made eye contact with me again as she continued trying to figure out my relationship with the guy with all the money. It wasn't that she was unfriendly or rude. She was not. It's just that I was a slight distraction, not the focus of her attention. The focus of her attention was the rich guy.

Walker said he'd also like some coffee. She excused herself, but in no time returned with two mugs of coffee, cream, sugar, and a plate of cookies. She asked Walker for identification and explained that she would return for his approval and signature after she had completed the paperwork. When she left, we both laughed. In the midst of grief, laughter is something else people do.

"I feel like a rich person," he said, laughing again.

"If you had walked in here with a check for fifty dollars and asked to open an account, you'd be out there balancing a clipboard on your knees without the coffee and cookies," I said.

"It's the way it is. The people who need the least get the most," he said.

We enjoyed the coffee and cookies, expounding upon the injustices of the world, as an account for half a million dollars was being opened in Walker's name.

Walker looked up from his coffee and once again spoke about the very unlikely but, to him, profoundly important fact that I had appeared without warning at the exact moment he needed me. He then said, "Are you supposed to be my true love, David? We must marry when they change the law." He smiled. "I know, sadly you really are a straight bastard. Still, I'm tempted to declare there is something sacred in our being together in this space and at this time."

He was, of course, right. I too was amazed that I had arrived at his door when I did under those circumstances. It was almost enough to make you believe in a loving god, or as Walker said, in sacredness. Fortunately, there is always Fyodor Dostoevsky's innocent child to pull you back from the brink.

Imagine for a moment that standing next to me is an innocent suffering child...No, no, let's make this specific and personal. Imagine that *Megan* is standing next to me, innocent and suffering—suffering despite confident prayers, fevered prayers, propositional prayers, and what-the-hell-I-might-as-well-give-it-a-try prayers. A god who allows and does not intervene in the suffering of an innocent child is offensive to the human soul and its commitment to love and justice. When I imagine the tension, indeed the contradiction, between the traditional understanding of God and our common human experience, I become angry. You can't have it both ways—an all-powerful, all loving, all good God and the suffering of an innocent child, or the suffering of Richard Eugene Moss, for that matter. If you insist on a god, then it must be either indifferent or powerless, or perhaps both.

The best I can do with a powerless god is at least give that god the chance that I gave Jessica and Walker, and the chance Walker gave Richard Eugene Moss, which was to be friends and companions through the suffering. In other words, I can accept love. If I hesitate, it is not because the ephemeral nature of a god denotes weakness. Beauty is ephemeral and can still knock you over. But given that Jessica was much more tangible (I could feel her holding me when I despaired), the god thing can be hard work. And there is an unsophisticated voice within me that never stops asking that if God, and it's *God* I'm talking about, *is* so powerless in this utterly indifferent universe, then what's the point?

Of course, many choose God anyway, most commonly appealing to arguments about human free will (God can't, due to self-imposed restrictions, save Megan or Richard Eugene Moss because doing so would undermine human free will and thus the potential of and for the divine-human relationship) and about God's mysterious ways (God won't save Megan and Richard Eugene Moss, the reasons for which will never be revealed, and even if they were, would be incomprehensible to human beings). There have been, no doubt, trillions of words written and spoken articulating complex theological constructs to explain and justify these two appeals. For others, well, for me anyway, the weight of nature's indifference, human brutality, and injustice render any notion of a god illogical, irrational, and offensive to human intelligence.

So, did an indifferent powerless god direct me to Walker's home? If you insist on my holding onto something, having faith in something, then I choose Love with a capital "L." It was Walker who washed Richard Eugene Moss's sheets and made his bed when he could not lift a feather. It was Walker who cooked Richard Eugene Moss a warm meal when he had no appetite. It was Walker who cleaned Richard Eugene Moss's body when he couldn't move and didn't really care. It was Walker who whispered in Richard Eugene Moss's ear when he was frightened. And it was Walker who said goodbye when Richard Eugene Moss's time came to die.

But here's the apparent contradiction. The innocent child, the suffering, even the death, may negate a god, but, interestingly, it does not negate sacredness. Perhaps Walker was right. Maybe for that long-ago, seemingly chance encounter between us in Alameda, there was sacredness. Perhaps the Love is the sacredness. Or the sacredness the Love. If so, then surely I must rely on those who love me, and perhaps even those who, for whatever reason, have a passing thought of my existence, if only for a moment.

# 51

# The Palimpsest and the Samantha Esther Cunningham Email

I HAVEN'T BEEN COMPLETELY honest with you concerning Samantha Esther Cunningham, which kind of defeats the whole purpose of this palimpsest reading-below-the-surface-of-my-life exercise. The thing is, I didn't sleep well on the night of *the kiss*, and the next day I went to her office at the university and said, "I feel kind of out on a limb all by myself." That was it. That's all I said. She didn't respond, so I walked out. The next morning, she came to my office and said, "You're not alone on the limb." I didn't say a word, and she walked up to me, hugged me—and I mean a full body hug—kissed me on the cheek, and then left the office. We never spoke of it again.

I think it's not insignificant to add that Samantha Esther Cunningham's husband was, and presumably still is, a big man with a big gun, and that this is, after all, the United States of America, where there are more weapons floating around than citizens, and that said citizens, at an alarming rate, enjoy shooting each other for any number of reasons and sometimes for no reason at all.

Still, I did a little research late last night and found Samantha Esther Cunningham's email address. I immediately wrote the following email:

*Hi Samantha,*

*I'm sorry if I hurt you. Do you ever think about me?*

*David*

I moved the mouse over the send button but hesitated. I thought it might be best if I let the message sit overnight, so I placed it in my draft folder. It's never good to send an important email late at night, and certainly not after a bottle of red wine.

I arrived at Paradise Café around ten this morning, ordered my latte and croissant, opened my laptop, and, after only a moment's thought, sent the email. Ah, the power of the morning.

I haven't received a response. It is possible she doesn't remember who David is.

# 52

# The Palimpsest, René Descartes, and the Elusive and Illusive Balance

WITHOUT THINKING MUCH about it, I have never been comfortable with the Cartesian bifurcation of the mind and the body, the rational and the emotional. It implies my existence is more mechanical than organic, more mundane than spiritual. I may be abusing the word "spiritual," which obviously refers to human spirit or soul, while here I mean that I am more than a piece of meat, more than the banality of everydayness, more than the routines of breathing and making the bed, but something loftier, something else, something worthy of existence—or at least I should be.

René Descartes's *I think, therefore I am*—or for those of you enthralled with dead languages, *Cogito, ergo sum*—creates empty spaces that demand filling. Changing it to *I feel, therefore I am*, as some do, simply creates a new set of vacant spaces also needing attention. Even embracing Søren Kierkegaard, with his concentration on love and all its many manifestations, cannot justify *I love, therefore I am*. Once again, empty spaces.

We humans are rational, emotional, embodied beings. To be rational, our mind needs to listen to our embodied emotions. Our mind and body are interconnected, and for us to think logically and function properly, we cannot separate the two. Put another way, emotions are vital to our mind's ability to function appropriately and to think logically. If you want to make a bad decision, allow your rationality to dismiss your emotions. If you want to make a bad decision, let your emotions ride roughshod over your rationality. When we feel emotions, our body is sending signals to our brain to let us know where to focus, what to think, what to do. Feelings play a role in our logical thinking. Rationality makes sense of our emotions. We are always both mind and body, mundane and spiritual, rational and emotional. To deny this is not only unhelpful but counterproductive. If you don't believe me, perhaps you should read more—I recommend Antonio R. Damasio as a starter. If you don't believe me, perhaps you should cry more *and* think more, or think more *and* cry more.

All of that is fine and good, and I believe it, but what I currently lack is the ability to maintain the balance which in turn nurtures my wholeness. Right now, I would say, it seems I am, *I feel (so overwhelmingly), therefore I am not.* Everything is being drawn into a black hole where neither feeling nor thought, once captured, can escape. My overwhelming feelings will lead to my eventual numbness. It is not a contradiction. I will become dead inside—nonfeeling and therefore rationally impaired. I am in danger of disappearing in my desperation.

What's interesting, and not a little disturbing, is that I can "see" the balance in my imagination and see it clearly. It's just that when I attempt to realize it in my actions, it dissipates and dissolves, and the "me" that results from the "me" who acts is not the me of my illusory balance. I don't know how to get what is "inside" into the "outside." The best I seem able to accomplish is a permanent balancing and unbalancing in which all my parts, all the parts that make me, are mixed, ordered, and remixed. But what I so profoundly need at this point is that the predicament I call my life should become the achievement of actualizing the balance. I need to release whatever is left of me now so that it is not sucked into my personal black-hole singularity.

Often when people fall in love, they *feel* as though their love is wonderfully unique, never having been experienced before, and so they *think* it is so. They may even *tell* each other it is so. It's nonsense, of course. Be rational in your feeling. There has never been a love that surpassed every love and certainly not Love itself. You will never hear me say that the love between Jessica and me, or between Walker and me for that matter, was a one-off, a love that astounded the angels who blushed before God when they had to report on our profound, overpowering, overwhelming, extreme, acute, beyond sincere, deep union. I know that on these coffee-stained yellow pages, I must have made it sound like Jessica and our relationship were perfection itself. They were not, and I am not capable of blissful naivete and foolishness to claim otherwise. But death can tempt even an unbalanced and balancing person such as myself, just for a moment, to imagine that it *was* perfect. Perhaps perfection is always in the past tense.

Years ago, when Jessica and I lived in London, I went to the pub with a friend. Jessica had just left on some assignment for a week, maybe it was two, and I said to my friend that I was really looking forward to the time on my own. He seemed surprised, as if I had denied some moral imperative that demanded I miss Jessica while she was gone and certainly not enjoy the aloneness. So I said to him, "I enjoy the time alone because I know she is coming back."

As I got older, I enjoyed those alone times less and missed her more. But now...now there is no joy in being alone. This time, she is not coming back. Walker is not coming back. And so I am in desperate need of Balance. In lieu of that, I am reduced to the tedium and the tyranny of everydayness. I brush my teeth. I walk to the café. I drink lattes. I go to the toilet. I write.

# 53

# Michael Andrew Walker Johnson, the Swirling Languages of Nature, and the Death

I'M SURE YOU'LL REMEMBER my dinner at Le Bateau Ivre with Sarah. And I'm sure you can't forget that toward the end of the evening, things got a little heavy, well a lot heavy, and I told her about Walker's death and the letter he wrote for me explaining why he chose death, the letter that drove me from Castine, Maine, to Paradise Café, where, of course, I now sit. Though Sarah asked me, pushed me, to reveal the content of Walker's letter, I refused, fatigue being my excuse, though my claim of weariness was a deception. I just didn't want to relive the letter.

The truth is, even while articulating my pretense, there was part of me that actually wanted to tell Sarah about the letter. It wasn't just that I wanted to tell someone, anyone; I wanted to tell *her*. And so I went round to her place last night after dinner with the letter in hand. I arrived after the time Megan would have gone to bed. I explained why I was knocking on her door unannounced, of course, and that I could not read the letter aloud to her, but if she wanted to read it to herself, she could. She nodded; I handed her the letter. She settled on the couch, and I sat across the room in the large, soft La-Z-Boy. This is what she read:

*Dear David,*

*By the time I was 13 I had received and believed the message that I had no right to exist. Indeed, my brother told me that I was a "nonentity." That named my feelings. I say, "by the time I was 13," because I was in transition from living in France for the previous 2-1/2 years. On our last night there we stayed with Army friends of my father's. (They drove us to the train station the next morning to catch the train to Paris, where we boarded the train to Leghorn, Italy, to catch the troop ship home to New York City. That was 1958.) Anyway, their son, also my age, and I slept together in the same bed that night. And we began playing with each other sexually. The precise feeling I had was of an anchor dropping to the base of my life and grabbing hold. But the world was different then, and coming out at that time was dangerous. So, instead of recognizing those feelings for what they said about me, about my own self-recognition, I pushed them away (into the closet, so to speak).*

*But lately I have gone back to that moment in time, in Toul, France, in a stranger's bed, and re-experienced that revelation as coming home to myself, as in retrieving my past from the claims of culture and religion about people "like me." In sci-fi terms, it's sort of akin to rescuing my alien body. This is important: to gather the loose, unhinged fragments of my past and welcome them home. You know, home is where we can gather in peace, even our parts.*

*This is totally true and experienced in my life. I used to think that this way of thinking arose from trauma. But the more healed I get, the more it seems to be right on. Anyway, here's the business: we are all made of parts. We are parts.*

*This description is not wrong. It's what is right. The parts are in constant motion. While it's true that sometimes one part is dominant, what is not altogether correct is to say that one of them is always dominant. Yes, a part can hijack the entire panoply—a complete and impressive collection and a splendid display of who we are. The goal is to bring the parts into a coherent dialogue with each other.*

*The parts can be seen (literally, visually) in simultaneous motion, especially within certain circumstances, often in medicine ritual and ceremonies. This is a quick nod to explain why I am always doing parts work in ritual—the parts show up, sometimes simultaneously.*

*The parts are not contained within one's skin, or brain cavity, or neural physiology. The "mind" expands outward and has fluid boundaries. The parts are in constant motion within the mind. They can be seen in simultaneous motion, in different places in space, each doing their "own thing." This is normal. This is normal people's behavior.*

*However, when parts are recognized, that describes ordinary reality among generally healthy people. "Void work" confronts the entire panoply with extinction. What is to be discovered when approaching and entering the Void? And what do I bring back? Remembering that all of the parts are living beings, not fragments, not detached or unhinged, what I have seen is that some parts do one thing, other parts other things, but they are not disconnected, except in trauma. In healthy persons, the parts work in conjunction with each other.*

*There is no mono-soul, no single soul from which the parts split off or emerge. The "soul" is within all parts. The witness, the speaker, the protector, etc., are within all the parts. There is no singular self to achieve. People are shifting all the time. What is wrong is to try to force anyone to have a Solo Soul, one mono-soul. That attempt to enforce mono-[anything]—like monotheism—mono-soul is a colonizing, militarized attempt to persuade everyone that there also exists a mono-ruler, a single head for everyone to submit to. So the whole structure is built top-down. In trauma therapy, the idea of a whole soul is frankly necessary. Internal Family Systems uses that to good end. IFS can be a powerful, transformative, evidence-based therapy, seeing the mind as naturally composed of many parts and our inner parts containing valuable qualities. When I see people's parts in time and space, I realize that the notion of a single, mono-soul has yet to tell the whole story of human potential.*

*Besides "dissociated," another word is necessary. We need a word that recognizes the multiverse composition of a human being. This describes nature, of which we are a part. Something akin to "animist" is the term I'm seeking.*

*The more I come home to myself, gathering all the disturbed bits and weaving it all, the clearer I get about what I see around me in other people. Really, sometimes it's hard walking around others when I sense their parts frisking around and jumping back and forth. Also, I don't know if I have told you this, I can smell fear on/emanating from others. It is really silly that I even try to make it through the subways. So, the more healed I become, the more sensitive I am to living in this fucked-up culture. Some parts are wonderful. I have some dear friends.*

*So, David, you are asking why I would walk away into the forest. I feel whole, and the more whole, the more information I let in, and the more information coming in, the more tired I am. My parts are weary.*

*There is a drive for peace in all living beings. Well, my grasp back when I was in seminary was that the "holy" spirit, or whatever is holy about it, will feed our intentions. I think the Spirit is rather unmoral, not immoral, about giving the gifts to whomever is asking. Which puts a huge responsibility on what we are asking to be enlivened. Which led me to say that the spirit even gave goodies to Hitler. No one liked that. But not all of our choices are good, so we humans do battle to preserve peace, sovereignty of consciousness, sacredness of home, etc. Hopefully the good wins, but it doesn't always. And so, this leads to some questions about the spirit of life. Is it possible to say the spirit loves everyone? Even those we say are evil?*

*The more an individual person looks like a living template of quantum mechanics, the more the situation becomes unstable, while at the same time external forces—and internal desires—are demanding stability, for all the reasons I have named. I suppose it's something like what the rightwing Christian factions want, stability when everything around them is shifting and becoming less of a mirror for them. From my perspective, with everything in motion and my getting tired, the more healed I get, the more nature is the only place I can seek to find my peace. I am not in despair. I am not running away, though some will say so. The world is no more treacherous than it has ever been, albeit it is far more capable of widespread destruction than ever before.*

*Why would I leave you? I know that where I want to be is deep, deep, and deeper into the dark language of nature, sinking into the humming of and into the background radiance of nature. I want to hear the "still small voice" amidst the clatter and neon clammers of storms and thunders.*

*This reminds me of the Pied Piper of Hamelin when the flautist took all the children with him into the mountain where they disappeared forever. Setting aside for the moment why he took all the children of the city, the point is that they, before they had lost the ears for it, heard the song of life and walked into the deep, deep, and deeper realms of the languages of nature. That is what made it possible to induce them to follow.*

*Well, something like that. I feel the pull into the swirling languages of nature, where constant, as it were quantum, engagement is the reality. It's what I see. That reality.*

*So, when my brother said I was a nonentity, and when I grew up feeling that I had no right to exist, and therefore inhabited an alien body, from my age now and looking back, I can believe (without any astrological nut job's input) that I have been in the wrong perceptual reality, the one promulgated for millennia, and which I see is tragic, treacherous, colonizing, and militarized and is no place for me. I don't mention love, because so often "love" has been colonized and is passive aggressive.*

*I'm not unhappy. I have rescued my flesh from the damages. I feel love from and for. There is no "right" time.*

*We are all seeking to arrive at the beginning. The beginning
is not what happened back there in the realms of myth and
finality. The beginning is ahead of us. It draws us. We set our
banged-up pots and rusted pans on the side of the road (like
why we go to therapy), no longer useful having loved what
we must leave and freed ourselves to make the last of our
trips to the beginning, where [it] is constantly originating,
in constant birth. We are going there. The* tohu v'vohu *of
Genesis 1 (formless and void) has never finished its work
over which the spirit hovers. And so David, you who would
not, could not, marry me, it is goodbye. I love you. Always.*

When Sarah had finished reading, she rose from the sofa, walked
over to me, handed me the letter, and said, "What are parts?"

"Me too. I had to look it up." Reaching into my coat pocket, I
pulled out another piece of paper and said, "Here. I'm not sure this
is exactly what Walker would say, actually I'm sure it isn't, but we will
never know, and it's a short summary. I wrote it down thinking you
might ask."

"Can you read it to me?" she asked as she walked into the
kitchen, grabbed the bottle of brandy, two glasses, and then returned
to the living room. I began reading as she opened the bottle and
poured the drinks. I read this from Internal Family Systems website:

*It is the nature of the mind to be subdivided into an
indeterminate number of subpersonalities or parts.
Everyone has a Self, and the Self can and should lead the
individual's internal system. The non-extreme intention of
each part is something positive for the individual. There are
no "bad" parts. The goal of therapy is not to eliminate parts
but instead to help them find their non-extreme roles. As
we develop, our parts develop and form a complex system of
interactions among themselves.*

*Subpersonalities are aspects of our personality that interact internally in sequences and styles that are similar to the ways in which people interact. Parts may be experienced in any number of ways—thoughts, feelings, sensations, images, and more. All parts want something positive for the individual and will use a variety of strategies to gain influence within the internal system. Parts develop a complex system of interactions among themselves. Polarizations develop as parts try to gain influence within the system. The Self is a different level of entity than the parts—often in the center of the "you" that the parts are talking to or that likes or dislikes, listens to, or shuts out various parts. When differentiated, the Self is competent, secure, self-assured, relaxed, and able to listen and respond to feedback. The Self can and should lead the internal system. Our goal is to achieve balance and harmony within the internal system.*

"Did you get that?" I said.

"Enough. At least, I think enough," she said. "But David, I want to read Walker's letter again now that I have some sense of the language. Do you mind?"

"Of course not. Do you mind if I look in on Megan?"

"She's asleep."

"I know. I won't wake her. I'll just peek in the room," I said.

"Sure, if you want. By the way, what did you say to her the other night? She stopped using her nightlight."

I just smiled and handed Walker's letter back to her.

What followed that evening isn't important here. Sarah read the letter again. We checked with my notes on "parts" again, and if I'm making it sound like a seminar about psychology on the edge, then I'm mispresenting the time. Mostly we talked about Walker and death. It seemed obvious to me that, at least at first, Sarah could not grasp why this letter had had such a profound impact on me. Walker's death, yes, of course, but this strange combination of confession and exposition?

Here's the thing. For one, and most obviously, I knew Walker, and she didn't. I had years with him, and she didn't. I was in love with him, and she wasn't. But also, the letter was pure Walker. I hesitate to call it his manifesto because it was not a public statement. It was his personal end of life...what? His philosophy? Spirituality? Psychology? Declaration? Perhaps strategy? Or maybe all of that. All I can say is that it was thoroughly Walker, and when I read it, grieving his death, it overwhelmed me.

At the end of his letter, Walker had written, "We are all seeking to arrive at the beginning. The beginning is not what happened back there in the realms of myth and finality. The beginning is ahead of us. It draws us." And then, "...We are going there. The *tohu v'vohu* of Genesis 1 (formless and void) has never finished its work over which the spirit hovers."

These lines reminded me of another Jewish concept introduced to me by a good friend, Joel Vaschel Dichter. The word is *teshuah*, which means "to return," implying, of course, a return to God. *Teshuah* has deep and ancient meanings in the Jewish faith, but I was taken by the simple notion of the permanence of returning, always in motion, never stopping, always going...where? Home. Joel Vaschel Dichter told me that in a more traditional sense it speaks to both the continued need for self-analysis and self-healing. It acknowledges our relationship to the secular, I would also say mundane, world and how within us all is the capability to push ourselves away from the spiritual and even from our very selves. *Teshuah* provides us the opportunity to confront ourselves and the Other. It affirms our ability for free choice and personal growth.

If Walker was always going back to the beginning, he was also always returning. He was always pushing himself away from whatever encouraged him to push himself away from himself. He was always self-healing and, though I don't like it, the walk into the wilderness to find that perfect tree, to hear swirling languages of nature, was his free choice. I'm guessing that in his mind, whirling with all his parts, it was also growth.

As for me, I'm in danger of stalling. My forever returning no longer knows where I'm going. What is "home" without Jessica and Walker? What is a home to me without companionship, conversation, silence, laughter, annoyance, embraces, shared meals, shared chores, background noise, and love? If there is such a place, why would I ever want to return there? I'm speaking metaphorically, of course, but as I write this in Paradise, my metaphor is slipping over into literalism, and I wonder, perhaps fear, that "our" house in Castine is a home I cannot return to. Whatever. This I do know: I need to decide soon, because the specter of Barry Patrick Olds and the Brotherhood of Christian Businessmen grows ever larger. I'm about to be kicked out of my paradise sanctuary.

One more thing. I'm deeply disappointed that Walker did not come and say goodbye. One last conversation, laugh, hug. I wouldn't have had to know it was the last of us, but it would have been nice to feel him again and to tangle with his mind. It just would have been nice.

# 54

# The Palimpsest, Megan Margaret Williams, and La Val's Pizza

I HAD QUITE THE ADVENTURE yesterday evening. Sarah and Megan came by Paradise Café at lunch and, of course, found me at my table hunched over my yellow legal pad. Megan did the quick run around the table and tried to hug me. I dropped my pen, turned to her, scooted my chair away from the table, picked her up, and plopped her in my lap. Sarah sat in the chair opposite. After the hellos and how-are-you's, we ordered sandwiches, lemonade, and two beers.

Surprises can sometimes be unwelcome. This was not one of them. Sarah did have an agenda, however. She asked me to babysit that very evening, apologizing for the last-minute request. I just laughed. As if I had something else to do. Apparently, Sarah had a surprise meeting with a "client" at Rose Pizzeria on University Avenue. I didn't ask about it as it was none of my business, but, of course, I agreed to take on Megan for the evening. Admittedly, I did so with some fear and trembling. Never in my life have I ever cared for a small child. At seventy-four years old, I was facing my first babysitting job.

We agreed to meet at the top of the hill where Le Conte Avenue, Scenic Avenue, and Ridge Road merge. I was standing in front of Pacific School of Religion. Sarah drove up, Megan hopped out, and I heard Sarah shouting thanks as she drove down Le Conte toward

Hearst Avenue. So there I was, Megan looking up with a big smile, and I said, "Do you like pizza?" The answer was, of course, yes.

I took her by the hand, and we walked down Ridge to Euclid Avenue and turned right. Our destination was La Val's Pizza on Euclid. I'm not sure it's the kind of place you should take a small child, but I got it in my head she would like pizza, and that's the pizza place I know.

The entrance to La Val's opens into an off-street patio-like area with several long picnic tables and a tree growing upwards, desperately looking for the sun. As we entered, we hung a left and went up to the counter to place our order. From the ceiling over the counter hung several large blackboards announcing the menu. Behind the counter was a chaos of restaurant necessities—a soda machine, several beer taps, coolers with a variety of canned and bottled drinks, signs, various messages taped to the walls, and behind all that, a large black and white photo of the University of California and the Berkeley football stadium surrounded by other university buildings. To the right of all this wonderful mess were stainless steel pizza ovens and tall racks of trays.

After I read Megan the list of pizzas on offer, and after rather long negotiation, we settled on a large pepperoni and two Cokes. I figured a beer was inappropriate for the evening, though I'm quite sure Megan wouldn't have minded. I figured that Sarah would, however, so Coke it was for both of us.

We walked away from the counter, past a pool table and down a few stairs into the main restaurant area. There were several red, faded leather booths along the wall, numerous large tables in the center, tables along the windows looking out at the central patio, and tables by the front window facing the street. The place was nearly empty, so we grabbed a window table. I asked if she wanted me to get a child's booster chair, and she shook her head "no" emphatically. So I helped her onto the chair, which was a little high for her. I wasn't sure what to say to her so was glad that she seemed contented looking through the big window at the people walking down Euclid. Eventually she turned back to me and said, "David, are you very old? You look old."

"Well, it depends on who you ask. To you, yes, I am very old. But to someone who is, say, ninety-four years old, not so much. Actually that person might think of me as youngish. Why do you ask?"

"Well, you're a lot older than my father would be," she said.

"Yes, I'm sure I am," I said and chuckled. "Where is your father? Do you see him?"

"I don't know where he is. I've never seen him," she said.

"I'm sorry."

"It's all right. I don't know him. I can't miss him."

I heard my name being called, told Megan to sit tight, and went back to the counter to get our pizza. We settled into eating with enthusiasm, though even with Megan scooted close to the table, it was a stretch for her to reach the pizza. I put a slice of pizza on a plate and slid it to her. "Thank you," she said with a smile. As we were eating, I learned once again how much Megan likes to ask questions.

"Do you know that Mommy likes you? She says you are a nice man."

"Well, I guess I hoped your mom liked me, but it is nice to hear," I said.

"Do you like me?" She asked in a simple straightforward tone that carried no challenge or manipulation.

"Yes, Megan, I like you very much," I said.

"That's good, because I like you a lot," she said, taking another bite from a slice of pizza. "So, we will be friends."

"Yes, of course. I think we are friends already," I said.

"And will you be friends with Mommy?"

"Yes, your mom and I are good friends, or at least I think so."

"That's good because we haven't known you for very long," she said.

"Well, you're right about that. But sometimes people can make friends very fast," I said.

"Yes, I make friends fast sometimes," she said.

There was a pause in our conversation as a golden retriever walked up to the window and looked in, at us or the pizza, who knows. Its owner had paused on the sidewalk talking into her cell phone. Megan climbed down from her chair, went to the window, and put her face right up to the glass at eye level with the dog. They both looked happy with the encounter. The cell phone woman started walking down the street, saw her dog and Megan doing their eye to eye, and paused. She made eye contact with me and smiled. Then she gave a tug on the leash. The dog started to walk away from the window but looked back as Megan waved goodbye. She returned to the table, accepted my help onto her chair, picked up her slice of pizza, and asked, "Why do you write all day?"

That question caught me by surprise, though perhaps it shouldn't have. Every time she sees me at the café, I'm writing, and after all, she is inquisitive.

"That's hard to explain," I said.

"Try," she said.

"Well..." I paused. "I'm trying to figure a few things out."

"What things?"

"Well, what I'm going to do next. Things have changed for me, and, well, yes, I need to figure things out," I said.

"Mommy said your wife died. Are you sad?" she asked.

"Yes, to be honest, I am sad," I said.

"And Mommy said your friend died, and that's why you are sad. I'm sorry," she said.

"Thank you, Megan. That means a lot," I said, looking at her.

"Does the writing make you happy?" she said.

"Well, maybe. Maybe not yet, but I'm hoping it will when I'm done," I said.

"Me too. I hope it makes you happy."

I didn't lie to her. I didn't say the writing made me happy, but neither did I say that some days it made me miserable. I was also struck by how much Sarah had told Megan, and I wasn't quite sure I approved of her disclosing such fundamentally important aspects of my life. However, the more I thought about it, I guessed that Megan had asked Sarah what I was up to, or why I was sad, or why I sat every day at Paradise Café, and she, Sarah, had opted for honesty.

This is not all that transpired between Megan and me at La Val's, but it does represent what is important in this my palimpsest quest. After the questions about my writing, Megan switched the conversation suddenly, without the need for any segue, to television shows she liked to watch, cupcakes she liked to eat, and games she liked to play on her tablet—that's right, she had a tablet! I was grateful for the change in direction.

I walked Megan back to her home, actually carrying her part way. Sarah had texted me saying when she would get home. Megan and I arrived a bit early, so we just sat on the front step and continued our nonstop conversation over a breathtaking range of topics.

Sarah offered to give me a ride home, but I told her the walk would be nice, and it was. I'm sure all children are amazing at Megan's age, but it was Megan I knew and Megan I was impressed with. My fear and trembling about "babysitting" were misplaced. We had a great time. It lifted my spirits. It gave me a break from despondency. And, I want to emphasize, Megan also had a fabulous time. I know because she told me.

# 55

# The Palimpsest and the Cacophony of Ghosts Past

I LOVE THE WORD "CACOPHONY." I love the way it sounds, the feel of it in my mouth when I say it aloud. It's from the Greek *phōnē* which means "sound" or "voice." *Phōnē* is joined with the prefix *kak*—from *kakos*, meaning "bad." Thus cacophony literally means "bad sound." The primary definition is a harsh or jarring mixture of sound, a dissonance. But don't forget *phōnē* also means "voice," so it's not improper to think of a raucous, discordant assortment of voices. Sitting at Paradise Café, surrounded by an ever-increasing gathering of palimpsest ghosts, or voices, from my past, I'm partial to a secondary definition: a striking combination, or an incongruous or chaotic mixture.

This mid-morning, as the marine layer dissolves above me, I have inadvertently, but inevitably, conjured a cacophony of ghosts from my yellow pad, resurfacing from beneath my parchment of a life. They have rather loud voices. Some of them are me, David Robert Bainbridge, in times past—indeed so past that they seem like strangers with only a vague connection to the person I am today. Some of them I have completely forgotten existed. I used to tell Jessica, and also Walker, come to think of it, that I only remember enough of my life to maintain a sense of identity through time, but that most of my memories have faded to nothingness as if they never existed. These Me's that insist on speaking now, seemingly happy in their chaos, are only tenuously my kindred, and yet they claim full-blooded brotherhood. Other ghostly spirits are of people I knew who, I must assume, have a legitimate claim on my time and life. Some I welcome with joy, some with surprise, some with reluctance, and some with disdain.

This is no *symphony*—a harmony or agreement in sound, the prefix *syn* meaning "together." Nor is it a *euphony*—a sweet or pleasing sound, *eu* meaning "good." No, this is a damn cacophony of ghosts demanding my attention, and even my commitment, each fighting for liberation from my yellow pad. And what makes matters worse, I brought this on myself. Sanctuary, my ass.

MY FATHER TAKES ME to my first day of school. I am approaching the threshold of my first classroom. As we reach the door, I stop and look in at the other children sitting on small chairs at small desks. I refuse to enter. My father kneels on one knee next to me and speaks softly. He asks why I don't want to enter, and I say nothing. He tells me I will have to enter, find a desk, and sit down. I say nothing. He asks if I want him to walk in with me. I turn to him and say that I will enter if I can sit next to the little blond girl in the front row by the window. My father has a quiet word with the teacher, who is patiently watching this scene, then I, by myself, walk boldly into the room and take the desk next to the little blond girl. We become friends. Years later, when we move, I say a painful goodbye to the little blond girl in the front row. Now I can almost see her face. Almost. I wonder what happened to her. I wonder if she ever thinks of me. I wonder, if I met her now and told her this story, whether she would remember me. I doubt it. Most certainly not.

The night of my first day of school I have a dream. I dream that I wake, get out of bed, go downstairs, and walk out the front door. On the front lawn is a row of naked adult women, and with them, the little blond girl, also naked. Of course, being a five-year-old child, I have no idea what a naked adult woman would look like, but there they are. It is clear to me that I am to choose one to return with me to my bedroom. I choose the little blond girl.

I am sad to say the little blond girl has no name, but she does have a vague young face.

I AM SITTING IN THE office of the owner of a furniture factory in San Salvador. He sits across the large desk, a large man with sharp, dark features and slicked-back black hair. He asks, surprisingly to me, if I had noticed his big slick black car as I was entering the factory. I say I had. In the back window of the car was one of those yellow signs, but this one didn't say, "Baby on board." It said, "I am angry."

The owner tells me, with more pride than seems warranted, that he keeps his workers just well enough to work, but unwell enough that they can't rebel. I am at a loss for words and so I just nod.

I AM STANDING IN A redwood forest picnic area with a bottle of beer in my hand. Samantha Esther Cunningham is standing in front of me, also holding a bottle of beer, looking up at me. I am talking, but I can't hear what I am saying. From the look on her face, the sweetness and the intensity in her eyes, this spirit visitation is obviously post-kiss. There she is, as if real. Her brown, wavy, almost curly hair settling on her shoulders. Her short-sleeved shirt hugging her body. Her bare arms bidding a touch. Her tight jeans perfectly suggestive. Her slim but wonderfully proportioned body asking to be embraced.

Now there she is looking straight into the camera, her right hand lifting her hair off the back of her neck, her left holding a cup of coffee. Her heavy sweater is both rustic and attractive. She has a slight smile on her face, an intimate smile, a smile that could only be meant for me, though that may be more hope than reality.

Now there she is standing behind me as I sit in a chair on an outside patio reading, reading what, I don't know. The sun is shining in her hair rendering it more blond than light brown. Her long-sleeved t-shirt is pulled up to her elbows and her hands are in the front pockets of her jeans. She is smiling widely, almost laughing. One would think she is in love. Next to her, also behind me, stands her husband, and he is looking at the papers in my hands trying his best to read along. Samantha Esther Cunningham is looking at me.

Now there she is in a museum looking at a Georgia O'Keeffe painting. I am looking at her from behind, at a slight angle. Her wild hair covers the side of her face so I can barely see her profile. She has a purse over her left shoulder, and her left hand is in her pocket. I can just see the silhouette of her breast.

I have searched out the painting. It is called *Flower Abstraction*. The painting, like so many of O'Keeffe's paintings, is extremely sensuous, even sexual. It should be called *Flower Distraction* because I searched for it to distract me from the implication of this particular voice, this particular ghost. This conjuring disturbs me. Everywhere, every time, it is after the kiss.

It is disturbing that Samantha Esther Cunningham is standing in front of the sensual *Flower Abstraction*. It is disturbing that I find her so attractive. It is disturbing that I imagine her naked. It is disturbing that I fantasize about our making love. It is disturbing that I think she may have loved me. It is disturbing that she may now be telling me just that.

I really don't want to know why Samantha Esther Cunningham visits me so often. Perhaps tomorrow. Perhaps an email wasn't enough. Perhaps I should try to find her.

I AM SITTING IN A VERY small Havana café—so small it is difficult to call it a café—looking out to sea toward Miami. I am alone. I am younger. At the next table is a young—younger than me—man looking at me and sketching. He gets up and hands me the piece of paper, a caricature of me. It's really good and makes me smile. He wants one US dollar. I refuse and hand the caricature back to him. Little did I know so many years ago that I would regret that decision for ever. It was just one dollar.

Now I have disembarked once again at the Havana airport, or to be authentic, La Habana airport. I am changing US dollars into Cuban pesos, and for some reason, I put the cash in my jacket pocket instead of the travel wallet in my briefcase. I walk through security and enter the main hall of the airport, and a man approaches me and asks if I need a taxi. I do.

As we walk to his car, he asks if I speak Spanish. I do not. He insists I put both my suitcase and briefcase in the trunk. I always keep my briefcase by my side, but this night I do as he asks. He further insists I sit in the front seat, which is not unusual in places I travel. I sit in the front seat.

As we speed down a highway, he asks if I mind if he puts on some Cuban music. I do not, and he blasts it out at discomforting decibels. But it is night, it is Cuba, it is warm, the windows are open. I am free.

Suddenly his cell phone rings. He talks, in Spanish of course, and then asks me if I would mind if he stopped to pick up a friend at the side of the road. I do mind, but say no. The friend gets in the back seat, they talk in Spanish, the music blasts away.

We arrive at the at the Hotel National de Cuba, the hotel with memories and history. I get my suitcase and briefcase, pay the driver, and check in. I am in my room unpacking, retrieving my laptop from my briefcase, and I realize I have been robbed. They only took cash, not credit cards. I sit on the bed feeling like a complete fool. Do you speak Spanish? Do you mind some loud music? Do you mind me picking up a friend? Once I calm down, I realize it was a damn good theft. The friend obviously reached through a cutout hole in the back seat into the trunk. No more said.

Now I'm taking a coco taxi to Plaza de Armas. It is afternoon. I sit on a bench among the palm trees and large plants looking at the statue of Carlos Manuel de Cespedes, one of the people instrumental in the struggle for Cuban independence. All around me is the sound of Cuban music, and there are books, dozens and dozens of tables overflowing with books. I am at peace, if only for a moment. And then a beautiful woman sits down beside me and asks if I desire a friend. I wish I did, but I say no, no thank you, and get up and leave the plaza.

Now I am sitting by a large window in the Hotel Ambos Mundos in old Havana drinking a Cuba Libre. I'm there only because Hemingway lived in this hotel for a time, in room 511, to be precise. An old man walking along the sidewalk stops and looks in at me. We make eye contact. And then he gives me the finger and moves on.

I HAVE TO GO TO THE bathroom, but it's my turn to read aloud. I am reading the sentence, "The dog chased the cat down the road..." As I get to the word cat, my eyes stop and so does my voice. I know the word "cat," but I am stuck and cannot say it. The teacher comes up to me, hits my hand with a ruler, and shouts, "Cat! You are so stupid!"

The teacher moves on, and I still need to go to the bathroom. I raise my hand and ask. The teacher tells me I can wait. I shit in my pants.

As I walk home, I hope my school bag covers the stain I assume is seeping through my pants. I stink. The liquid shit is running down my left leg. When I get home, I go directly to the bathroom. I undress and throw my clothes in the corner. I get into the tub and wash myself and then go to my bedroom and slide under the covers.

My mother comes in and asks me what happened. I tell her. She loves me. She is my rock.

KELLY FAY POOLE AND I are standing by my locker in our high school. She is holding my hand and telling me what our plans are for the evening. Her father is away for the week on business. She assures me she has the condoms, and I don't have to steal some from my father. This is a great relief to me. Tonight is the night, the first night, and anyone observing us in the bureaucratically two-tone painted school hall could have guessed the truth. We're both excited and scared shitless. Kelly is the first woman I have sex with, but not the first woman I kiss.

Now Kelly Fay Poole is sitting on her front porch complaining about her father and crying. There is something oppressive about their relationship, but she does not tell me what. However, I know the tears are genuine. He father, while not evil, is not a nice man. She says she is going to shut her eyes and walk across the street in front of her house, an often-busy street. She does just that, and I don't stop her.

Now Kelly Fay Poole and I are at Great America, two young people having the fun of children while pretending to be adults. I doubt I have ever seen her laugh so much. I try to win her a huge stuffed lion, but I fail. The next day, I drive back to the amusement park and buy the damn thing. Kelly is thrilled when I show up at her door with a huge lion in my arms, orange with a pure white mane.

Now Kelly Fay Poole is standing by the closed door of my bedroom telling me that while I was on vacation with my family, she had sex with Paul Bradley Jones, twice. I tell Paul Bradley Jones to go fuck himself later that day. A few weeks later, I forgive Kelly Fay Poole. It makes me feel good, though if truth be told, my young heart never completely recovers.

Now Kelly Fay Poole and I have driven to a park with a large, wooded area. We have walked into the woods for privacy. She is lying on the ground and asking me to punch her in the stomach. I do so reluctantly. She tells me with a fieriness in her voice that I have to punch her harder, I have to punch her very hard, or it will not work. She is convinced she is pregnant. She unzips her jeans and pulls up her shirt, exposing her bare abdomen. I punch her very hard.

Now Kelly Fay Poole is dumping me at a summer party in the back yard of one of our rich friends. It is very sunny and warm, and everyone is having a good time. These things happen.

I AM SITTING IN FRONT of three drunk Thai men sharing a bottle of Scotch on the Chao Phraya. Across the river is the Wat Arun temple. A longtail boat, serving as a river taxi along Klong Man Canal, sits quietly to my left, its huge car engine and long tiller system at rest.

I watch my meal being cooked right in front of me in large woks heated with gas cylinders. Water is heated to cook meats, vegetables, rice, and noodles, and it is never dumped or replaced. Small fish swim below the cooking area where they throw food scraps over the railing. Sitting there I can smell the food cooking. The air is hot, but the Singha beer is cold. Some men come in and buy whiskey, water, and rice. An Anglo sits down to my right. He orders rice and vegetables and proceeds to pull out his own chopsticks. Monks from Wat Arun come across the river on a Chao Phraya express boat and find a table in the restaurant.

The riverside restaurant on Tha Tien Pier is run by one family. The son cooks the meals. The mother and daughter clean and buy supplies. The father sits, always with a happy, surprised look on his face, not judgmental or mocking, just good natured, as if life is always a wonder to him. Behind and slightly to my right are stairs leading up to the family's living quarters. The youngest child, a beautiful little girl with a bright smile, is forever running up and down those stairs.

I AM SITTING ON MY bed. Next to me is my mother. In her hand is a volume of the *Little Red Science Books*. She reads a paragraph aloud, and then I read a paragraph aloud. She whispers to me that I am *not* stupid. She is saving my life.

I STOP AT A RED LIGHT downtown at night. Suddenly two men open the car doors. One pushes me away from the steering wheel. The other takes his place in the passenger seat. I am surrounded. It's a carjacking, way before carjacking was a thing.

They drive at speed to the flats. They each get out of the car. One opens the back door and tells me to lie on the seat face down. I assume he is going to hit me in the back of the head. He does not. We spend the next three hours or so riding around the city. From time to time, I lift my head to look at the face of the driver in the rear-view mirror. He smiles at me.

The car stops, the back door is opened, and I'm told to get out of the car with my eyes closed. I do what I'm told. One of the men leads me to a parking meter, places my hands on the meter, and tells me to keep my eyes closed. And then he whispers that the car is pointing to the city center. I stand there for quite some time, and no one stops to ask what I'm doing. I finally open my eyes, and I'm alone. I drive home and tell my parents everything.

The police come and take me out of school. I am sitting at a table in a dingy small room in the downtown police station. I'm confronted by good cop bad cop right out of a cheap television show. They eventually ask me to look through numerous books of photos—mug shots. From time to time I pause as if I might have found my muggers. But no, I move on.

No one to blame. No one physically harmed. No one caught.

I AM SITTING IN MY study at my computer at home alone. Jessica has flown off to Boston on a job. I hear a ping. There is an email, and this is what I read:

*Dear David,*

*I am so in love with you tonight that I don't know how I'm going to bear the separation. I want to hold you and kiss you and wrap myself around you all night. I want to find a hundred ways to tell you how much I love you—just a hundred for tonight and more for the nights after.*

*If I had my calculator, I'd be counting the minutes till I am home. As it is...I want you!*

*Jess*

I AM ON A FROZEN FOOTBALL field. A light snow is falling. We are home from college for the Christmas break. In the huddle, Gerald Schumann Ruprecht is telling me to run straight down the sideline for fifteen yards and then to cut into the center of the field. I do as I am told. I run as fast as I can. I cut into the middle, and as

I do, several things happen simultaneously. I turn my head toward Gerald Schumann Ruprecht, who has dropped back to pass, the throwing motion just ended, and we make eye contact. While I am looking into his eyes, I also see the ball which cradles between my arm and chest. And at that very same moment, I am tackled to the ground. I look up while on my side, and Gerald Schumann Ruprecht is smiling. It is pure perfection.

IT IS A BEAUTIFUL DAY, and I am at a summer party of a friend whose family has much more money than mine. The large attractive house with the spacious back yard has a view of the lake. The lake is nowhere to be seen from my house. Three girls, all friends of Catherine Dimitra Drakos, have pinned me to an outside wall of the house and are telling me, with great sincerity and urgency, that if I do not kiss Catherine Dimitra Drakos soon, and they mean very soon, Catherine Dimitra Drakos will dump me with a harshness reserved for losers in cheap B-movies. Her patience has run clean out. I have never kissed a girl before in my life, and the three friends are making it clear that as I am already in the eighth grade, I'm late to the game. This I sadly know.

Now I am standing with Catherine Dimitra Drakos behind the school. It is dusk. It is warm. I am frightened. Catherine Dimitra Drakos is standing with her back against the school's red brick wall. I am standing very close to her, but not leaning against her body. I place my hands on her arms. We look into each other's eyes, I lean forward so, yes, now our bodies are touching. I kiss her. She kisses me. Her lips are full and soft and sweet. Her hair smells like spring. Her skin is smooth. I like it. I intuit that I will never forget this moment. We do it again. And again. Catherine Dimitra Drakos did not dump me that summer.

I AM IN PAI, THAILAND. It's a small and quiet crossroads town on the journey north toward Myanmar. I stay at the Chez Swan Guest House, a modest place with a nice café and bar. My room is clean and neat and has a large banyan tree outside the window.

The café bar has a brick floor in a chevron pattern, a bamboo roof, and walls held in place by wooden poles that look to be small trees cut down for the purpose. Outside are two picnic-type tables under a corrugated steel roof supported by similar tree poles. Across the street is a wood and bamboo hut built around a tree, the tree actually growing through the roof of the hut. There is a chair literally carved out of a tree trunk upon which an old woman sits selling banana milkshakes. A single corn stalk grows in the corner of the hut.

Now I am checking out of the guest house and going to the bus station where I buy a ticket to Mae Hong Son. The bus to Mae Hong Son is not a bus at all but a flatbed truck with a tin roof and two benches running along the sides of the bed. I tuck my leather bag under the bench and sit near the back of the truck. Eventually I give my seat to a woman and child who join us as we pass through one of the numerous mountain villages along the way. I spend most of the trip standing on the back step of the truck, holding on to the metal pole that supports the roof. A young couple climbs into the truck with their baby. It is an endearing sight. The husband's obvious affection for his child is moving. The child is wrapped in dirty cloth and is breastfeeding against the cold.

As we pass through village after village, women and children climb onto the flatbed. The women smile at me and touch my hands. Their smiles are always red lips and red-blackened teeth from chewing "betel nut," the nut of the Areca palm, which isn't really a nut at all but a drupe. The smiling children, not yet on betel nut, are shy and laugh behind their hands as they look at me. Apparently, I am the only white person in the northwestern mountains of Thailand.

Mae Hong Son, the City of Three Mists, is located in a beautiful valley between high mountain ranges near the Myanmar border. I stay in the Piya Hotel, which is not the best in town but is located on the lake with a wonderful view. Just outside my window is the mist-covered lake with palm trees and large ferns on its shore. There are houses on the other side of the lake and hazy mountains beyond. To the right of the hotel is the local wat.

Now I leave the hotel and sit in a café by the lake. It is incredibly beautiful. A man and woman pass in front of me pulling a cart with over-large wheels. The cart is filled with ceramics of different styles, functions, sizes, and colors. Hanging from the cart is a bell on a string announcing its presence.

I am, for the moment, at peace.

MY FATHER, PATRICK Daniel Bainbridge, is telling me the story again as we are sitting on the front porch on a summer evening. The doctor is informing him that he has to choose. Either my mother, Mary Anne Bainbridge, or the child, who is me. The doctor insists he cannot save us both—labor has gone on too long, the child does not want to come, Mary Anne Bainbridge is exhausted. Without hesitation, my father demands with a moral and commanding authority that both shall live! Indeed, we both do live to hear the story again and again. As he rocks back on the chair, my father is saying to me, "Dave, you sure didn't want to come into this world. You almost killed your mother." Those were the days before cesarean became the go-to solution.

That's me, David Robert Bainbridge. Slow to enter the world.

I NEED TO PUT MY PEN down. Perhaps I need to forget all this palimpsest stuff and go back to Castine, Maine. Perhaps the void cannot be filled. Perhaps there is no one to find and no one to save. Perhaps John Winston Lennon was right when he wrote "all you need is love." I always thought that was extremely naïve, if not downright wrong. But take away the love, and there's not much left over. Just a black hole.

# 56

# The Palimpsest, the Father, and the Concept

WHEN MY FATHER DIED, I went to his office at the university with my mother. It was a simple job—clean out the office, decide what was going to be trashed and what would go to my mother's home. The details of that day are not important. What is important is that in the back of a tall filing cabinet, I found an old manilla folder, browning with age, with bent corners and small tears, containing a manuscript. The manuscript had ten chapters, 146 double-spaced pages. The first half was fading blue carbon-copy pages, the second, black originals.

As you know, Patrick Daniel Bainbridge had abandoned Jesus to become a Joycean scholar. What am I saying? He was a Joycean nerd. He wrote many academic articles, mainly about *Ulysses*. But this manuscript was something different. It was old! He must have written it when he was young, perhaps in his thirties or early forties. It certainly was not about Joyce. A cursory glance determined that.

I walked over to my mother. "What is this?" I asked, holding the folder in front of her. She took it from me, glanced at the first page, and said, "Oh, this. It's your father's book. He wrote it years ago. I had no idea he kept it."

"His book! What book?"

"It's not important. It never got published. He only showed it to me. No one else read it," she said.

"What's it about? I asked.

"Oh, I don't know. I don't remember. It was his philosophy, his spirituality, how he thought things should be, how he thought people should live."

"Dad had a spirituality? He wrote a book about spirituality?" I was stunned.

"It's more philosophy. But why would you be surprised your father had a spirituality? He did do Jesus before Joyce, remember."

"Yeah, but he never talked about it. Hell, when I told him I was going to seminary, it took him two weeks to even respond, he was so disappointed."

"He wasn't disappointed. He was worried. You know what the church can be like."

My mother handed me the manuscript and returned to clearing out his desk. I simply asked, "Can I have it?"

"Of course. He'd be pleased."

After we cleared out the office, after the memorial service, after I was confident my mother was okay, I got on a plane to London. With ten hours ahead of me, locked up tight in that metal and fiberglass tube flying at great speeds and heights, I lowered the tray table, placed the manuscript in front of me, and began reading.

The book is terrible. I could only read the first few chapters. I skimmed through the rest, except for the conclusion which I read in full. It seemed only fitting. I was disappointed it was not a great work, or even an average work, of philosophy. Why? I'm not sure. Just because he was an excellent Joycean did not mean he was a great philosopher or rocket scientist. Patrick Daniel Bainbridge was what he was. I was also surprised about the poor quality of the writing itself—the mystery of why this manuscript was so poorly written, while his articles on Joyce were not, was never solved. To make my point, here's the opening paragraph of the closing chapter, painfully obviously entitled, "In Conclusion":

*The concept has been stated. Several attempts have been made to demonstrate how it could be lived. It is now time for a short concluding statement.*

What was of importance to me, more important than his Concept, was his handwriting. The tab on the folder said simply: *Manuscript from Patrick Daniel Bainbridge.* The first page of chapter seven, entitled "In the Spirit," was positively covered in his writing, with corrections and additions to the text. Several sentences were crossed out, though I must confess they didn't seem any less worthy than the many that survived. But seeing his awful handwriting, much of which I could not read, helped me imagine him sitting at his desk at home typing away on his Concept, desk lamp illuminating the desktop, floor lamp by the big worn leather chair casting friendly shadows across the room. Patrick Daniel Bainbridge writing philosophy, spirituality, and a Concept for all to read: Who would have thought? Certainly not me.

I've told you how *Chapter Ten: In Conclusion* begins, but then he wrote:

*I wondered as I read over this work, just how would it be received. We live in a nominal world. For anyone to want to be other than nominal, he makes himself an obstacle.*

I am fascinated by the word "nominal." Of course, what he meant was, "Existing or being something in name or form only." Or "Someone or something supposing to have a particular identity or status, which in reality does not have it." Apparently, my father believed the world was something in name only, that whatever status or identity it claimed to have, it did not, and that if a person wanted to be other than nominal they would become—no, it was more active than that—they would *make themselves* an obstacle. But an obstacle to what? Or to whom? He continued:

*For anyone to want to be anything other than our present day understanding of what a person ought to be and ought to do, that person makes himself an obstacle. They must acknowledge that the concept of this book in reality is the way we want to live. If acknowledged, you admit you do not have peace. Herein is the purpose of this work. But herein also is the failure of this work. For this book can only go so far in presenting the challenge for you. With the words of disturbing significance you may have read, you may have seen the shortcomings which are peculiarly yours. But this book cannot make any of these monumental, eternal decisions for you. I conclude by pointing out that you have one choice to make. You must choose either the way of nominality or reality. If you choose nominality, I will admit failure. I will recognize that you would not be embarrassed, for with you will be the great majority. But if you choose the experience and possibility of living in reality, then I will have succeeded. It is my sincere hope many of you will choose the fullest concept of this book. It is my hope that you will choose to be different, to be an obstacle. My sincere hope is that you will not be swallowed up, but you will prove the concept. Dare to be different.*

I'm guessing, or hoping, that my father himself never reread his conclusion—there are no handwritten corrections—but that the manuscript was locked away in the manilla folder before his final editing. He does not, at least in these concluding pages, define what he means by "reality," though I'm guessing it has something to do with living right, abandoning the status quo, and embracing his Concept in the hopes of obtaining peace. Obviously—hopefully—he must have defined reality in the text, and I'm sure his Concept becomes clear in the reading—and let me be clear, I didn't understand the Concept after reading chapter one, which is actually entitled, "Understanding the Concept."

You can't be faulted if you are at this moment objecting that becoming an obstacle to the continuation of the status quo doesn't seem to guarantee a peaceful life. But perhaps this is where my father's spirituality comes in. Perhaps a deeper understanding of the meaning of the word "peace" is necessary. Perhaps the Concept is counterintuitive. Or, perhaps, Patrick Daniel Bainbridge is delusional.

Again, the writing is abysmal, but there is something there, at least for me. Somehow, through the awkwardness of the prose, you can sense, almost feel, an urgency, something approaching a pleading, but stopping at the precipice. He wants so much for the readers to embrace the Concept so they are not swallowed up but become obstacles, because it is only then that the Concept is proven and the author avoids failure.

It is only in becoming an obstacle that we can find peace, or so my father claimed. If he was correct, it must be admitted that I am living a nominal life and that I have not become an obstacle, for peace is a foreign land to me. Let's hope he was wrong. Or that I can change.

We have nominal, obstacle, reality, peace, the Concept. To this he added, in his closing four sentences living, hope, and freedom.

*Living, a constant process, cannot and will not be stopped by the lack of peace. We simply go on living but without our desired hope. If we had implicit faith in reality, this would result in a new way of life, freedom from a chaotic, uninspiring system of life. Our resulting cry of thanksgiving would acknowledge our newfound freedom: freedom from systems, freedom from guilt, freedom as a gift of peace.*

*We simply go on living but without our desired hope.* Perhaps the most important words in the entire manuscript. Perhaps the most important words Patrick Daniel Bainbridge ever uttered. And perhaps the words themselves are nothing less than profound. They almost break my heart.

There is no title page in the folder, just the ten chapters, each held together with now-rusted paperclips leaving their brown, stained image on the paper. Given the pedestrian nature of the writing, I wouldn't be surprised if he called his book simply, *The Concept*. Perhaps. But for me? I'd entitle the book, *Living on a Broken Mirror*.

# 57

# Michael Andrew Walker Johnson and Singing the Great Enfolding

A FEW WEEKS BEFORE I left Castine for Berkeley, and obviously before Gregory Stuart Peel called me to tell me Walker's remains had been found in the Adirondacks, I received an email from Walker. It wasn't long but it was poignant and moving. We had not been in contact for some time, so it was also surprising. The email began with these words:

> *After all these years I read the speech you gave at my ordination, and it hit me again with a force of truth. I had started reading it twice before, but every time I got to "At first glance it is a dark photo of death—it is after all a grave marker in a graveyard. At first glance, too, your ministry is one of death, of dark days, and with people who have been largely ignored or forgotten by our society and our churches" I started crying. Really, I'm not sure exactly why, but most likely because I remember the feeling of love in the midst of some awful times.*

To be honest, at first, I didn't know what to think. I was surprised that he had read the charge I gave at his ordination. I was shocked he even had a copy. He continued:

*The words you spoke at my ordination have come into a similar space. Maybe I have already told you this. At the beginning of every medicine ceremony I lead, I sing words (while eating the sacrament) that translate "help me help you help me help you help everyone." As I tell everyone, the song anchors the medicine ceremony in service. Everyone is everyone—non-human and human, the whole deal, the consciousness of Being there to benefit others from the benefit we gain from the ceremony, to let ourselves be affected in such a way so that others are affected by healing and being woven back into nature and a Great Enfolding.*

I never heard Walker sing the ceremony. I wish I had. It's obviously too late now. Perhaps if I could somehow magically conjure his presence so he could sing to me, I would benefit. Maybe I'd be anchored. Maybe the consciousness of Being would touch me. Maybe I would become everyone, the whole deal. I don't know what the Great Enfolding is, and I ache that I cannot ask him, but right now, sitting here in the sun, pen at work on a very common legal yellow pad, I think I would like to be enfolded. Yes, someone, wrap me in your loving arms and don't let go.

# 58

# The Palimpsest, the Brotherhood, and the End of Sanctuary

HOW DOES A PERSON KNOW when they reach self-understanding, self-knowledge, self-completion, self-actualization through the act of palimpsest? Do you measure it in time? In pain? In tears? In blood? I'd really like to know. It's important because Barry Patrick Olds has been very nice to me over the past five days. Melissa Jennifer Davis has been distant.

Barry Patrick Olds and his Brotherhood gang have been coming to Paradise Café quite a lot lately. He carries a briefcase and references Jesus. He quotes scripture and walks with arrogance. He buys me a latte.

Two days ago, he sat at my table, as usual, uninvited. He put that latte on the table and said, "How's the writing going? You must be on your second yellow legal pad by now. Am I right?"

"What do you want, Barry?" I asked, while accepting the latte.

"Nothing really. I'm curious what you've been writing so faithfully each day," he said.

"I'm writing the definitive work on Joshua ben Joseph. The theme is: Jesus went into tomb and Christ came out. A man went into the tomb and a metaphor came out," I said. "What do you think? Think I'll find a publisher?"

"Oh, I have no doubt," he said, with a mean-spirited smile. "But I don't believe you. You're writing something much more personal. Or at least, that's my guess."

"Barry, what can be more personal than Jesus?"

"David, you don't like me, do you?" Barry said as he stood up.

"I don't know you, but I abhor most everything you stand for and believe in."

Barry Patrick Olds's question was a fair one, and the truth is, no, I don't much like him. However, in the palimpsest spirit of surface truth, underlying truth, scraping, x-raying, hurting, and bleeding truth, Barry Patrick Olds may not be quite as despicable as I have no doubt made him appear on these yellow sheets of paper. On the other hand, perhaps he is.

This happened the next day.

Barry Patrick Olds and his Brotherhood crew came out of the café and stopped at my table. Barry Patrick Olds looked down at me with a broad smile and said, "You've got two weeks."

"What happens in two weeks?" I asked, though I already knew the answer.

"In two weeks you lose this table. And if I'm honest, in two weeks you will not be welcome here, though I guess I can't stop you from coming. But in two weeks, this café will be for true believers and genuine seekers. You are neither. Have a nice day, David."

It was like someone had taken a hammer to my heart. Yes, in part it was the bitterness of losing to a person I hated, but the loss of my sanctuary was more devastating. Paradise Café had been my safe place, my comfort place, my friend place. Jessica and I had spent immeasurable hours sitting at Paradise Café. I met Walker at Paradise Café, right here at this table. I spent days of my life sitting at Paradise Café reading, writing, thinking and, most recently, trying to fill the black hole that is David Robert Bainbridge. And in two weeks, it would be gone.

I set my pen and yellow pad aside and waited. The café was somewhat busy, but I knew in half an hour or so things would quiet down, and Melissa Jennifer Davis and I would have a little chat.

Each time she passed my table she refused to make eye contact, but I looked her in and out of the door without fail. To her credit, I didn't have to tackle her. When things had emptied out, she sat down at my table with two glasses and a bottle of red wine. Without speaking, she poured the wine. I looked her in the eyes and said, "Melissa, what the hell have you done?"

"Drink the wine, David. It's on the house," she said, taking a healthy drink from her glass.

"Melissa, you didn't sell Paradise Café to those fundies?" I said.

"Well, they made me an offer I couldn't refuse, as the saying goes," she said. "I know it's a cliché, but in this case it's true. They offered me way more than the café is worth on the market. It leaves me sitting very pretty."

"Of course they did. They want the location. This location is at the bottom of Holy Hill. Up the hill are seven seminaries and theological schools. This is an invasion. You let them in! You gave them a foothold!"

"I'm sorry, but I'm tired, and I can now retire more than comfortably."

We both grew quiet. My heart had sunk to the place where all defeated hearts go. Even the wine tasted bitter.

"You know what they're going to call the place?" she asked.

"No, of course not. But I have an idea. It should be called, 'Paradise Lost Café,'" I said.

"Very clever, but no. The café will be called the Christian Community Café," she said, sitting back in her chair with a smirk on her face.

"You've got to be kidding me," I said.

"Nope. I call it the Three C's. But it's got a kind of subtitle. The Christian Community Café: A Place for Believers, Seekers, and Friends of Jesus. And David, you will not be welcome here," she said.

"So I've been told by Barry Patrick Olds himself. And he did enjoy telling me."

"I bet he did," Melissa Jennifer Davis laughed. "Here's the deal. We've got two weeks. For those two weeks, you order whatever you want, as much as you want, and it's on Paradise Café. Whatever you want."

"Well, I won't say no to that, but Melissa, this place was my sanctuary," I said.

"Sorry, but I need to get out and move on."

"What are you going to do?" I asked.

"I don't know, but I'm not going to be doing it here. Finish the bottle. You look like you need it," she said and disappeared into the café.

It felt like the warm sun was mocking me. My God, she sold Paradise to a bunch of Christian fundamentalists. The symbolism was maddening and painful. The Brotherhood of Christian Businessmen indeed. Somebody save me.

# 59

# The Palimpsest and the One Good Thing

MANY YEARS AGO, A COLLEAGUE and I, actually a friend by the name of Nigel Terence Thompson, traveled by road through a part of India that I can no longer remember—meaning I can't remember where in India we were traveling—but I do remember the journey. It was both fascinating and terrifying. I once told Jessica that if I were to die during my travels, it would most likely be in a vehicle accident and not in a plane crash. This was particularly true in India. Our destination was a small Dalit community where we would meet a local bishop and some villagers.

We stopped twice on the way, first in a crossroads town where we purchased sweet brown sugary tea from a street vender. Next to the tea shop—I say shop, but it was really a large kiosk—was an old man sitting beside a tree making flower garlands. He had a huge basket of bright yellow flowers, and he hung the completed garlands on the tree. Our second stop was at a roadside café where we bought cold bottles of Coke and sat outside watching the cars and trucks speed by. As I talked to Nigel Terence Thompson, I noticed to my right, sitting at another table, a large baboon staring at us. India was the country that most reminded me that I am an animal sharing the planet with other animals—in India, the cows, pigs, primates of many kinds, dogs, cats, were forever underfoot, in the roads or sitting next to you at a café.

When we reached the Dalit village, we were greeted with a Tiger Dance, or Pulikali. Two men were entirely painted in yellow and red tiger stripes. They wore tiger masks on their heads. Each had a rope around his neck held by two other painted men in elaborate costumes. The tigers strained against the ropes trying to escape. It was quite the spectacle.

We were ushered into a humble church where we found approximately three hundred men and women crowded together on the floor. At the front, a man with an Indian drum was playing as we entered. Men came to us and placed three garlands around each of our necks, honoring our visit.

It was my job to bring greetings, so I stood up and said the words I had said so often in so many places. I looked out at the gathering of people sitting on the floor, felt the heat radiating upwards toward the ceiling, breathed the scent of the garlands beginning to overwhelm, and then I said six simple words I had never included before. I said, "We are all equal in Christ."

It seemed to me a good thing to say in an extremely poor Dalit church in a village probably not noted on a map, whether or not I actually believed it. Goodness knows, I would not have told them what I meant by the word "Christ." You have heard me say it before: Jesus, the man, went into the tomb, and Christ, the metaphor, came out. If Christology meant anything and was not just an esoteric theology of counting the number of angels on a pinhead, then it seemed good to me to say, "We are all equal in Christ." After all, the metaphor supposedly destroys the walls that divide us, those walls we build so high and thick and strong. In Christ there is neither Jew nor Greek, male nor female, slave nor free—the dividing walls of race, gender, and economics come crashing down. Or so we like to say. I thought I needed to proclaim that we all *are* Christ, or at least invited to become so. If that is too blasphemous for you, then how about, we are all capable of being Christ-like. But if I'm going

to blaspheme, I might as well go big. Surely if we are all Christ, or
Christ-like, or possess the spark of the metaphor that escaped the
tomb and breaks down the dividing walls, it is important to say, "We
are all equal in Christ."

And so I said it.

I spoke in short sentences, and the man standing next to me
translated my words in equally short sentences. But after I said the
metaphorical words of wonder, he went on and on and on. I actually
turned to him and watched. When he had finished, he turned his
head toward me, and I asked, "What did you say?" He said, "I was
explaining to them what the word 'equal' means."

This threw me for a moment, reminding me that no matter how
long I travel, and no matter where I go, my US American naivete
never seems to disappear completely. His comment also angered me.
I turned to look at the bishop sitting behind me. I had not taken
to him when we first met, and now I was positively unimpressed.
*What the hell is he teaching them*, I thought, once again spewing forth
naivete. I turned to the translator and told him to translate again,
"We are all equal in Christ." I did this three times and he translated
three times. Then I told him to ask the drummer to stand.

The drummer must have been approximately forty years old,
though he could have been older. Jet black hair, a mustache, deep
dark skin, and worried eyes. I'm sure he was wondering what I
wanted. I walked up to him, took a garland from around my neck,
lifted it over his head and unto his neck, and said, "We are all equal
in Christ!"

The poor man was horrified. He quickly took off the garland and
placed it on a small table to our left. I asked the translator to tell him
that I apologized for embarrassing him and wanted to speak to him
after the service. The translator did so, and the drummer just looked
at me.

After the service, I ended up in the van without having made contact with the drummer. The van was surrounded by men, women, and children from the church ready to wave us goodbye, when suddenly he appeared through the crowd, walked up to the window of the van, looked me in the eyes, crossed his arms, not in insecurity defense, but in confidence and bravery, and smiled for all the world to see. It was a glorious sight. I smiled back. The van slowly moved away.

So, do I believe what I just said about "Christ"? Yes and no is the ambiguity I'm looking for. I have no Christology to speak of, no orthodoxy that would be acceptable. Now in my seventy-fourth year, they'd never let me in the club. And I must confess, I have a hard time getting my mind around the idea that Barry Patrick Olds is Christ-like. And yet, if the idea of Christ is anything beyond a god seeking a subordinate's worship, or simply an imitation game cloaked in sacredness, the idea has to be accessible. Actualization has to be possible.

I remember Walker writing, *For me, god is the luminous background to creation but not a monotheistic luminosity.* From there he could see no way to a Christology of any value because there was none. From there he could not call himself a Christian. I'm inclined to agree with him—God as a luminous background. Incandescent. Radiant. Shimmering.

Perhaps Christ, at least for some, could be a luminous background to the human soul. But not a distant, untouchable luminosity. An incandescent force. A radiant metaphor. A shimmering invitation.

Would I stand up today in front of a crowd of people and say, "We are all equal in Christ"? Certainly not. And yet, through all the years, doing so in that village and gifting the garland may have been the boldest thing I've ever done. It may have been the one good thing I've ever done.

# 60

# The Palimpsest and the Ontological Crisis

OF COURSE I'D READ about it, the protagonist having an ontological crisis, but I had always somehow assumed that such things were the remit of literature. I've never seen myself as the main character in a fiction, or in life for that matter. I've since learned that an ontological crisis and being a main character should both be avoided if at all possible.

I struggle to think you will understand what I'm going to tell you. You've already heard my sad story about receiving Walker's email, forwarded by his partner Gregory Stuart Peel. I thought, and no doubt you thought, that that moment, the reading of the letter from Walker explaining why he would walk off into the wilderness to die without a word of goodbye, was my ontological crisis. Hell, it drove me from Castine, Maine, to Berkeley, California. But no. Here's what happened yesterday.

When I left Castine, I arranged with a neighbor, Sally Louise Lessing, to forward any mail she thought looked important to my Berkeley apartment. She was hesitant at first, fearing she might not be able to discern what was important and what was not. I told her to do her best, but bottom line, I really didn't care one way or the other. All I wanted to do was get to Paradise Café as soon as possible.

Yesterday morning, before heading off to the café, I collected half a dozen envelopes that had been forwarded to me by Sally

Louise Lessing but had been sitting on the small, inadequate desk in my apartment for a couple of days. I planned to read them over lunch.

Arriving at Paradise, I went through my normal routine—placed my yellow pad and pen in front of me on the blue and white checkered tablecloth, put my laptop in the top left corner of the table in case remembrance or research was demanded, and had a good morning chat with Melissa Jennifer Davis as she brought me my latte and croissant. The letters remained forgotten in my bag.

At the end of my café day, I returned to my apartment, had a light dinner and a beer, and settled in to watch a little TV. At about nine in the evening, I suddenly remembered the damn letters. I got up, grabbed my bag from the desk, and retrieved the letters. I went back to the couch and began going through the mail. The largest envelope contained two items. The first was a short note from Gregory Stuart Peel, the second an unopened, normal-sized envelope. The note told me that Gregory Stuart Peel had been emptying out Walker's desk and files, something he was loath to do right after Walker's death, and he had found the accompanying envelope addressed to me. In fact, the envelope said, "To be mailed to David Robert Bainbridge upon my death." Under those words was written in red, "Private and Confidential." Gregory Stuart Peel explained that he thus had not opened the envelope and had no idea what it held. What it held was a poem written to me by Walker.

I know what you're thinking. We've been through this before. Why wasn't the poem sent with the letter Gregory Stuart Peel had scanned for me? Well, I'll tell you why. Because that is Walker! He liked doing things like this—hiding something away with the possibility that one day it would be found. He did it all the time. Once we were taking the ferry from Fionnphort, Mull, to Iona. About halfway between the two islands, Walker reached into his backpack and pulled out a heavy iron pipe, eight inches long and sealed at both ends. I, of course, asked him what it was, and he told me the pipe contained a poem he had written about the sea and Iona. He then proceeded to drop the pipe and poem into the water and said, "It will probably never be found, but if someday a long, long time from now it is, and if someone for some crazy reason decides to break the seals and finds the poem, it will be one damn mystery. I haven't signed it."

He reveled in this sort of thing. It is not at all surprising to me that he had hidden the letter and the poem in different places, assuming they would be found at different times. It's not unreasonable to think there is something else tucked away, waiting to be found with the instructions to send it to me urgently. The bastard is going to drive me crazy, and he did it on purpose.

I was so angry at him in that moment that I could barely read the poem. I loved him dearly, but now that he's dead, I could almost hate him. Nonetheless, here it is:

*Wanderer*
*riverspeaking*
*telling endtime to trees and scat*
*wordleaking*
*take givenbody eat*
*tongueflinging forests onto soil*
*seedseed drop wordseed*
*here, rootrot, take my pauses*
*here, fallen log, eat my gerunds*
*eager outgo lungsqueeze*
*wordwinds breathing*
*wanting empty*
*burthenfree*
*words carry memories, you know*
*like viruses*
*hooking brainwise docking sites*

*reactivating my mouthspew*
*agonist for release take and eat*
*gave out lots I did, before*
*in the big sucking city taking*
*volumevalued*
*saw alltosee in the big seehereopportunities*
*they demanding make more*
*make more they said, saying saying*
*I said I'm tired*
*I want to empty the youtake and youeat*
*but cannibal it is mustmunch*
*shall keep eating*
*and making more of the making of them that feed*
*that it keeps eating the more that it needs*
*then*
*wanderer made breathturn*
*speaking trees and scat onto wide fields*
*syllableforest planted word by word*
*dolloped onto the soil*
*because wind and water, bird and bush*
*speaking the same language*
*absorb it all having the grammar for it*
*blood birth hum and flesh into the earth*
*then*
*when the last word outgo is outgone*
*I will have given myself away entirely*
*word by word, comma by comma, footnote by footnote, moral by*
*moral, endless endless endlessly pattern by pattern, library by library,*
*bibliography by bibliography, yesterday's leaves, this morning's leaves,*
*papers pads staples scripts newspapers blogsites film scores, enfolders*
*regulators measures moments miniscule curls of wondering the last few*

*coughs of sound of a soft gurgle maybe? maybe? love by love, intimacy*
*by kiss by kiss given love by love, then*
    *thinned out*
    *ghosting disappeared*
    *from particles into energy waves*
    *that's how to imagine it*
    *and the imagining of it also gone*
    *whisp away my final [ ] to be empty*
    *last word being [ ]?*
    *any idea of anyone's last [ ]?*
    *then, self-ghosted, gone?*
    *what reservedword poised [ ]*
    *at the threshold*
    *the carapace of soul*
    *fleshmelted into mist in the godbreeze*
    *a word known only to creosote caverns*
    *crystals and wolves*
    *even I do not know the last [ ]*
    *because*
    *when I say [ ] I will not be there*
    *to have known to say*
    *Aha! So that's what [ ] was*
    *surprised with joy even I do not know*
    *to have told whom I love or handed you*
    *[ ] of my unfurling-into-forest wordnotes*
    *having left my mouth*
    *[ ] cradled [ ] [ ]*
    *your caring, cupped hands*

UPON READING THE POEM, I sat frozen for a few minutes. The poem had clearly been written for me. It speaks of shared memories and was written in an almost brother-like, lover-like, friend-like, never-married-like, intimate language shared between the two of us. "Brother" is not right. "Lover" is not accurate. "Friend" is not enough. But I am at a loss for a word that describes who we were together. What do you call what was between this straight man and this gay man? He was part of my soul in a fundamentally different way than Jessica was. The poem is very private, just for the two of us. Upon reading it, perhaps you felt a bit lost, like you were eavesdropping on a conversation that began a long time ago. Perhaps I should not have included it here in my palimpsest contemplations, precisely because it is so intimate and private. However, I thought you needed to read it if there was going to be any chance of your understanding what happened next.

To me, the poem is incredibly visceral and direct. It is pure Walker. I can hear him, feel him, smell him. It is a poem about death, or rather the break between the living and the dead. It is evocative. It is beautiful. It is Walker. It is a beloved man sitting with his back against an old and great tree, away from people, but in harmony with a different reality, breathing his last.

I don't believe in ghosts. I have no idea what happens to human beings when we die. I don't even know if we have a soul, that *something* that can be distinguishable, divergent, discernable, from what we call mind and consciousness. But for a moment, Walker was in the living room of my small Berkeley apartment. He was there. No, I didn't believe he was there, but he was there. Walker was there in the apartment with me. My breathing quickened. Tears started to form in my eyes. I began reading the poem again but could not see through my tears. And then, suddenly, my world collapsed. My sense of who I was disintegrated. The black hole within me grew exponentially and threatened to overwhelm me. It was eating me whole, and I became frightened—a deep terrorizing fear. Without really thinking, I left my apartment and literally ran to Sarah's house.

It must have been approaching ten at night, but there were lights on. I banged on the door. It took forever for Sarah to come to the door. When she opened it, I just began to weep. She must have been shocked, but she took me by the arm, led me into the living room, and sat me down on the sofa. She settled next to me and began asking me what was wrong. I tried to speak, but simply fell onto her, my head in her lap. She stroked my head with one hand and held my shoulder tight with the other.

I kept saying over and over again, "I can't do this! I can't do this!" To her credit she didn't ask what I couldn't do. Perhaps somehow, somewhere inside her, she knew. She cradled me closer. I put my arm around her waist and just wept.

At some point, I fell asleep exhausted—not just from the weeping, but from the years alone, the deaths, the losses, the failures, lovelessness, the everything I was not, the everything without Jessica and Walker.

When I awoke, it was after 3:00 a.m., and Sarah was still sitting there with my head in her lap, I now stretched out on the couch. I slowly sat up, numb, emotionally shell-shocked, and yes, embarrassed. Sarah simply said, holding my hand in hers, "What happened?"

I told her about the poem. I tried to explain why the poem had set me off but failed, because I myself didn't actually know. I told her about Jessica. I told her about acute panmyelosis with myelofibrosis. I told her about my father's love for Joyce and his terrible book. I told her about Russian tanks. I told her about meeting Walker. I told her about my dyslexia and science fiction. I told her about not having children. I told her about the kiss—Walker's kiss, not Samantha Esther Cunningham's kiss. But then I told her about Samantha Esther Cunningham. I told her about escaping my family. I told her about Walker and the Mother God. I told her about seeing Jessica sitting in lamplight through the window and falling in love all over again. I told her about my fear of the dark. I told her about being hated. I told her about starry starry nights and aliens. I told her about dinosaur tracks. I told her about Walker and Old Compton Street. I told her about the cacophony of spirits. I told her about the corduroy jacket. I told her about being planted in the soil of one's home. I told her about magic mushrooms in Amsterdam. I told her about shapeshifting. I told her about the dead plants and the ghost. I told her about failing the murderer. I told her about Megan's smile. I told her about the swirling language of nature. I told her about everything. I told her about me. And when I was done, the sun was coming up on another beautiful Berkeley day.

I was a mess, to say the least. Sarah suggested I take a shower, even though I would have to get back into my wrinkled, yesterday clothes. The hot water on my face and running down my body felt good. As I was drying myself, I looked into the mirror and saw a weary old man. But inside, I felt lighter. No, my cathartic confessional release had not resurrected me into a world made new, but the black hole no longer threatened. Indeed, it seemed to have diminished some. So I ventured toward the kitchen where I heard voices. As I entered Megan said, "David, good morning. Did you sleep over?"

"Yes, honey," Sarah jumped in. "David and Mommy had a lot to talk about last night and it got late, so David slept on the couch."

Sarah looked tired, but focused. I couldn't blame her for her weariness. When we made eye contact, she smiled. It helped.

"What did you talk about?" Megan asked.

"Just things," Sarah said.

"What kind of things?"

"Just things, honey."

Megan looked thoughtful for a moment and then, apparently, decided to drop the interrogation and said, "David, do you want some breakfast? Mommy's making pancakes!"

"That sounds good, Megan. Thanks," I said.

"Come sit with me," she said. And so I did.

After breakfast, when Megan was getting dressed, I started to apologize to Sarah for crashing in on her the night before. She told me to shut up and hugged me. Then she added, "But we do have things to talk about when you're ready. You scared me."

"It's a deal," I said. "And don't be scared. I mean, I get it. A crazy old man spent the night on your couch crying! But...Well, don't be scared. Perhaps I'm not done yet."

I went home, changed, and started the short walk to Paradise Café.

# 61

# The Palimpsest and the Decision

THIS IS MY LAST DAY at Paradise Café. For the last time I am sitting at my table, leather bag on the ground to my left, the sun casting ribbons of light and shade, my yellow legal pad in front of me, my medium-blue ballpoint pen in hand, latte and croissant before me. My sanctuary has come to an end. My palimpsest endeavors are finished—this is my last entry.

Tomorrow Barry Patrick Olds and the Brotherhood of Christian Businessmen take over Paradise. Their sign is already inside the café leaning against a wall: *The Christian Community Café: A Place for Believers, Seekers, and Friends of Jesus.* Melissa Jennifer Davis has been spreading the word up and down Hearst Food Court that the café's new name is the *Three C's.* As you know, I have renamed it *Paradise Lost Café.* Sometimes the bad guys win. Melissa Jennifer Davis has gifted me the café's original sign, simply: *Paradise Café.* I have accepted the gift. It will go home to Maine with me.

Within the week, I will be leaving Berkeley. It's time to go home, though the word "home" is deeply complicated. Was my palimpsest experiment a success? It's hard to tell. If by success we mean healed, then no. As Walker would say, my parts are not yet in "coherent dialogue," and my "entire panoply" is not yet fully reconnected. In fact, writing on my yellow pads has left me feeling bruised and, yes, scraped bloody. But I think it's important to report that I have made a decision. It frightened me at first, but now I feel a calmness, though

I do not yet entirely trust it. The calmness feels good. It's been a long time since something of substance felt good.

This morning before coming to the café, I stopped by Sarah's place with an offer, a proposal. I pointed out to her the following. She needed to leave her house or find a roommate to help cover expenses. Given her line of work—basically digital work in a virtual reality—she could live wherever she wanted. Megan could start school anywhere in the country.

I asked if Sarah and Megan would like to live with me in Castine, Maine, as family. I have never had a daughter or a granddaughter, but having both might be just the thing. And even if we came to call ourselves family, I would expect everyone to pull their weight—meaning this would be no free ride. I would expect payment of a mutually agreed rent.

Sarah's immediate response was shock. She asked if I had thought it through. She asked if the house in Castine was big enough for a "daughter" and "granddaughter." I assured her it was, that each of them would have their own bedroom and that she, Sarah, could have a study. She asked if the schools were good in Castine, and I said I thought they were. She said Maine was a long way away, and she had never been there. To this I remained silent. Finally, she asked what would happen if it didn't work out, and I said I would pay to relocate them to wherever she wanted to go. What I didn't say was that this old fart of a man would be willing to change his will if it did work out. I have no one else, after all.

I have this image of the three of us climbing into Sarah's car, pulling a small U-Haul, the Paradise Café sign roped to the roof, and driving across the country. I picture their other belongings traveling by a commercial mover. I fancy it could be good.

You, no doubt, think I'm crazy. You will tell me I should take more time, think it through, be cautious, be smart. You are thinking that I am so traumatized that I'm selfishly latching on to Sarah and

Megan. Perhaps you are right, but perhaps you are wrong. However, if my house were just around the corner from their present home instead of three thousand miles away, I'm quite sure you wouldn't object so strenuously. I ask you to not let geography frighten you. For a digital nomad and a preschool child, geography is nothing.

I am closer to the Balance than I was even a few days ago. Perhaps my parts are indeed approaching coherent dialogue, and the self of my panoply has emerged from the black hole. If so, no small accomplishment. No, of course, I may not be there yet, and I may have a long way to go, but am I expected to achieve profound healing in isolation? Can I find wholeness alone? We human beings are not built for alone. So I'm taking a chance. Perhaps at this late date—third act and no encore—I can learn to be a good father and grandfather. Perhaps not. But now all there is to do is wait for Sarah's and Megan's answers.

Resurrection has always been and always will be a metaphor—a man went into a tomb and a metaphor came out. But the word can also be used to describe a transformation and the renewal of a human spirit. I believe it takes time. No flash of light to fashion David Robert Bainbridge into a new man. Still...

Perhaps the angels will reappear and sing.

# Acknowledgements

I want to thank James Lawer for his collaboration on ideas and especially for the poems. All the poems in *Paradise Café* were written by him. The poem in Chapter 60 was specifically written for poor David Robert Bainbridge, the protagonist in our story. This book has been many years in the making, meaning many years sitting on my hard drive, and Jim never forgot or lost interest.

Thanks to Teresa Fernandez, editor and proofreader of $Er^2$ at www.er2pro.com[1]. And thanks to Kevin Ydhistira Alloni for the cover photograph.

---

1.    http://www.er2pro.com

# Also by Dale Rominger

Fiction
*Alien Love or Thank You Alpha Centauri*
*The Poetry of Being Human*
<u>Drake Ramsey Mysteries</u>
*The Woman in White Marble*
*The Girl in the Silver Mask*
Nonfiction
*Midnight Memories Inside the Back Road Café*
*Notes from 39,000 Feet*
*Dis-Ease: Living with Prostate Cancer*

# Notes

Chapter 1

I first encountered the word *palimpsest* when reading *Palimpsest: A Memoir* by Gore Vidal. Here is what Vidal says at the beginning of his book:

> A memoir is how one remembers one's own life, while an autobiography is history, requiring research, dates, facts double-checked. I've taken the memoir route on the ground that even an idling memory is apt to get right what matters most...

> Title: *Palimpsest*. For years I've used this obscure word incorrectly. Worse, I've always mispronounced it, not sounding the second *s*. I had thought that the word was applicable only to architecture, lie the wall of San Marco at Venice with its fragments of bas-reliefs, bits of porphyry, shards of ceramic, all set in plaster to form a palimpsest.

> I have just now looked up the earliest meaning of *palimpsest*. It is even more apt than I thought: "Paper, parchment, etc., prepared for writing on and wiping out again, like, like a slate" and "a parchment, etc., which has been written upon twice; the original writing having been rubbed out." This is pretty much what my kind of writing does anyway. Starts with life; makes a text; then a *re*-vision—literally, a second seeing, an afterthought, easing some but not all of the original while writing

something new over the first layer of text. Finally, in a memoir, there are many rubbings-out and puttings-in or, as I once observed to Dwight Macdonald, who had found me disappointedly conventional on some point, "I have nothing to say, only to add." (Vidal Gore. *Palimpsest: A Memoir*. London: Andre Deutsch, 1995, pp. 5-6.)

While I too can barely pronounce the word *palimpsest*, I do love it and the ideas it generates—both the literal and the metaphorical. When I first started thinking about David Robert Bainbridge and first meeting him at such a crucial point in his, I knew the only way for him to tell his story was as a *palimpsest*.

Chapter 4

"...banquet table seemed to sag under the silence and loneliness."

Theodor Storm, *The Rider on the White Horse*, New York Review Books Classics, 1964: 226.

Chapter 12

"He was the gay friend and I was the straight friend."

Geoffrey Duncan, ed, *Courage to Love* (London: Darton, Longman and Todd Ltd, 2002), 151-152.

Chapter 19

"And {And] mx [matrix] 3; and 0-1} ^[that scholar] (2[this scholar]..."

Danis Rose, *James Joyce Ulysses: A Reader's Edition* (London: Picador, 1997), lxxviii.

"*He entered Davy Byrnes. Moral pub. He doesn't chat...*"

Wikipedia, s.v. Davey Byrnes pub. Last edited 11 March 2021. https://en.wikipedia.org/wiki/Davy_Byrne%27s_pub.

Chapter 24

"Even as we speak, the work is being done, within. You were born to heal."

Olds, Sharon. *Stag's Leap*. New York: Alfred A. Knopf, 2012, p.67.

Chapter 25

"The person who looks in through an open window never sees all the things that are seen by someone who looks in through a closed window."

Roberto Calasso, *The Ruin of Kasch* (Cambridge: Carcanet Press Ltd, 1994), 290.

Chapter 27

"STOP IT!" The sound ceases. The lights come on. And Eleanor realizes that Theodora is on the other side of the room just awakening. Eleanor screams, "Good God—whose hand was I holding?"

Shirley Jackson, *The Haunting of Hill House* (New York: Penguin Press, 2019), 178-180.

Chapter 52

Internal Family Systems Therapy from: *Psychology Today*, s.v. Psychology Today Staff. Last edited 20 May 2022. http://www.psychologytoday.com/us/therapy-types/internal-family-systems-therapy.

# Don't miss out!

Visit the website below and you can sign up to receive emails whenever Dale Rominger publishes a new book. There's no charge and no obligation.

https://books2read.com/r/B-A-FMQW-WGWEC

**BOOKS 2 READ**

Connecting independent readers to independent writers.

# About the Author

Dale Rominger has been a minister, educator, speaker, world traveler, and consultant. He has traveled extensively assisting in development projects and creating education and encounter programs with international partners. Now retired, Dale lives in Seattle with his wife, Roberta, reading, writing, and cooking.